KAREN SANDLER

CLEAN BURN

EXHIBIT A
An Angry Robot imprint
and a member of Osprey Group

Lace Market House,
54-56 High Pavement,
Nottingham NG1 1HW
UK

www.exhibitabooks.com
A is for Arson!

An Exhibit A paperback original 2013
1

Copyright © Karen Sandler 2013

Karen Sandler asserts the moral right to be
identified as the author of this work.

A catalogue record for this book is available
from the British Library.

UK ISBN 978 1 90922 330 1
Ebook ISBN 978 1 90922 332 5

Set in Meridien and Franklin Gothic by EpubServices

*To Gary,
my sounding board and
one-man support group.*

PROLOGUE

Mama was busy in the alley when the car pulled up to the church next door.

It wasn't a proper church, not a real place of worship. No towering steeple, no stained glass, nothing but an electronic keyboard for music. The stucco one-story had been a dry cleaners until some prideful mail-order minister came in with a few folding chairs and a podium and declared it a place of God.

Mama knew better. God's glory didn't reside in so humble a place as that ramshackle storefront on Sanchez. As His instrument, Mama took it upon herself to purify and clarify God's message in this place. To make clear the folly of sin.

Which was why she was busy in the alley when the car pulled over to the curb.

Mama shrank back behind the dumpster, squeezing between it and the church wall. She'd worn sturdy shoes and blue jeans to protect her feet and legs. If she was quick with a kick, the rats wouldn't bother her much.

It was a fancy car, a Mercedes or maybe a Lexus. Shiny silver gray. The passenger side door opened and a girl put her feet out onto the pavement, something cradled in her arms. The girl had skin the color of milk chocolate, and her pretty face was tired and drawn. She looked barely older than Angela, Mama's thirteen year-old.

The girl rose carefully and walked toward the front step of the church, holding what looked like a mass of blankets held close to her chest. She looked up and down the street. At one point, Mama thought the girl saw her and she retreated into the shadows and held her breath.

By the time Mama dared look again, the girl had set the bundle down on the steps and was pressing a button beside the door. The girl probably thought that would call the minister, but Mama knew he didn't stay overnight on Thursdays, which was why Mama was here. He wouldn't be back until the morning when it would be too late.

After a moment's hesitation, the girl dashed back to the car. She slipped inside and the car roared off down the street.

Mama counted out ten breaths before she crept out of the alley to the front step of the church. She peeled back the pale pink blankets the girl had left, her hand trembling when she saw the brown stain of blood. Then she saw the milky brown eyes gazing up at her and she couldn't breathe at all.

It was Lydia.

Tears filled Mama's eyes as she picked up her infant daughter. Lydia had been gone so long. Mama held the sweet weight close to her breast, praising God, reveling in His magnificence. Confirming the righteousness of Mama's mission with this gift.

Cradling Lydia against her hip made it harder to finish the work she'd come out to do. But she'd performed the task so often now, she managed it one handed. Then she dashed up Sanchez the two blocks to her apartment.

The next morning, the minister found his church engulfed in flames. By the time the fire department extinguished it, there was nothing left inside but sodden ashes.

CHAPTER 1

9am on a Wednesday morning. While I slurped up a triple-shot latte in my San Francisco Excelsior district office, the past tapped me on the shoulder with a sledgehammer.

Not to say the past ever left me completely alone. Tommy Phillips made sure of that. Even now, he lurked in the back of my mind, sad-faced and accusatory, the twelve stab wounds in his small body red and lurid in my imagination.

Sometimes, I ignored him, blanking away the image. Sometimes, like now, I let him stay, due penance for my sins.

My very soul screaming for caffeine, I'd gulped a mouthful of latte just as my assistant, Sheri Proud, buzzed me to announce an unexpected visitor. "Ruth Martinez is here."

The latte burned my tongue as my throat refused to swallow. I set the cup down and my hand crept of its own accord toward the box of matches tucked beside a stack of client files.

I dropped my hand in my lap. "What does she want?"

"To talk to you." The couldn't-care-less tone of voice was vintage Sheri, but I'd bet Watkins Investigations's every last receivable she was itching to know Ruth's business with me.

I'd just as soon the diminutive Hispanic woman would drop off the face of the earth. Because she'd walk through the door of my office with enough emotional baggage to outfit an around-the-world tour, and a sizeable portion of the contents of those metaphorical suitcases would be given to me.

Without conscious thought, I swept up the box of matches and closed my fingers around it. Okay, I'd hold them. I just wouldn't open the box.

In my mind's eye, Tommy just stared at me. He never spoke, but I could imagine him saying, "Yeah, right."

I turned slightly to block him from my peripheral vision. "Send her in."

It was too damned early to face bogeymen. I'd run a surveillance the night before, snapping digitals of a sicko creep violating his marital vows with two blonde bimbos. When I crawled home at 2am, exhausted and disgusted, I spent five restless hours in bed entertaining dark dreams.

Sheri opened the door to let Mrs Martinez into the closet that passed for my office. I clutched the matches tighter, feeling the corners of the box bite into my skin.

The manila folder under Mrs Martinez's arm didn't bode well. I creaked to my feet, gulping back a yip of pain as my left calf cramped. As I shook her hand in greeting, Mrs Martinez glanced down at my arm. Even though all my secrets were hidden by my long-sleeved T-shirt, I had to resist the impulse to tug the sleeve farther over my wrist.

She'd scarcely aged over the last decade, a little more gray in that jet black hair, the lines in her face a shade deeper. Her waking nightmare fifteen years ago transformed her from a youthful forty-two year-old to a middle-aged dowager overnight. Her face had marked time since then and only now matched her age.

The gaze of her dark brown eyes strafed me from head to foot. "Janelle, you look like crap."

No use denying the honest truth. I gestured toward a visitor's chair wedged in a corner. My desk was jammed into a third corner beside a tiny window with a view of the adjacent building. Still seated, I could turn from my desk to rifle through the filing cabinet that occupied the final corner.

In desperation, I could brew my own java in the geriatric Mr Coffee that sat on top of the filing cabinet.

Mrs Martinez ignored the chair, instead squeezing past me to examine the photo gallery I'd posted on the scrap of wall between desk and filing cabinet. A bittersweet reminder of my days with the San Francisco Police Department, the faces of my successes smiled at me from school photos framed in cheap plastic. Underneath the pictures of smiling boys and girls, their name and a date – when I'd found them and reunited them with their parents.

Not always unscarred, physically or mentally. But alive at least and back in loving arms.

Mrs Martinez zeroed in on the sweet young face of a dark-haired girl. Touched a finger to the tacky plastic frame.

"How is Teresa?" I asked.

"Married last year. Which you ought to know since I sent you an invitation."

Those canny eyes spotted the framed photo face down on my desk. Before I could scoop it into a drawer, she snatched it up, gazed down at the smiling towhead.

"Tommy Phillips," she said softly.

I wanted to shut my eyes, to forever banish that face from my consciousness. Why did I keep the damn photo any-way?

Mrs Martinez set Tommy's picture back on my desk and edged past me again. We seated ourselves and she set the folder in front of me.

No way I was stepping into that briar patch. I slid the folder toward her. "I handle domestic cases now, cheating spouses, that sort of thing."

She slid it back, opened it. The sweet face that smiled up at me from the folder could have been one of those hanging on my wall. "His name is Enrique Lopez," Mrs Martinez said. "And he's missing."

My fingers prickled with the urge to open the matches still cupped in my hand. "My office isn't equipped to handle the missing kids cases."

Mrs Martinez barreled on ahead. "Enrique's three and a half. One of my Head Start clients. His mother was an addict, coke at first, then meth. Clean off and on, but she was on the drugs more than off. Felicia tried, but she was stuck in the Tenderloin with all the other addicts on Jones Street."

"I know a great PI who can help you, Sheri will get her number for you." I said it loud enough for Sheri to hear me through the paper-thin dividing wall.

"About four months ago Felicia told me she'd be sending Enrique to her mother, that she'd found a rehab facility that would take her. She had it all worked out." Mrs Martinez finally took a breath. "A month later, I go down to her apartment to check on her."

Damn, this woman had *cojones*. I tended to avoid that part of the Tenderloin. If I had to traverse Jones or Eddy Street, it was in my car with doors locked, praying for green lights.

But Ruth Martinez had shown her mettle fifteen years ago when her seven year-old daughter, Teresa, was kidnapped. Tempered in that forge, she wouldn't back down from anything if it involved someone she cared about.

"I find out from one of her sleazy buddies Felicia died of a drug overdose a few weeks before. No sign of Enrique."

I blanked out the image of that small boy abandoned in his apartment, sobbing over his dead mother's body. "Social services got there before you. He's probably in foster care."

"Social services has no record of him. The landlord found everything still in the apartment – Enrique's clothes, his toys, his blankie. Vandals had set fire to the sofa, but all the boy's things were still there."

"Then he's safe with his grandma," I told her. "Give me her number. I'll call her for you."

"Don't you think I tried that?" Mrs Martinez speared me with that knife-sharp glare. "It was a cell number. It belongs to someone else now."

I forced myself to maintain eye contact as I shut Enrique's folder. "Sheri will give you Patti's number. She's a fantastic investigator. The best." I held the folder out to her.

She didn't take it. "I'd go see the grandmother myself if I could, but my dad's got the Alzheimer's now. I take care of him. I don't know when I'd be able to get to Greenville."

A chill burned down my spine, roiled my stomach. "Greenville."

"That's where the grandmother lived. It's up in the foothills," she told me helpfully. "Off Highway 50."

"I know where it is." Sixty miles west of South Lake Tahoe. A locale that featured prominently in my nightmares.

"The grandmother's last name is Lopez, same as her daughter. I don't have a first name." Mrs Martinez rooted around in her purse. "I won't be able to pay you until Friday, but I have an extra twenty I could..."

As if I'd take money from her. "Let me call Patti. She owes me a few favors. I'm sure she'll do some pro bono work for you."

"I don't know this Patti. I know you. You found my Teresa. You found those others." She gestured at my gallery.

She'd propped Tommy's photo up, angled toward me. He grinned, maybe one of the last happy moments of his short life.

"I haven't done that kind of work in years. Patti would be better at it."

"Please, Janelle." Her face softened into a vulnerability that frightened me even more than her unshakeable self-assurance. "I know he's not my responsibility anymore. But there was something about him – maybe because he reminds me of my Teresa, what happened to her. I just can't let him go."

The impossibility of saying no left me breathless. Yet saying yes brought its own agony. There was no way I could jump into another investigation of a missing child without revisiting the emotional landmine of my failure with Tommy.

"Let me make a few phone calls, poke around on the Web," I said finally, hedging. "See what I can find out." Who needed the legwork to Greenville with the internet close at hand?

As I walked Mrs Martinez out, her gratitude sent off knives of guilt into me – the freeform variety with no discernible source. I'd quit SFPD because a friendly-fire bullet in my left calf, and the surgeries that followed, had chained me permanently to a desk. But even before that rookie's dropped gun sent a hollow .22 through muscles, nerves and bones, Tommy's death had sent me on a downward spiral. I was spending far too much time contemplating the damage a Sig Sauer P229 could do to the back of my head.

I was arranging the particularly juicy shots of last night's freakshow when Sheri came in without bothering to knock. I kept my eyes glued to my computer screen. "Pretty busy here."

Young, black and drop-dead gorgeous, Sheri didn't suffer fools gladly. Scary smart and the daughter of a judge, she was only biding her time with me until she graduated law school at Hastings, when the world would kneel at her feet.

Sheri loitering in my doorway like a supplicant didn't auger well. I tried to keep my focus on my laptop display, but with a six-foot-one goddess looming over me, my attention finally strayed.

"What?" I asked, one hand still on the keyboard.

"You're going to track down that kid for Mrs Martinez?"

"Just making a few phone calls." Although I'd already compiled a mental list of databases I'd search and the connections at Social Services I'd tap.

"What about Mrs Madison?"

My brain chugged along for several moments trying to recall which client she was. The wife of the guy who dated cheerleaders? Or the one whose husband had absconded with his secretary and all the marital assets?

Sheri's glower finally jiggled the right brain cells. "Your mother's friend," I said.

"You passed her off to Patti two months ago. Didn't want to be bothered investigating it yourself." Sheri drew herself up, growing an inch in her Prada flats. "James is still missing."

I remembered Glenda Madison now – a petite black woman in her late thirties. A teacher at the middle school where Sheri's mother was principal.

"If Patti came up empty, there probably isn't much I can do."

"Just talk to her again. Maybe there's something Patti missed."

A burning erupted in my gut, crawled its way up my throat. "You know damn well why I can't do that."

But Sheri had little patience for my ugly history and nasty scars, emotional or otherwise. "It's been six years, Janelle. It's time you stopped treating that dead little boy like a damn albatross around your neck."

That's what a college education gets you, a snotty attitude and Samuel Taylor Coleridge references. Even though she was right about Tommy, that wasn't why I considered giving in. Sheri, once she sank her teeth into something, had more perseverance than a pit bull. If I said no now, it wouldn't be the end of it.

"Can she come by late this afternoon?" I asked. "I should get back from the Inman surveillance by four."

I'd like to say Sheri skipped off, happy as a clam that I'd seen the light. But she still eyed me with suspicion. "She'll be here."

The surveillance went as well as could be expected. I wasn't made by the target, I got plenty of photos and only had to limp along on my gimpy leg two blocks to and from the BART transit station. I was downloading photos of Mr Inman feeling up the Other Woman when Sheri announced the arrival of Mrs Madison.

She was well dressed in a decent quality, but not expensive suit, her hair soft and feminine around her dark face. She toted a large, practical handbag with a manila envelope peeking out.

She shook my hand. "I'm Glenda Madison. We spoke a while ago about my son, James."

I gestured her toward the guest chair. "How long has he been missing now?"

She took the envelope from her purse, then seated herself. "Since December 29th."

Three months ago. A stone cold trail. "If Patti couldn't help you, I'm not sure what I can do."

"The police won't do anything. They say he's a runaway."

And he probably was. "Tell me again what happened."

Mrs Madison clutched the envelope to her middle. "He was having a hard patch with his stepfather and they weren't getting along. They fought over a New Year's Eve party James wanted to attend. My husband lost his temper and James ran out of the house."

Tears shone in her dark eyes, but she didn't let them fall. "He was last seen at an Arco station in Emeryville." She took in a shaky breath. "It was the middle of the day, so I thought he'd be okay. That he'd come back when he cooled off."

"You have to understand, as long as it's been, there's probably not much I can do."

Before I could stop her, she spilled the contents of the manila envelope on my desk. She pointed to the top photo. "This is James's first baby picture."

I stared for a moment at the scrunch-faced infant in a hospital cap. "Mrs Madison..."

Setting aside the baby picture, she indicated the next in the stack. "Here's James at his first birthday party." Whipped cream frosting smeared across a grinning toddler face. "Here's his kindergarten picture." Tossing that on top of the first two, then held out a folded crayon-scrawled piece of construction paper. "That's his first Mother's Day card."

As her hand trembled, glitter floated from the construction paper onto my desk. She carefully slipped the keepsake back in the manila envelope and held out two small plastic bags. "Here's the first tooth he lost. That's hair from his first haircut."

I stared at the white enamel fragment and the curls of black hair. Sweet baby James smiled up at me from my desk.

She put away the artifacts of James's babyhood. "He's eleven years old and an A student in school." She handed over a report card, followed by an eight-by-ten of a grinning boy with his mother's eyes.

"The police won't do anything," she repeated. "No one else cares. Even my own husband thinks he's dead."

She wouldn't want to hear the truth, but I had to deliver it anyway. "You might have to accept that he is, Mrs Madison. A kid like him, unprepared for life on the streets, it's a reasonable conclusion."

Her fingers crumpled the edges of the envelope. "But Sheri says you found so many children." She glanced up at my photo gallery. "All those kids. She said if anyone could find my James, you could."

I contemplated all the ways I would torture Sheri before I killed her. I had no magic bullet to finding lost kids. It took time and damn hard work, the kind of energy already expended by Patti and the police. To say no would crush Mrs Madison; to say yes would fill her full of cruel hope.

But her silent plea stabbed me more deeply than the final cut to Tommy's small chest. I would hate myself later – hell, I already hated myself – but I nodded. "Let me see what I can do."

The tears did spill from her eyes then, despite the tremulous smile on her face. I closed my ears to her thank yous as I rose to escort her from my office, focusing instead on the slash of pain in my calf.

Mrs Madison let me keep the photos – scanned copies of the originals. I stuffed them into Enrique's file folder, then dropped into my chair, slapping shut the lid of my laptop. Sheri still lurked in the outer office, but I didn't give a damn. I grabbed a fresh box of matches from my drawer – I'd gone through the others riding BART to my surveillance – and dumped them on my desk.

The temptation to light them all at once surged through me, never mind the tinderbox status of the rattletrap building I leased space in. I hadn't given in to that impulse since my teen years, had grown a little maturity along the way. And with Sheri only feet away, I would have to save my other, more perverse habit for later.

I picked up a match and with a deft twist of the wrist snapped off the head. The sin of cowardice. I still lived in terror of the evils from my childhood, even though my own personal monster was dead.

I set the head to my right, the stick to my left, and picked up another. Snap. The sin of guilt. When I lacked the courage to do, I justified my inactivity with remorse. All these years chasing philandering husbands when I could have saved lives.

Snap. The sin of despair. I clung to blackness the way others clung to faith. Because it was easier than to hope.

I went through the entire box of thirty-two. When I exhausted my transgressions, I continued to decapitate matches until all the blue and red heads sat stacked in their neat pile. I tossed the sticks in the trash and crumpled the heads in a tissue. I'd drop them in the toilet on my way out.

I was nothing if not a sucker for empty ritual.

That night I holed up in my tidy studio apartment off Mission Street, lining up burnt matches like miniature firewood on the coffee table. New red marks joined the dozens of others dotting my arms from wrist to elbow, one for each burnt match.

I'd just struck another when the phone rang. I blew out the flame and grabbed the portable. Didn't recognize the caller ID. "Yeah?"

"This is Mrs Madison." I heard the excitement in her soft voice. "I have a lead."

A faint adrenaline edge from my recent catharsis lingered, befuddling my brain. "A lead for what?"

"Someone thinks they saw him. Saw James."

I'd done nothing since this afternoon, not so much as a Google search for James Madison. Guilt had me itching for another match. I nudged the coffee table farther away. "Tell me."

"I got a call," she said. "Friend of a friend. Her daughter works at a McDonald's near Greenville. That's about thirty miles east—"

"I know where Greenville is." Damn, what was this? Old home week for all my personal ghouls? "When was this?"

"Right after James disappeared. Three months ago."

A damn long time. "How sure is this girl that it was James?"

"She seemed sure." Now doubt seeped into her tone. "Could James be in Greenville?"

"He could be anywhere." Or nowhere. Dead like her husband said.

"A black kid in South San Francisco wouldn't stick out," she pointed out, "but Greenville's as white as Beverly Hills. If he's there, someone's seen him, noticed him."

I couldn't deny that. Greenville's minority population consisted of a few enclaves of Mexican immigrants who worked the orchards and vineyards and the handful of upper-middle class Asians and African-American transplants from the Bay Area.

"What if you went up there?" she asked.

"I have a business to run, Mrs Madison." Even as I said it, I didn't give a damn about whatever miscreant spouse I was scheduled to chase that week. The dual link between James and Enrique intrigued me, made me want to put the pieces together. Even if it meant returning to Greenville.

Fending off a sense of doom, I told her, "I could probably go over there for the day."

My stomach clenched at her profuse thanks. I'd likely be destroying that happiness soon enough. Before she signed off, she gave me the girl's name – Emma – and her cell number.

Since Sheri had delivered this problem to me, I had no qualms about calling her this late at home. "What have I got tomorrow?" I asked without preamble, then waited while she fumbled for her iPhone.

"The Billings surveillance, then you're meeting with Mrs Spitzer."

I picked up a matchstick, jamming it in my mouth instead of lighting it. "Try to reschedule Mrs Spitzer. Call Patti and see if she has someone to cover for me on the surveillance."

"Should I say thank you?"

"You damn well shouldn't," I told her. "This will probably end badly."

If not for Mrs Madison, then certainly for me.

CHAPTER 2

James scrunched deeper into the corner of the basement, the cinderblock cool against his back, the thin mattress barely padding his butt against the concrete floor. The candle he held tight in both hands had burned within an inch of the bottom. The heat from the flame wasn't quite hot enough yet to burn him, but the melted wax was. If he wasn't quick enough to tip the candle when the wax spilled over, he'd end up with blisters again.

Like he had the first time Mama had made him hold a lit candle. That had been before he'd learned it was best not to fight Mama, best to let her do exactly what she wanted.

The day she'd taken him, they'd driven for what seemed like forever until they were far away from the city. After bouncing around on an old dirt road in the middle of nowhere, Daddy had stopped the car and told him they had to walk the rest of the way to the cabin.

James knew once they left the road, he might never find his way out again. So he'd tried to escape, taking off into the trees, running as hard as he could. Mama had caught him, then hit him so hard, it had knocked him out. He woke up in the basement the next morning. Soon after, Mama brought the candle.

She'd wrapped his fingers around it and lit it, then sat on the stairs watching him. She never moved, even when the baby cried, even when Sean tried to climb in her lap.

He remembered everything about that first time – the nasty smell of the basement, the way the window up near the ceiling hardly let in any light. How hot the drops of wax had felt on his fingers. When the candle had burned half-way down, Mama finally blew it out. The wax had only dripped on James's fingers twice before he figured out how to tip the candle.

He tried hard to be good so Mama wouldn't get out the candle again. But it seemed he always needed punishment, because he hadn't changed the baby's diaper when she needed it or because Sean wet his pants during the night. Other times, like now, Mama made him do it just to make him stronger, better able to fight the sin. And she let the flame burn lower each time before she blew it out.

He didn't know what time it was. Night-time, but not too late, since Mama was still here. The candle's glow lit enough of the darkness so he could make out the baby in the playpen on the other side of the basement. He thought she was sleeping, but sometimes Lydia would just lie there, her thumb in her mouth, awake and staring at him.

Mama was on the stairs. He couldn't see her, but he knew she was there. Sometimes, the candlelight caught her eyes as she stared at him.

The candle was nearly to his fingers. Melting wax dripped down and onto his skin before he could tip it away. Tears filled his eyes from the pain.

He tried to be quiet, to endure the pain. But the words slipped out. "I want to go home."

He held his breath, waiting for Mama's wrath. But she didn't speak, didn't move. Her inaction made him brave. "I won't tell anyone if you let me go home now."

Still no response from Mama. Was she still there? Had she somehow crept up the stairs without him hearing her? The door was noisy, but maybe she'd found a way to open and close it without making a sound.

"I don't want to do this anymore!" he called into the darkness. He blew on the flame and it went out. The tip glowed a moment more, smoke drifting from it, then the room went black.

James had only an instant of joy before the slap of Mama's feet across the concrete floor sent terror crashing down on him. She grabbed his ankles, yanking him flat on the mattress, his head banging against the cinderblock wall as he went down. Her hand on his chest made it hard to breathe.

"I'm sorry, Mama. I'm sorry," he gasped out.

He thought he'd die right there. Mama's rage burned him like a white-hot flame.

But after what seemed like forever, Mama let him go. She fumbled around for something, then the bright flame of Mama's lighter blinded him in the darkness. She lit the candle in her hand, watched its flame for a moment.

Then she wrapped his fingers around it and returned to the stairs.

CHAPTER 3

Thursday morning, with the decks finally cleared for a day away, I went into the office to tie up a last few loose ends. I wasn't in a rush to get an early start. My meeting with the girl at McDonald's wasn't until one, but I wouldn't be lollygagging either, not with Sheri glowering at me and checking her watch every two minutes. I's dotted and T's crossed, I left at ten, stopping in Emeryville on the other side of the Bay Bridge.

As expected, I didn't learn much at the Arco. Rodney, the greasy-haired attendant, vaguely remembered James coming in for a candy bar around noon on December 29th. Rodney saw him eating the candy bar over by the pumps one minute; the next, James had vanished. I left my card with a request that he call if he thought of anything else.

Back on the road with a coffee refill and a fat-laden cinnamon roll, I hit the Yolo Causeway east of Sacramento around 11.30, then stopped in Rancho Cordova for lunch. After the cinnamon roll, I didn't have much of an appetite for the coffee shop burger and fries I ordered, although the three glasses of Coke I downed polished my caffeine edge nicely.

The Micky D's where Emma worked was another half hour up Highway 50, ten miles southwest of Greenville. I'd called her last night to arrange our little gab fest, the crack of her chewing gum pinging in my ear with every other word. Since it was her spring vacation, she was working the day shift and would take her break around one.

My mental picture of sixteen year-old Emma proved accurate – spiky black hair, seven earrings lined up along the outer edge of her left ear, only two in her right. I saw the faint mark of a brow and lip piercing, but apparently Emma had made some effort to uphold the McDonald's image by leaving those adornments at home. She'd covered most of the tattoo on her neck with a T-shirt under her uniform shirt.

A light drizzle had started up as we stepped outside the restaurant, the parking lot misted with moisture. I would have suggested we sit in my car, but I saw that pack of cigs in her hand. No way was I sullying my upholstery with tar and nicotine. Not to mention that temptation to brush against that searing heat in the close quarters of my Escort.

Instead we sat on the edge of a planter spilling over with impatiens and pansies. The building's overhang did a half-assed job of keeping us dry.

Her cigarette lit and dangling from her right hand, Emma took a look at James's photo. "Yeah, that's him. They were calling him Junior though, not James."

"Then how do you know for sure it was him?"

Emma studied the photo again. "I'm ninety-nine percent sure. Thing is, it was weird seeing a black kid with a white family. He stood out. Kinda stuck in my mind."

"So what did you see?" I took a notepad from my pocket.

"I was taking a smoke break, you know? We get ten whole minutes. Big deal." She took a long drag, then blew smoke from the side of her mouth, away from me. "I saw the whole thing."

"Saw what?"

"There was like, a fight or something."

"James was fighting?"

She flicked an ash. "Well, he like, got out of the car, started to walk away."

"What kind of car?" I asked.

"I don't know. Maybe a Honda. Dark. It had four doors, cuz the kid got out of the back seat. Anyway a lady in the car yelled, told him to come back."

"What did she look like?"

"Couldn't see her. Just heard her hollering. Mostly I saw the guy. He was older, like your age."

I wrote, white male, late-thirties. "Describe him."

"Kind of like... I don't know." She stared at the burning tip of her cigarette for inspiration. "George Clooney in that brother movie. The one he sang in."

I had to scratch my head over that one. *Oh Brother, Where Art Thou?*"

"Right. The guy had long raggedy hair and beard. I didn't like that movie. Too weird." She rubbed the empty hole of her lip piercing.

"About how tall, do you think? Dark or light hair?"

"Kind of average." She shrugged and the two-inch long pendant hanging from her right ear swayed. "Brown hair, brown eyes."

"But you didn't see the woman."

Down to the filter, she lit another cigarette with the butt of the first. "She never got out of the car."

"What did the bearded guy do when James took off?"

"He goes and talks to the kid." She ground the spent cig into the dirt of the planter.

"Did James get back in the car?"

"Didn't look too happy, but he did."

I fished Enrique's photo out of my pocket, shielded it from the drizzle as I showed it to her. "I don't suppose he was with them." It wasn't even a long shot. It was mere whimsy. But as long as I was here...

Emma took a look. "Nah. Just the baby the guy had."

"He had a baby?"

"Yeah. Like, I don't know, eight, nine months old. The baby was black, too."

I didn't know what to make of that little oddity. Was the baby adopted and they snatched James to give her an older brother? That was just plain goofy. "You're sure they were headed to Greenville?"

"Heard the lady ask the scruffy guy how much farther it was." She pinched the end of her half-smoked cigarette. "Oh, yeah. One more thing. It was beyond strange."

"What's that?"

"As they pulled out, I saw fire in the back seat."

A tremor shivered down my spine. "The car was on fire?"

She shook her head. "Just a flame. Like a lighter or candle or something."

"Could the lady have been lighting a cigarette?"

"If she was, it took her an effing long time. I could see the flame burning all through the parking lot. And they drove slow." She got to her feet. "I gotta go."

I dug a twenty from my pocket, handed it over. "Thanks."

"Hey, anytime." Emma grinned as she stuffed the money down her bra. There wasn't a whole lot there to hold it in place.

I climbed back into the Escort, relieved to be out of the wet, and grabbed my cell. As I punched in my office number, I tried to ignore the sense of impending doom. "Sheri? I need you to check on any missing six- to ten-month olds in the Bay Area and greater Sacramento area. African-American."

"Is this where I talk you down from the ledge?"

"Just do it." I chewed on the inside of my mouth, too damn intrigued by the puzzle Emma had laid out for me. I pressed a thumb to the bridge of my nose. "Don't give me any crap," I said preemptively.

"What?"

"Get me a room in Greenville. The Gold Rush Inn isn't a complete dump."

"What happened to just one day?" She was laughing at me. Silently. I could sense it.

"The day's half over. I need a little more time."

I hung up before she started snickering, then switched off the phone and tossed it back on the seat. Besides the emergency mini-toiletries bag I kept in the trunk, there was a plastic Safeway bag stuffed with old T-shirts I'd planned to take to the thrift store. They were stained and full of holes, but there might be one decent enough to wear tomorrow. I could rinse my unmentionables in the bathroom sink.

Done ruminating on my wardrobe, I twisted the key in the ignition and backed away from the Golden Arches. As I drove back onto eastbound Highway 50, I could feel Greenville sucking at me like some evil Klingon tractor beam. With any luck I'd still be in one piece when the old hometown spit me out again.

I'd expected the Sacramento Valley suburban sprawl would have spread to Greenville in the twenty years since I'd escaped. It had nibbled at the edges a bit, creeping up the foothills starting at the western edge of the county, filling the empty rolling hills between oak trees. But the cookie-cutter housing developments with inspiring names like Valle Verde Vista and Sunset Equestrian Ranch petered out at about the 2000-foot elevation mark. Nothing competed for the space between oaks except a few scrub pines, some redbud and manzanita and the occasional rustic log home.

Oddly, Tommy receded in my mind not long after I'd crossed the Sac County line into Greenville County. Maybe he'd been elbowed out by the innumerable other ghosts that haunted my psyche now that I was on home turf. Knowing what kind of dark memories lurked deep in my brain cells, I wasn't sure Tommy's absence was a good thing.

I avoided Main Street once I'd passed into Greenville city limits, unwilling for the moment to confront that blast from the past. Instead I took the back road to the Greenville County Sheriff's Office, a familiar track from days of old when Sheriff Kelsey caught me breaking windows or committing other minor acts of chicanery.

As I pulled into the parking lot, my ruined calf muscles sent a warning shot across the bow. Long car trips wreaked havoc with my leg, set off breath-stealing spasms. The dull ache I felt when I swung my foot to the pavement was only a precursor to the agony I'd feel when I tried to straighten and stand.

Hooking my fingers over the car door, I pushed myself up with my good leg and gritted my teeth as I unbent my left knee. I stood there, eyes shut as my knee throbbed, praying no one was watching. When the pain receded from excruciating to bearable, I shut the car door and made my way across the parking lot, pretending I wasn't sweating from every pore.

Although the low-slung brick building housing the county sheriff's office hadn't changed a whit on the outside, it looked like the interior had been spruced up with another coat of beige paint. The chipped Formica reception desk in the lobby looked like the same one Miss Gladys Woodward had hunched over in my wild adolescence. Since Miss Woodward had been requisitioned from the same era as the desk, I half-expected she'd still be there, her pruney face even more convoluted than it had been two decades ago.

But instead, a young woman with a bad-hair-day coif smiled as I approached. "Can I help you?"

"Where's Miss Woodward?" I looked around. Maybe they had her preserved in alcohol somewhere.

"I'm afraid she's passed on." Her smile faded for an appropriate moment, then she turned up the wattage again. "How can I help you?"

Julie Sweetzer, her name tag read, her badly fitting red and white striped shirt telling me she was a civilian. An evil impulse in my brain immediately labeled her Miss Sweet-as-pie.

"Is Deputy Ken Heinz in?"

"It's *Sheriff* Heinz." She looked offended in Ken's stead. "I'm afraid he's out. Can I take a message?"

"Where is he?" I looked past Miss Sweet-as-pie to where a female deputy sat behind a desk, a metal detector wand at the ready. Homeland security had even reached its tentacles here to Greenville.

She kept that smile fixed on her face. "I'm not at liberty to divulge Sheriff Heinz's current location. But I'd be glad to take a message," she told me cheerily.

I rarely let myself be thwarted by cheer. I leaned close to the reception desk and kept my voice low. "I'm sure you know Sheriff Heinz was with the San Francisco Police Department." She nodded. "He's my former partner. I drove over from San Francisco to discuss a case with him."

"You're a police officer?"

I always try to avoid the direct lie. "I really could use Ken's input on this case."

She stared at me, washed out blue eyes looking deep into my soul. She'd have a hard time finding one.

"He's at the Jansen place." She pulled a sticky pad over and scribbled an address. "You take Rock Creek Road out past County Line–"

I snatched the slip of paper from her. "I know where the Jansen place is." Although since Bart Jansen had been older than dirt when I left Greenville, I doubted he was still in residence.

By continuing on the access road out of the sheriff's headquarters, I sidestepped Main Street again as I cut over to Rock Creek. I caught a glimpse of Holy Rock Baptist church, its steeple still the highest structure in downtown Greenville. I had only the dimmest memories of walking into that church with my mother, sitting in a well worn Gold Rush era pew and admiring the particularly gory stained glass rendition of the crucifixion over the altar.

The Jansen place was three or four miles out of town, back in off Rock Creek a good mile or so. The fact that I could picture nearly every winding turn along the way before I hit it wasn't comforting. Two decades should have obliterated the familiarity.

Anticipation of my upcoming reunion with Ken added to the anxiety stewing inside me. He'd been the perfect partner, damn near reading my mind when we were investigating a scene or interrogating a suspect. We could still be mowing down evil-doers in San Francisco if I hadn't stepped over the line with him.

I nearly missed the turn into the Jansen's driveway, despite the massive stone and concrete mailbox that had been installed there. Old Mr Jansen's mailbox had been standard gray metal on a four-by-four; this new one was five feet tall and topped with the name *Markowitz* in six-inch-tall letters. Old Mr Jansen was used to finding his mailbox broken off at the base Sunday mornings after young Greenville miscreants such as myself cavorted through the countryside on Saturday nights with baseball bats in search of mailboxes to flatten. He had a stock of four-by-fours in his shed, ready to repair the damage.

Local juvenile delinquents wouldn't put a dent in the Markowitz mailbox with anything short of dynamite. I guess big city transplants have no sense of humor.

The Markowitzes had also paved old Mr Jansen's pothole pitted gravel drive, smoothed it out with a sheet of high-dollar asphalt. It would make the trek up the driveway less messy when the winter rains hit, but considering the lack of a culvert at the halfway point where heavy storms always laid a ribbon of rushing water, the drive would be impassable with the first winter deluge.

I pulled around the last turn into a clearing and my heart went pit-a-pat at my first view of two pretty red fire engines.

Parked alongside were a fire truck, fire department SUV and an EMT rig. They'd apparently already quenched the blaze, leaving in black sodden ruin an out structure too big to be a shed, too small to be a barn. A detached garage maybe, a guess that was confirmed by a glimpse of what appeared to be the skeleton of a car under the collapsed roof.

The two-story behemoth that had replaced Jansen's tidy frame house seemed untouched by flame. Lucky Mr Markowitz. As I did a U-turn in the driveway, parking my car off to the side to give clearance for the fire rigs, the EMT pulled out, no sirens, no lights. Apparently no injuries for the Markowitzes either, another stroke of good fortune.

I drew my creaky body from the Escort, a matchstick in my mouth to work off some of my nervous energy. As I tried to work some flexibility into my calf, I spotted a Crown Vic and Ford Explorer, both emblazoned with the Greenville County Sheriff emblem, parked over by the house. The fire companies were stowing their hose back in their engines, the captain chatting with a kid way too young to be wearing a deputy's uniform. If Ken was here, I didn't see him.

A skinny, prematurely bald guy that was no doubt Mr Markowitz emerged from the house. A little girl, maybe six, trailed behind her father, clutching a teddy bear. Markowitz looked around him in agitation, then started toward the burned out garage.

I couldn't help myself, my attention strayed to the ragged, charred edges of unburned siding. In my twisted mind, the only thing more enthralling than fire was its aftermath. It had taken a heap of self-discipline over the years to resist the urge to move into arson investigation. Nevertheless, I'd dabbled in it on an amateur basis over the years, buying books off Amazon, all but drooling over the photographs.

Then when someone torched the Sudsy Clean Laundromat across the street from my apartment, I'd watched avidly behind the limits of the crime tape. Once the arson investigators finished their work, I'd volunteered to help the Nguyens clean up the mess. I didn't even bother to tell myself I was only being neighborly. I knew what impulse sent me slogging through that sodden, blackened mess.

But unlike the Nguyens's Laundromat, where much of the rubble had already been cleared away before I could get my mitts on it, the fire in the Markowitz's garage was newly extinguished. It would still hold a fascinating treasure trove of clues I itched to decipher.

Before I could take a step toward the ruins, Ken rounded the front of the garage, coming into view. And I completely forgot about the fire.

I had maybe a thirty second grace period before Ken noticed me. Time enough to take in the fact that in three years, he really hadn't changed much. He'd let the buzz cut from his SFPD days grow out, his sandy hair now long enough to curl behind his ears. The khaki shirt didn't fit as well as the blues we wore in San Francisco during our beat days, but even at 45, he looked damned good.

When he first saw me, his gaze rolled right past without recognition. Then he lasered back on me, something flickering in his face he would have killed me for if he'd known I'd seen it. An instant later, that light doused and I saw nothing but disinterest in those blue eyes.

He sidestepped Mr Markowitz and headed toward the Explorer. The riled-up homeowner started to follow, then stopped to answer the summons of his cell phone.

I moved on an intercept course, more unsettled by Ken's dismissiveness than I wanted to admit. I pasted a cheery grin on my face. "Ken!"

As he turned toward me, a twitch in his jaw told me his self-control wasn't quite as all-encompassing as he might want me to think. "Did you make a wrong turn somewhere?"

"Good to see you, too." I tapped the sheriff's badge on his chest. "So you're already running the place. What happened to Sheriff Kelsey?"

"Heart attack."

"Dead?"

"Retired."

"Too bad." There was no love lost between Kelsey and me. He and dear old Dad had been thick as thieves way back when, drinking buddies, hunting and fishing partners. Kelsey knew what my father was doing to me, had seen the marks on my arms. At best, he pretended not to notice; at worst, he thought I must have deserved the punishment.

Kid Deputy made his way over to us, oblivious to Ken's and my little drama. He gave me a puppy dog smile. "This a friend of yours, sheriff?"

"Janelle Watkins," Ken said, the words dragged out of him. "My former partner at SFPD."

Kid Deputy thrust out a hand. "I'm Alex Farrell."

I shook his hand, keeping my attention on Ken. "Pleased to meet you."

Alex pointed at the matchstick I was chewing to shreds. "You just quit smoking or something?"

I pulled it from my mouth and shoved it in my pocket. "Or something."

He grinned at his boss. "Didn't she do profiles for SFPD? Maybe she could do one for us on our arsonist."

"How do you know it was arson?" I asked. "Maybe Mr Markowitz was cooking meth in his garage."

"Nah. It was arson," Kid Deputy told me. "We've had a string of them. I bet you could figure out who."

I risked a glance at Ken. He stared off into the middle distance, his jaw working.

"I don't profile anymore," I told Alex. "I'm a private investigator."

Alex's radio squawked and he excused himself, moving to the far side of the Explorer. Ken bent his head, lowered his voice. "We had an agreement."

I remembered all too clearly when it had been struck, the verbal missiles we'd lobbed at one another. "It's been three years, Ken."

"'Stay the hell out of my life' didn't have an expiration date."

Guilt slashed me at the raw expression of pain on his face. "Can't an old friend drop by to say hello?"

"We're not friends, Janelle. Not since that night, anyway."

Our first night, I wondered? Or the final night, when the truth blew up in all our faces? Or maybe the night a week later, when I abandoned all shame and called him, but Tara picked up the phone instead? He might not even know about that night.

I realized Alex had returned. He may not have heard our exchange, but he had to feel the weight of the rough silence between Ken and me. In typical small-town fashion, he no doubt hankered for all the details. I wasn't about to add any fuel to that fascination.

I was almost relieved to see Markowitz hot-footing it over to us, oblivious to his daughter still dogging his heels. As she trotted along behind him, she used the teddy to swipe at the tears running down her face.

Markowitz blustered up to Ken. "I need a police report. The insurance company won't process my claim without it."

Ken shifted his attention to Markowitz. "I told you before, it'll take a few weeks."

"That was a cherry ragtop '65 Mustang," Markowitz said. "I just had it transported up from LA."

"Tough luck," I told him, although I couldn't muster a whole lot of sympathy for a man who was as negligent of his kid as this one seemed to be. "What's the problem with your daughter? Was the car a favorite of hers?"

"Her cat was locked in the garage when it burned. I told her I'd get her another one," he said with a dismissive shrug. "She's just a crybaby."

I took a deep breath, squelching a number of creative possibilities that would make this man cry. "You, on the other hand, are exhibiting tremendous bravery in the face of such a catastrophic loss."

Markowitz stared at me, wheels turning as if he was trying to figure out if I'd just insulted him. He sneered at Ken. "Get me that police report. ASAP." He stomped off back toward his house.

"Real neighborly guy," I commented. "I can see why you prefer Greenville over the city."

"Sheriff tells me you're from here," Alex said. "Was Clement Watkins your daddy?"

I forced myself to count to five so I wouldn't chomp Alex's head off at the shoulders. Not his fault he'd innocently conjured the Source of All That Is Evil. "Yes."

Ken knew a little bit about my "daddy". "What was the call?" he asked Alex.

"Ruckus at the high school."

Ken gave Alex a nudge toward the Crown Vic. "Get over there."

Before Kid Deputy folded his lanky body back into the car, he grinned at me. "How long are you here for?"

"Just the night. I'll be driving home in the morning."

"See you later, then." He dropped into his patrol car and cranked the engine, then roared out with youthful enthusiasm.

"You have a reason for being here?" Ken asked. "Besides stirring up the Greenville rumor mill?"

I should have whipped James and Enrique's photos from my back pocket, asked my questions of Ken, then continued on my merry way. But here I was, just steps from a freshly suppressed fire scene, a likely arson. This wasn't photos from a book; it was the real thing.

My feet moved of their own accord toward the garage. Ken dogged my steps. "That's a possible crime scene, Janelle. You need to keep the hell away."

"I'll stay on the perimeter," I told him, still limping toward temptation. "I just want a closer look."

Except he knew about my history with fire. "I'm not letting you feed your damn compulsions, Janelle."

"It's not that." I stopped and turned, forcing myself to meet his skepticism eye to eye. As if that would make my lie less despicable. "I have the chance to pick up a couple of new clients if I get some background in arson. You know fire investigation inside and out. Maybe you can give me a few tips."

Ken had worked arson with the state before he joined SFPD. He'd had a scientific instinct that made fire investigation an irresistible game. I hoped that drive to solve puzzles still lurked inside him. At the same time, I prayed he wouldn't be able to see through my bullshit.

He fixed me with his hard blue gaze and I knew he saw right through me. "You get that sick look on your face and I'm marching your ass out of here."

Shame burned in my gut. He'd caught me more than once burning myself, knew that look of blissful agony.

Leaving me feeling knee-high to a cockroach, he turned toward the burned out shell of the garage, giving the structure a wide berth. He greeted Ed, the fire investigator, as he came around the back of the garage with his camera. Ed was in turnout gear, including helmet and boots, and was starting his documentation of the fire by photographing the exterior.

We stopped on the far side of the garage, its wall burned down to blackened stubs of two-by-fours. The leaves of the oak tree overhanging the structure, usually bright green this time of year, had faded to brown from the fire's heat. From our vantage point, we could view the entire interior.

Seeing the destruction, familiar excitement squirmed inside me. I struggled to keep it from showing on my face. Watch Ed, I told myself. Focus on his process, not what the fire has done.

I narrowed my gaze on the investigator, imagined myself in his boots. He had to be careful not to contaminate the scene. Trace from outside the structure might confuse the investigation.

On the other hand, the amount of water dumped on the structure during suppression could wash away signs of ignition source or whatever accelerant might have been used. On top of that, a dozen firefighters likely had been tromping all through the garage. Their job was to knock down the fire, not preserve evidence for investigation. And after suppression came overhaul, where the firefighters moved or removed the contents of a structure to eliminate any hidden flames, glowing embers, or sparks to prevent the fire from rekindling.

All that aside, Ed would wash his boots before entering. Dawn dishwashing liquid was the only thing approved to clean equipment in California. He'd use a separate pair of latex gloves for each sample he took. He'd also sometimes sample where he entered and exited.

Ed had finished his photo circuit and started back toward his Expedition with the camera. I swept a hand toward the garage and asked Ken, "So what do you think happened?"

"What do you see?" Ken asked.

Everything I knew about incendiary fires, I'd learned in a book, so I had none of the practical knowledge that Ken had. I scanned the mess, tried to compare what I was seeing to the pictures from the books. "Everything inside's pretty evenly burned," I ventured.

"What about the interior walls, particularly down close to the floor?"

I scanned the sheetrock, soot-covered from the ragged upper edge to its junction with the concrete foundation. Rifling through my memory of the pages of *Kirk's Fire Investigation*, a light bulb went on. "If it's an accidental fire, you won't see fire damage clear down to the bottom of the interior wall. There'll be an unburned swath along the floor."

He nodded. "You see anything else?"

I compared the destruction on the nearest side to the less-scathed opposite wall. "I'd guess the fire started over here."

"Possible. But you don't want to start with assumptions."

Which I knew well enough from my work as a detective with SFPD. You start assuming things and you run the risk of trying to fit the facts to your theories instead of the other way around.

"It also may not be an incendiary fire at all," I said.

"Maybe not. Before you think seriously in that direction—"

"—you want to find at least three signs of arson," I finished.

Ed had entered the scene wearing latex gloves. With a trowel in one hand and a quart-sized paint can in the other, he moved through the debris, away from the location I'd guessed as the point of origin.

The point of origin might seem like the obvious place to start sampling, but I knew you generally started at the area of least fire damage. Then you work your way backwards from there.

Ed scooped up ash into the can and shut the lid, then scribbled on a tag he adhered to the can. He set the can down where he'd taken the sample, then stripped off his gloves and dropped them beside the can. He would set an identifying number beside each of his samples, then take a photo of the can, gloves and number.

"Could it have been an electrical fire?" I asked as Ed moved off to his next sampling spot.

"You heard Markowitz," Ken said. "He wouldn't trust his baby to anything but the best. It was a brand new garage. All the electrical was pristine and to code."

"Could the bastard have torched it himself for insurance?"

"Possible. But as pissed as he is, I doubt it. Although..." Ken rubbed his chin, a gesture I remembered from our time together. I always teased him that that was the way he activated his brain. "Markowitz is a recent divorcee. Nasty custody dispute."

"So this could be the ex-wife's revenge."

Ken's gaze slid over towards me. "She'd know where to stick the knife."

Like I did. The message seemed to dangle in the air between us. He turned away, retracing our path around the front of the garage. "If you have a reason for being here, get to it."

I hurried after him the best I could, limping along on the uneven ground. "I just had a couple of questions."

As I caught up with him at the Explorer, I reached in my back pocket for the photographs. He put out a hand to stop me. "This better not be about some damned wayward husband."

"It's not a divorce case."

"Cheating spouses hit a little too close to home."

"It's kids. Missing kids. Two boys."

There was a time, before we lost our grip on the grenade that destroyed our partnership, I would have had him hooked, just like that. He'd been even more of a sucker for the lost kids than I'd been. He'd actually had a heart, as opposed to the chip of ice lodged in my chest.

Considering I'd let my fixation with fire completely sidetrack my supposed goal here – discovering what had happened to James and Enrique – I had no right to judge Ken for his disinterest. Even still, seeing not even a flicker of reaction in his face surprised me.

He wrenched open the door to the Explorer. "Take it up with one of my deputies."

I wedged myself in front of him before he could climb into the Ford. "This is James Madison. Eleven years old. That's a pretty recent photo." I pulled out the other picture. "And this is Enrique Lopez. Three and a half. He was two here."

Ken shouldered me aside and slipped past me into his truck. "I have a half-dozen runaways of my own on the department bulletin board."

Blocking him from shutting the door, I shoved James's photo under Ken's nose. "Have you seen him in Greenville?"

He gave the picture a cursory glance before pushing it aside. "No."

I pushed it back in his face. "He's been gone three months. He was last seen on his way to Greenville."

"I haven't seen him, Janelle." He started the engine.

Still standing my ground beside the open door, I switched to the other photo. "How about him?"

Ken barely looked at it. "Nope."

"His druggie mother supposedly sent him here to live with his grandmother. A Mrs Lopez."

"Damned common name." He tried to reach the door handle.

I planted my butt in the way. "A town this small, you know everyone. Is there a Mrs Lopez in Greenville who might be the boy's grandmother?"

"If I tell you, will you let me shut the damn door?"

"Yes." I didn't bother to cross my fingers.

He glanced down at the photo of Enrique. He was trying not to show it, but I could see that sweet baby face had tugged at him. "There was a Mrs Lopez living in the Stuarts's place. But she's gone."

"How long ago?"

"It's been three or four months. The Stuarts said they went to check on her when she was late with the rent and she'd cleared out. Their daughter lives in the house now." He reached for the handle again.

I kept to my post by the door. "Where'd Mrs Lopez go?"

Ken gave me a not so gentle tap with his elbow. "Out of Greenville, that's for sure."

"You don't know where?"

"I'm not the post office, Janelle." That elbow dug in a little deeper.

"Someone must know. A neighbor. Someone she went to church with."

"You know how it is around here. People pretty much keep to themselves."

I knew that all too well. "Did she have a child with her?"

"As far as I know, she lived alone."

He was really starting to piss me off, and not because of that elbow drilling into my ribs. There are barriers you put up in the City, self-defense against the crap you see there. This wasn't protective walls I was seeing in Ken, but the development of small-town mentality after only three years living in Greenville.

If he didn't actually see it happening he could ignore it. Sheriff Kelsey had been a master at closing his eyes to unpleasantness. I wouldn't have thought Ken would have fallen in that trap.

I leaned into the Explorer. "How would you know she lived alone? She could have kept a kid locked in the basement, could have beat him every night and you wouldn't know the difference."

Ken got the bulldog look I remembered from San Francisco. "If she'd had a boy living with her, I would have known."

I stuffed the photos back in my pocket. "Not much has changed here, has it?"

Ken angled from the Explorer. "What's that supposed to mean?"

"You and Sheriff Kelsey, I bet you're good buddies. I bet the pair of you yuk it up about wife-beating husbands who keep the little woman in line. Who pound their kids into a bloody pulp in the name of discipline."

Color purpled Ken's face. "Now wait just one damn minute–"

I flung an arm in his general direction. Left leg begging for mercy, I ran toward my car.

I don't know what I thought I'd accomplish by cranking the Escort's wimpy engine and tearing out of there. Just being in Greenville made me twitchy, and Ken's transformation into a Sheriff Kelsey clone just about put me over the edge.

I knew I wouldn't get very far. Ken's souped up Explorer could outrun my puny Escort without even trying. I'd just fishtailed onto the county road back toward town when he hit the siren. I kept going another half-mile, the wig-wags glaring red and blue in my rearview mirror. Not exactly a high-speed chase, since I barely broke fifty in the forty-five mph zone.

I wrenched the wheel right into the next turnout and killed the engine. I felt prickly all over, about ready to run screaming from the car and into the surrounding oaks and pines. With my luck I'd hit a patch of poison oak and be itching for real before the day was out.

Just to be perverse, I grabbed my registration from the glove box and tugged my license out as Ken came up alongside my car. I rolled down the window and held my documentation out to him as he leaned down.

"Put it away," he told me.

"I was speeding."

"I don't give a damn." He held out his hand. "Show me the pictures again."

I retrieved them from my back pocket. He took one in each hand and gave them a good long look. In the end, he shook his head. "If they've been here, I haven't seen them."

I took them back. "Thanks anyway."

"Follow me into town. Let me see what I can find on Mrs Lopez."

I wanted to say no just for spite, but that would have been stupid. "Sure. Thanks."

I watched him in the side-view mirror as he ambled on back to the Explorer. Allowed myself the briefest flashback of the first time we met, shaking his hand, feeling the spark.

Then I squelched the memory like I would a lit match, blowing it out, mentally grinding it into the dirt. I had to keep that flame dead cold, or it would burn me as surely as a glowing match tip.

CHAPTER 4

Rule number one of police work – never get naked with your partner. If that's not the number one rule, it should be, especially if said partner is married.

Ken Heinz and I ignored the physical signals zinging between us for the first four years of our partnership. At first we were too busy hating each other's guts as new partners. I thought I knew everything, had no respect for the eight years Ken had on me with the department. To Ken, I was not only an idiot, I was a dangerous idiot, too stupid to know when I was putting myself in peril. I didn't do much to change his mind about that during our time together, but I at least curbed the urge to display those self-destructive tendencies.

Once detestation segued into grudging acceptance, hormones started their ugly dance. The attraction blindsided me – I usually hooked up with men from the bottom of the barrel with souls as sick as mine. Ken was actually a pretty nice guy. But a *married* nice guy, which was probably what got my twisted psyche worked up.

I liked to tell myself it had just been physical between us. The sex *had* been phenomenal, even though it had only lasted a couple of months. But I would have laid down my life for that man, on and off the job. I couldn't say that about any of the sleazeballs I'd played mattress tag with in the years since Ken left.

For two months, the nightmares vanished. I put away the matches. The sounds and sights of fire engines barely raised an antenna. I let myself believe that Ken had healed me.

Then his wife Tara arrived home early from a trip to her mother's in Petaluma. And there we were, violating Ken's marital vows on the living room sofa.

After the disaster of that one desperate call to Ken, I shut him out. Barely spoke to him as we worked, avoided him completely during our off hours. The final blow, I requested a change of partner, taking on a rookie when I despised rookies. After three weeks of the cold shoulder from me, Ken had applied for a job with Greenville county sheriff's department. A month after that, he was gone, Tara with him.

I pulled into the sheriff's office parking lot the second time that day, still marveling at the novelty of driving up to the low, brick building voluntarily and in my own set of wheels. A refreshing change from two-plus decades ago, when my usual mode of transport was the back seat of the sheriff's car, with my wrists jammed behind me in cuffs.

Ken waited for me by the entrance, got to enjoy the sight of me grimacing as I unfolded my leg from the car, then hobbling along those first ten, twenty feet until the worst of the knots released. Considering the animosity he still harbored toward me, I'm sure he was enjoying every excruciating step I took.

He pulled the glass door open for me. "How's the leg?"

I sucked in a breath. "Functioning. Most days it doesn't hurt like hell." Except like now, when a white-hot knife blade was slashing its way through my calf as I followed him past the receptionist.

"I thought about calling you when I heard."

"Just as well you didn't. I wasn't in a frame of mind to talk to anyone." Besides which, his wife Tara was probably checking their phone records.

He waited while the deputy wanded me. The metal detector went wild when the young woman waved it over my left calf.

I hiked up my jeans to show her the scars. "Bionic leg," I explained. I had a card from my doctor I used when going through airport security, but with Ken's blessing I didn't need to produce it.

We continued on through a door labeled "No Admittance" and down a long hallway carpeted with mushroom gray indoor-outdoor. Ken's office was the last one on the left, his name on an engraved plastic placard by the door.

"I bought a card," he said. "Never sent it."

"I was pretty inundated with that crap." Not entirely a lie. The department sent me flowers and a single card signed by most of the detectives. At that point in my career, I'd alienated pretty much everyone in the squad.

He motioned me to a chair. "I was surprised to hear you quit."

I sank down on the molded plastic chair, barely holding back a moan of relief. "Being chained to a desk and shuffling paperwork was a real dream job, but it was time for the party to end."

I looked around at the cluttered space that passed for his office. The dimensions were barely bigger than the shoebox I worked in, and he'd managed to crowd in even more furniture. Besides the desk, piled high with reports and miscellaneous paperwork, he had a computer desk with a desktop model tucked beneath it, a printer/fax/scanner combo beside the monitor, twice as many file cabinets as I had, and a waist-high refrigerator with a microwave on top of it. The coffee maker sat on the microwave.

"All the luxuries," I noted.

"Some perks in being top dog."

An array of photos on the wall above the computer caught my eye. I recognized the smiling woman in the leftmost picture as his sister, her long blonde hair brushing the cheeks of the towhead baby girl on her lap. Next to that one, Ken's niece looked to be about six years old and his sister's smile wasn't quite so enthusiastic. The remaining three in the gallery featured the niece by herself, progressively older in soccer and baseball uniforms. The last photo was a school shot of a defiant adolescent.

As Ken moved toward his desk, I blocked him. "Something I need to say." I'd rehearsed on my way over here and had to get the words out before I wimped.

He eyed me suspiciously. "What?"

"I'm sorry."

He looked confused for a moment, then pushed past me to his chair. "I called on the way here. There was no forwarding address for Mrs Lopez at the post office."

"Let me finish. I screwed up your life. Your marriage. Was an asshole afterward."

"Have you been watching *Oprah*?" He pushed back in his chair as if he didn't like being so close to me. "Is this some kind of 12 Steps crap?"

"Can't a person just be sorry? If I hurt you–"

"I'd have to care about you to be hurt, Janelle."

That knocked the wind out of me, left me struggling to get my bearings again. Ken avoided my gaze, cutting me even more adrift.

"Anyway..." Damn it all, my voice was quivering. "Sorry."

Silence stretched until I thought its weight would crush me. I focused back on the lifeline of Mrs Lopez. "Was there any mail left in her box?"

Ken still wouldn't look at me. Anger warred with a nagging ache.

"You want me to take back the damn apology?" I asked him.

Finally he turned toward me. "I want you to drop it. I'd like it better if we'd never..." He shook his head. "Mrs Lopez didn't get her mail here in Greenville at all."

"Not even general delivery?"

"They had no record of it."

Was the woman hiding? With a daughter involved with drug dealers, maybe that was how she kept herself safe. "Would the Stuarts know where she went?"

"Maybe. They're in South America for most of April. Their son's on a mission in Peru."

I dug my fingers into the clot of pain in my calf. Better that than what I was feeling inside. "The neighbors?"

"The Stuart place is on ten acres at the end of a dirt road," he said. "The nearest neighbor is a quarter mile away. The only reason I remember Mrs Lopez at all is that she called about an intruder. Turned out a raccoon was digging through her trash."

A paranoid woman might interpret marauding forest creatures as a threat. "Could she have moved down into Sacramento?"

"She could have moved anywhere." He turned toward his computer and typed. I got to my feet stiffly to check out the display over his shoulder. "Over six hundred Lopezes in the Sacramento area."

Talk about chasing wild geese through haystacks. It would likely be fruitless, but I could have Sheri start down the Lopez listings, making calls in between legitimate work. It would serve her right for roping me into the search for James.

Hoping to narrow down the legions of Lopezes, I asked, "Would the Stuarts's daughter know Mrs Lopez's first name?"

"I can call and ask her." He flipped open a Greenville County phone book, then punched out a number on his desk phone. "Hey, Trish. It's Sheriff Heinz."

I only half-listened to the conversation as I took a closer look at the photos on his wall. Somewhere between that eleven year-old picture and the most recent, something had taken the smile off Ken's niece's face.

Ken hung up. "Trish never knew the woman. She'll ask her folks next time she calls them."

I nudged the soccer photo straighter. "Is that really Cassie? How'd she get so grown up?"

"She lives with me now."

"What happened to your sister?" For the life of me, I couldn't remember her name.

"Cassie got diagnosed with diabetes two years ago. Melinda... she's just not equipped. She asked me to take Cassie for a couple of months, then never came back to get her."

"Where's Melinda now?"

"LA, last I heard. She doesn't keep in touch."

That explained the anger in the thirteen year-old's eyes. Moms that didn't hang around. We had that in common.

Reading from the phone book, Ken scribbled on a piece of paper. "The Stuart place is out on Black Oak Road. Trish said you can drop by later today, but she doesn't think she'll be much help."

"I might be able to cross-correlate the former address. Use it to narrow down the Lopezes." That is, if Mrs Lopez used the address on another rental application. If she was running from someone or something, she might lie about a former residence to cover her tracks. "What about local sex offenders?"

With more and more laws in place preventing molesters from living near schools and parks, the sickos got forced out of congested urban areas and into rural towns like Greenville. Offenders could live on the fringes, out of sight. More insulated from the kind of degenerate worms that populated big cities, small town kids tended to be less wary, more vulnerable when a molester crept out of hiding to make contact.

"You already checked the Megan's database for local offenders?" Ken asked.

"Yeah. Are all four still in the area?"

"Two of them moved. I can take you out to talk to the other two." He typed at his keyboard and the printer spit out a sheet of paper.

"I can handle it." I tried to grab the paper.

He held it out of my reach. "My jurisdiction. You go with me."

"I already looked those names up on my own computer. No reason I can't go out on my own."

"But you won't. Because I'll be with you."

He didn't seem in a mood to argue. He walked out of his office without so much as a look over his shoulder to see if I was following. When he did check on me as he reached the end of the hall, he took in my slow progress as my leg refused to unknot and waited until I caught up.

"Need anything from your car?" he asked as we headed for the Explorer.

"Let me grab my computer bag."

After a trip to my Escort, I settled in the front seat of the Explorer with my laptop balanced on my knees. I hadn't entered my notes yet from my conversation with Emma at the Golden Arches. I could type what I knew into my database and keep my hands busy while we drove.

"Who first?" I asked. "Paul Beck or Chuck Pickford?"

Ken gunned out of the parking lot. "Paul Beck. He's farthest out, at the Pine Hill Mobile Home Park."

As I pulled out the laptop, I found a stash of matches in a side pocket. Figuring it was fate that had put them there, I fished one out and tucked it into the corner of my mouth.

Ken glanced at the matchstick then glued his eyes on the road ahead. When he didn't seem inclined to make further conversation, I waded into the minefield on my own.

"So how's Tara adjusting to country life?" I asked as I waited for the computer to boot.

I figured the man must have lockjaw, considering how stiff his face got. "She lasted a month. Moved to Reno to be near her folks."

That lent a new perspective on his reaction to my apology. I bent to my keyboard, and mumbled out, "Sorry to hear it."

He narrowed his gaze on me. "Are you?"

"It's not as if you and I were going anywhere." I put just the right cavalier tone in my voice.

"But we sure shot the hell out of my marriage." He might not have cared about me, but matrimony meant something to him.

Still, I had to wonder just how strong his marriage had been, considering everything Ken had done to fix his short-lived mistake. Privately, I doubted anything would have satisfied Tara.

As we climbed a bit into a more alpine elevation, the foothill oaks gave way to ponderosas and white fir. I rolled down a window, took in the fragrance of pine. For a long time, the slightest whiff of that thick scent in a car air freshener or kitchen cleaner and I'd be back in the cabin with my father.

I rolled up the window again, refocusing on what Emma had told me. "Pretty ironic. Of all the places you could have gone."

"I needed a change. So, what happened to your father?"

"I understand he left Greenville six or seven years ago. Died in his sleep a couple of years after that. A real shame." I banged a little harder on the keyboard. "He should have suffered."

As he slowed to turn left, he took in the display on my screen. It was the start page of ProSpy, the profiling software I'd used in days of yore. This version was souped up and far superior to what I'd used at SFPD, but familiar enough that Ken recognized it.

"I thought you weren't profiling missing kids anymore."

"ProSpy is useful for more than missing kids." Although despite keeping up with upgrades, I'd had no use for the software since I'd quit SFPD. "I'm just trying to get some information on James and Enrique."

"And just how's that different?"

I was saved from having to formulate an answer by our arrival at the mobile home park. I shut my laptop and slid it back into the black bag as we slowed for a speed bump just inside the entrance. It seemed far too idyllic a place for a molester to call home, with the tidy little mobile homes tucked between tall green pines.

Beck's place was in the back corner of the park, a single-wide crammed between two double-wides on a cul de sac. Unlike the well kept homes bookending it, Beck's mobile screamed neglect from its peeling exterior to its weedy little plot to the rusted out carport that ran alongside.

A rusted out *empty* carport. Ken parked across the driveway and we got out of the Explorer. "Is he at work?" I asked.

"He works nights at the Hangman's Tavern."

Ken climbed the stairs and pounded on the door. "Paul Beck! Open up, it's the sheriff."

The mailbox at the street was overflowing with junk mail. "Is he out of town? Or is he gone?"

Ken peered into the window. "If he moved, he left everything behind."

My hands in my back pockets, I perused the circulars and loan offers jutting from the mailbox. "Maybe because he had something that meant more to him than his crappy furniture. Something he had to hide."

Ken tromped through the weeds to the nearest neighbor and pounded on the door. I did the same at the mobile on the other side. No answer at either one.

We met back at the Explorer, Ken looking none-too pleased. "I'll give the tavern a call. See if they know where he is."

The bartender at the Hangman's Tavern didn't know much other than that Beck had told the owner he would be gone for a few days. As we made our way back toward town and our second quarry, Chuck Pickford, Ken called Miss Sweet-as-pie at the county sheriff for a lead on Beck's next of kin. If Greenville had actually entered the 21st century and had reliable wireless, I could have documented the molester's entire family tree on my laptop before the admin put fingertip to keyboard.

"Damned system's down," Ken said as he dropped his cell in the center console. "She'll call when she has the information."

Chuck Pickford had put down slimy roots in one of those three-story Victorian monstrosities that Greenvillians had been so fond of constructing around the turn of the last century. This one was a little worse for wear, the blue paint faded and peeling off the clapboards, the dirty white gingerbread trim ravaged by age and dry rot. The steps of the front porch looked pretty iffy and I took care to test each tread before I put my full weight on them.

What might once have been a gracious front parlor now served as entryway, mail center and last resting place for cast-offs. A bicycle missing its seat and both pedals, an inverted umbrella and the remains of innumerable emptied six-packs littered the space. Obviously not a place for recovering alcoholics.

Six of the twelve postal boxes on the wall hung open and vacant, the curling strips of paper identifying former occupants barely readable. Pickford must have been a fairly recent arrival, since the black ink on his tag was still vivid. Room number eleven. On the effing third floor.

Up to now, I'd been doing a credible job of gimping along in a way that wasn't completely pathetic, and Ken had been polite enough to pretend my left leg wasn't useless meat. But those two narrow flights of stairs would strip away any dignity I might have hoped to retain.

There wasn't a trace of pity in Ken's expression. "I could carry you up."

"I could rip your face off and make it into a purse." I waved at the stairs. "After you."

He started up. He didn't wait for me at the landings, didn't look back over his shoulder to check my progress. He didn't say a word when I finally dragged myself next to him outside room eleven, sweat soaking my long-sleeved T-shirt. Although my leg still whined, the exercise had actually loosened it up a smidgen. The easing of the pain didn't do a damn thing for my mood.

Ken pounded on the door. Muffled footsteps from inside, then the door swung open. With his gentle green eyes and thinning hair, Pickford looked like everyone's favorite uncle, the one who gives you a dollar every time you see him. Of course, that wasn't all Chuck Pickford would give a kid.

He smiled, those guileless eyes widening. "Sheriff Heinz, what a pleasure." If I hadn't read his entry on the Megan's law database – lewd or lascivious acts with child under 14 years – and if I wasn't such an inveterate skeptic, I might have believed the man was as harmless as he looked.

"I'd like to ask you a few questions, Mr Pickford." Despite Ken's courteous tone, the corner of his mouth twitched down. I guessed that beneath the polite sheriff's veneer, in his heart of hearts, Ken harbored a secret wish for an excuse to pound Pickford.

I longed to flatten the slimeball myself, just because. The satisfaction would be worth the possible assault charge.

Pickford glanced over at me, nothing but soft innocence in his green gaze. I did my best to transmit into Pickford's warped mind my hopes for his demise.

Still smiling, he stepped aside, opening the door wider. "Come on in, Sheriff." I hobbled in after Ken.

The room had a similar decorating scheme as the lobby downstairs. All the furnishings looked as if they'd been diverted from a dump run to the local landfill. Chips and cigarette burns marred the aged Formica countertop in the postage-stamp kitchen. Beside the kitchen island, a scarred dinette table featured a single ladderback chair with a rung missing. A sprung easy chair with a mismatched ottoman and a hideously ugly coffee table comprised the living room set.

"How may I be of assistance, Sheriff Heinz?" Pickford's soft voice matched his pleasant smile, a civilized façade papered over his depraved soul.

"This is Janelle Watkins, a private investigator. She has some pictures to show you. A few questions to ask."

As I pulled out the photos, Ken's attention fixed on the doorway that led, no doubt, to the bedroom and bathroom. He moved toward the opening like a labrador scenting a bird. "Mind if I take a look around?"

I watched Pickford closely for a reaction. Only the faintest flicker of concern, gone so quickly, I might have persuaded myself I'd been mistaken.

His smile broadened again. "Go right ahead, Sheriff. Look anywhere you like. Now, how can I help you, little lady?"

My skin crawled as I held out the photo of James. "Have you seen him?"

He briefly studied the picture, then shook his head. "Can't say that I have."

I traded James's image for Enrique's. Fascination kindled in Pickford's eyes, although he immediately squelched it. With a wistful smile, he stroked a blunt fingertip across the boy's sweet face.

I snatched the photo out of his reach. "Did I say you could touch?"

His sweet smile didn't waver. "I hope those two youngsters aren't in any trouble."

"They're missing."

"Did they wander off?" he asked, those vivid green eyes generous and kind.

"Someone took them." Maybe someone like you, you sick bastard.

The empathy in his face looked so genuine. "Their parents must be heartbroken."

Like the ones whose kids' lives you tore apart? That I saw none of Pickford's vileness in his face made me feel sick. The exterior ought to match the black corruption of the interior, ought to mark his flesh with oozing, gaping sores, a warning to the innocent.

Swallowing back the acid in the back of my throat, I waved the photos in his face again. "Take another look. Are you sure you haven't seen them?"

His gaze slid from the photos to my arm and before I could stop him, he took my hand. "You've hurt yourself." He took my arm. His gentle touch on the red, puckered scars dotting my inner wrist roiled the contents of my stomach to a crisis point. I tried to tug my hand away, but he wouldn't let go.

"An accident," I said. He clearly didn't believe me, and I was horrified by the urge to justify myself to Pickford the way I used to with my father.

He patted my hand. "When I sense someone in pain, I feel I have to reach out."

My skin crawled. "Is that what you tell the kids?"

"I love children." He gave me a sad, wounded look. "I don't know why anyone would think otherwise."

Pickford's touch, like an echo of my father's few tender moments, made me so sick I was about to lose my lunch on his cross trainers. Desperate, I balanced on my gimpy leg and stomped on his instep. Pickford jumped back in surprise, setting me free.

"Sorry, sorry, sorry!" I could hear myself say to my father. I managed to bite back an apology to Pickford.

Ken returned from his foray, meeting my gaze with a slight shake of his head. In that moment of distraction, Pickford plucked Enrique's photo from my fingers. "I know him."

I tugged my sleeve back down, my jaw clenched and aching. "From where?"

"Not sure." He stared at the picture. "But I've seen that face." He fixed those bright green eyes on me. "I hope you'll let me know when you find him."

Not in any universe, real or imagined. I retrieved Enrique's picture, tucking it into my back pocket. "Thanks for your cooperation."

My queasiness persisted during my painful descent back down the stairs. Whatever the impetus that had brought me here to Greenville, it evaporated, drowned by impotence.

"Did you find anything in the bedroom?" I asked.

"Neat as a pin. No pictures, no toys or games, no suspect magazines. Certainly no sign that a boy's been here recently."

"What about a computer?"

"I can't see this place wired for internet. In any case, not so much as an iPad."

"The library have internet?"

Ken nodded. "I'll check with the librarian. See if Pickford's been in."

As Ken started the engine, I shut my eyes, gritting my teeth against a serious jonesing for a lit match. "Damn," I muttered. "I should just go back home."

"I don't know what you expected."

I opened my eyes. Ken was about to make the last turn toward the sheriff's office. A black impulse sank its teeth into me. "Go back," I told him.

"What?"

"Go back to Pleasant Creek Road."

He gave me a long look, then made a U-turn. We traveled in silence until I saw the familiar side road. "There," I told him. "Make a right on Lime Kiln."

He did, then slowed on the pothole pocked asphalt. Even though he crept along at twenty-five, I missed the marker and we rolled right past it.

I spotted the faded sign in the side view mirror. "Stop."

He did, backing up as I craned my neck to see behind me. I pointed wordlessly at the weed-choked gravel drive. "Watkins" was spelled out in pallid gray letters that nearly matched the weathered wood of the sign.

As we jounced down the washboarded surface of the driveway, the past dropped over me, clinging like the sticky strands of black widow webs. Still, I slouched toward my past like Yeats's rough beast, and with no better sense than that pitiless sphinx.

CHAPTER 5

The clearing was gone, choked by manzanita, the cabin itself overwhelmed by blackberry vines. Ken drove up to the wall of red, twisting branches as far as he could, then cut the engine. He angled his body toward me and watched as I stared out the windshield as keenly as a lookie-loo at a multi-car pile-up.

This was my legacy, the only thing tangible left to me by my father – except for the scars, that is. I owned this wreck of wood and nails and the acre of land it sat on. It was the first time I'd laid eyes on it in twenty years.

I grabbed the handle and wrenched the door open. My left leg had cramped up again, but I ignored the pain as I limped up to the tangle of manzanita. There was just enough space between clumps to pass through, although I'd have to do some fancy maneuvering to avoid the poison oak that wound its way up the thicket.

I dimly heard the ding-ding-ding as Ken opened his door, then the clunk as he shut it again. I was focused on the overgrown greenery, trying to make out the front porch under all those thorns. The blackberries hadn't quite enveloped the front door, or maybe someone had been here recently and had pushed them aside, because the door yawned open. Maybe it was my father's ghost coming and going, forging a path for me in anticipation of my return. Not a cheerful thought.

The front porch steps had rotted away. I had to pick my way along the supports, using blackberry vines for balance, jabbing my palms with the wicked thorns. With that pinprick pain, I was seven years old again gathering ripe berries in the stifling July heat. The sweet-tangy taste of blackberry juice settled on my tongue.

I'd torn my shirt once berry picking, giving my father justification for punishing me. Of course, he could find justification in the phase of the moon or the color of his morning piss. There was nothing I could do to please him, and far too many ways to incur his wrath.

I stood now in the center of the cabin's main room, the late afternoon sunshine nearly obliterated by the dense vines shrouding the windows. Broken furniture littered the floor. Spiderwebs draped the remnants of the sofa. Blackberries intruded through holes punched in the walls, whether an act of my father or rowdy teens using the cabin to party I didn't know.

The place shouldn't have smelled the same, but somehow it did, stale, sour beer permeating the sofa, the reek of cigarettes still clinging to the walls. Like a key thrust into a rusty lock, the scents, whether real or imagined, opened the lid on old memories. I stood there, helpless, while they pulled me back in time.

Dimly, I heard my name called; Ken, I realized later. But in the throes of flashback, his voice morphed into my father's. Thirty years vanished and I was that little girl again, as defenseless as a kitten.

"Janelle!" Daddy shouted, cigarette bobbing in his mouth. "Where's my damn beer?"

"Right here, Daddy," I told him, the can clutched in my hand. I'd torn off the tab just the way he liked me to, had kept it very still so it wouldn't fizz over.

I made my way toward him, the room an obstacle course of upended ashtrays and discarded wine bottles. I had to be very, very careful, because Daddy liked his beer just so.

I nearly made it to the sofa, was just about to reach out to hand Daddy the open can. I didn't see Daddy's feet near mine. He might have moved them into my way; sometimes he did that just because. I tried to keep the beer from spilling, would have turned myself inside out if it would have helped. But a fountain of foamy wet spurted from the can, landing on Daddy's lap.

With a roar, he jumped up, a dark avenging monster. I screamed and dropped the beer, tried to run as it rolled across the floor, emptying its contents. I didn't get more than a few feet away before Daddy grabbed my arm.

Even though I knew it would make it worse, I screamed and struggled to get away. Daddy pinned me against the sofa. He took his cigarette from his mouth.

"Daddy, no. No!"

He lowered the glowing tip toward my arm. I screamed again as I felt the pressure of it against my skin...

"Damn it, Janelle!"

Ken's voice finally registered. His hand was wrapped around my arm; it was his gripping fingertips, not a burning cigarette I felt digging into my skin. I wrenched myself free of him, and stumbled from the cabin.

On the porch, thorns hooked my T-shirt, catching me up short. Panic flooded me – it was my father reaching out, digging in to keep me from escaping the cabin. His clawed fingers raked an old burn scar on my belly, the one he'd given me for tearing my shirt as a seven year-old.

All sanity lost, I fought back, a scream as corrosive as acid at the back of my throat, barely contained. I would have wriggled free of the shirt, abandoned it, but I knew that would enrage Daddy even more.

I finally pulled free, blind from pain real and imagined. Tripped on a broken step, went down to my knees in the dirt. It felt as if someone had staked my left leg to the ground.

One breath, two, then I pushed to my feet, woozy and sick. Became aware of reality again, bit by bit. The ramshackle cabin, the thickets of twisted manzanita surrounding it, the Explorer parked nearby. Ken standing beside me, a witness to my disintegration.

I wouldn't think about that. Angling away from him, I tugged up the hem of the T-shirt to check for damage. Red streaks criss-crossed my stomach. I wondered vaguely if my father's poison had infected them.

I tried to cover up again, but Ken hooked his fingers in the knit. "Maybe you ought to have a doctor look at that."

"A little Neosporin and a bandage and I'll be fine." My voice shook. "I've patched up worse than this after Daddy got finished with me. He wasn't much on doctors." Heal or die was his unspoken motto.

Ken tugged on the shirt again, pulling me closer, wrapping his arms around me. I grit my teeth so tightly my jaw ached, trying to fight back the weakness I felt lapping at me. If my father truly rose from the dead in that moment and flayed me alive, it wouldn't have hurt as much as it did accepting Ken's comfort.

I thought I could hold it inside, could keep the agony at bay. But it erupted like the worst kind of nausea, when you're empty inside but your body still convulses. My eyes were dry and I didn't make a sound, but I thought my sobs would break me apart.

And he just held me. Matched my silence, kept his large hands spread across my back while emotions gushed from me like blood from an open wound. I just wanted to die, to be seared to ashes on the spot. Anything but feel the pain burning inside me.

When it was finally finished, I pushed away from him, keeping my head down as I headed back toward the Explorer. My hands shook as I swiped at my cheeks, the dampness telling

me a few tears had escaped after all. Ken kept his distance as
he followed me and I almost hated him for that kindness.

Once I'd fumbled the seatbelt around me, I opened my
laptop again. "We ought to check Greenville Hospital and the
local doctors. Could be James or Enrique were brought in to
be seen."

He stared at me. "The cabin... that was where–"

"My own personal hell." I'd tried for a light tone, but my
throat was in shreds. "Could we just not..."

Quiet ticked away for several long seconds. I squeezed my
eyes shut, imagining myself suspended by a thread over a pit
of excrement. If I stayed motionless, I wouldn't fall. But one
word, one touch from Ken would sever the thin support. I'd
have to count on him to catch me. I wasn't sure he'd even try.

Finally, he started the engine. "We'll stop by the hospital,
make some calls from there."

Once he had his driving to focus on, I grabbed my cell and
nearly dropped it when my fingers refused to work. With
slow, deliberate stabs, I dialed my office.

Sheri didn't pick up, and my mangled brain recalled she
was in class. She'd be pissed if I called her mobile. That anger
would throw her off the scent, keep her from sensing my
current fragility.

I dialed her cell number. She picked up after four rings.
"Hello?" she whispered.

"I need some info," I told her.

"It couldn't wait?" I heard muffled voices in the background,
then footsteps and a slamming door. "What?" Sheri spat out.

"Find everything you can on Paul Beck and Chuck Pickford.
And start checking Lopezes in the Sacramento area, see if you
can find someone who'll claim Enrique." I felt steadier now,
almost myself again. "Anything on the eight month-old?"

"I left for Hastings a few minutes after you called. When
have I had time to check?"

"Thanks anyway." I said it politely as I could just to tweak her some more, then pressed the disconnect.

"Is Fred Sykes still running that arcade in town?" I asked Ken as I stuffed away the cell.

He gave me a once-over, maybe to assess whether my sanity had returned. "Fred filed for bankruptcy a few years ago. Then about a month after he died, the place burned down."

"Where do the kids go now?"

"Greenville Electronics. They sell TVs, cell phones, home electronics. Owned by an out-of-towner. A guy named Rich McPherson runs it."

"What's the attraction for the kids?"

"They stock all the latest phones and tablets and run demo versions of the latest apps and computer games. The junior high set congregates there after school." He pulled up to a stop sign and waved the cross traffic on. "Hospital first? Or the electronics store?"

"The hospital can wait. Tell me about McPherson."

As we made our way back to town, the Explorer exceeded the speed limit by a good twenty miles an hour. "He's from somewhere in Southern Cal. I think he's married, but I've never met his wife. No children, but the kids seem to like him."

I narrowed my gaze on Ken. "Could he be a member of Pickford's club?"

Braking at the stop where Pleasant Creek crossed Main, he turned to me. "If McPherson was taking anyone into a back room, I'd know about it."

"Things could slip under your radar. You can't be everywhere at once."

"I'd know," he said again, goosing the accelerator and turning onto Main. "Cassie hangs out there in the afternoons."

"But would she tell you?"

"Of course she would," he said with all the confidence of the completely clueless.

"How old is she?"

He parked the Explorer in front of the electronics store. "Thirteen last month."

I managed not to laugh, although he may have caught my smirk. I scanned the length of Main Street as I climbed from the Explorer. The Greenville Pharmacy still shared space with the post office and Greenville Gazette. Mel's barber shop had survived the passage of time, although it looked as if Mel hadn't. A Korean woman swept the sidewalk out front while her husband snipped hair inside. Emil's Café still promised the Biggest Burgers in the West, the neon hamburger in the window sputtering as it always had. And the National Hotel, a Gold Rush-era holdout, had a new coat of brick red paint.

Greenville Electronics had taken the place of the hardware store, a town icon that had no doubt been erased out of existence by the big box home improvement store just twenty minutes down Highway 50. The front window displays of shovels, pickaxes and gold panning pans had given way to smartphones, iPads and Android tablets. Posters hawked cellular service and equipment.

Five boys and one girl – Cassie – clustered around two giant HD TVs and the massive display of a computer, zapping space aliens or kung fu fighters or whatever video-game demons they battled. Cassie had commandeered the computer, her blonde hair pulled back in a ponytail, a small black box strapped to her waist.

The man behind the glass sales counter – Rich McPherson, I presumed – looked to be about my age. He was a clean-cut Everyman with neat brown hair and a red "Greenville Electronics" polo shirt. When a kid went over to ask for change for the soda machine in the back, McPherson smiled at him and looked him in the eyes.

Ken headed toward his niece. McPherson likely wasn't going anywhere, so I figured I'd talk to the kids first. I zeroed in on a skinny, pimply-faced boy on the Xbox to Cassie's right. "Do you know either of these boys?" I asked, waving the pictures in his field of view.

His dancing thumbs never stopped their jig as he gave the photos a once-over. "Nope," he said eloquently.

I flapped them in his face again. "Are you sure? You barely looked at them."

He jabbed at the buttons, right-left, in quick succession. "Black kid, maybe eleven, twelve years old. Short hair. Scar above his left eye. Hispanic kid, two or three, a booger in his nose."

I scrutinized the picture. Damn it, the kid was right. I'd just thought it was a flaw in the photo. "Thanks." I walked behind Cassie to the boy on her left.

As I interrogated the heavyset kid, Ken and Cassie started a ping-pong match. "Is your homework done?"

"Why are you always hassling me?"

"Did you finish your homework?"

"I don't have any."

"Don't have any because you finished it?" Ken's voice rose. "Or because you'd rather play video games?"

"There's one little page of math. I can do it later."

As they continued to bicker, I moved along the line of intrepid game players, striking out at each one. Cassie had fallen into sullen silence by the time I turned to her. She flicked a cool glance in my direction before focusing on her game again.

No smoke pouring from Ken's ears, but it was a near thing. "I asked did you check your blood sugar?"

She stamped her foot when her gambit with a nasty puce space alien failed. "It's fine, Uncle Ken. I just tested it. Lay off."

"Turn off the game a minute, Cassie. I want you to meet someone."

She huffed with impatience. "You can't just turn off the game, Uncle Ken. I have to get to the next level first."

"Pause it or I'll pull the plug."

She scowled, but she did as he asked, turning toward us to give me a dismissive examination. "Finally picking brains over beauty in your girlfriends, Uncle Ken?"

Ouch. Before Ken could scold, I smiled and put out my hand. "Janelle Watkins. I was your uncle's partner in San Francisco."

"She profiled the Samantha Trenton kidnapper," Ken told his niece. "Caught the SOB an hour before he would have killed her."

Cassie shook my hand, faint interest glinting in her blue eyes. "Cool."

"I'm looking for a couple of missing kids." I held the photos out.

"How about a missing grownup?" Cassie asked, chin tipped up, mouth set as stubbornly as her uncle's. "My mom's MIA."

"Have you seen them?"

Her gaze skated over the photos an instant before she turned back to her video game. "No. I don't hang out with little kids."

I could see Ken getting wound up again, and decided it would be best to give them a little family time. I moseyed over to the sales counter where McPherson had a phone tucked against his shoulder, a catalog open on the glass display case. He smiled and held up a finger as I approached.

He wasn't much taller than me, maybe five-nine, and slightly built. He had one of those kind faces that always seemed to be looking the other way as I was growing up. I caught the faintest whiff of alcohol mixed with breath mints wafting from him.

He hung up the phone. "Can I help you?"

"I'm looking for a couple of missing boys. James Madison and Enrique Lopez." I laid the photos on the counter. They were already dog-eared from handling. "Any chance you've seen either one of them?"

I watched for a reaction as he carefully studied James's and Enrique's pictures. I saw nothing but honest concern and genuine sympathy. Damn, where was this guy when I was a kid?

"I know I haven't seen the older boy," he said finally, pushing James's picture toward me. "The little one... Have you asked Cassie? She does some babysitting. Maybe she's seen him."

"Did you know Mrs Lopez?"

Something passed across his face, a moment of confusion. "No, I don't think... Wait, I've seen her name in the files. Hang on."

He opened the bottom drawer of a filing cabinet behind the counter and dug through the tightly packed files in the back. I could see the neck and cap of a gin bottle near the front of the drawer.

Unearthing an invoice, he set it on the counter. "She bought an HD TV and Blu-Ray player." He scrutinized the order then set it on the counter for me to see, a cloud of minty gin mixing with the paper and ink of the hardcopy. "Looks like she paid extra to have them delivered and set up."

I scanned the faint writing on the NCR paper form. "Did you do the work?"

"That was before I moved here. We contract that work out anyway." His gaze flicked down to the invoice, fixed briefly on something on the bottom. What looked like a phone number was written there, the digits barely legible. I could make out what could have been the prefix – 306 – but before I could decipher the rest, Rich took the paper back.

He returned the invoice to the file. "Anything else I can do for you?"

I wanted another, closer look at the invoice, but the phone rang and he excused himself to answer it. Ken had taken a time-out on his harangue of his niece and ambled over.

"Find out anything?"

"Mrs Lopez bought a television and a Blu-Ray. Had it delivered to the same address as the one you gave me."

"I don't suppose she paid by check or credit card."

"Cash." I tried to catch McPherson's eye, but he was engrossed in his conversation, his back to me. "How old was Mrs Lopez?"

"I only saw her in town a few times," Ken said. "Sixty, maybe?"

We moved back toward Cassie and her fellow game fiends. "Why would a sixty year-old woman suddenly buy a new TV and player?"

"For her grandson, maybe?" Ken suggested. "Enrique may well be with her."

"But the timelines don't mesh," I pointed out. "The woman from Head Start said the kid was gone as of three months ago. You said Mrs Lopez moved a month before that."

Ever vigilant, Ken kept one eye on Cassie. "So Enrique went to his grandma's new place."

"But his mother said he'd gone to Greenville."

"She got it mixed up. You said she was a tweaker."

The box on Cassie's waist started beeping, a red light flashing. Ken moved in for a closer look. Cassie tried to sidestep him, but he hooked a finger in a belt loop on her jeans.

"Your insulin cartridge is low. Where's your spare?"

Cassie tried to wriggle free. "You're messing up my game."

"Is it in your backpack?" He picked up the vivid purple book bag at her feet and got the zipper half open.

Cassie snatched the backpack from him. "I forgot it, okay? I don't have my spare."

He grabbed her arm. "Then we'll have to go home."

"I'm not done playing."

Ken plucked the controller out of her hand. "Next time you'll remember to carry a spare."

Ken perp-walked Cassie from the store and out to the Explorer, the kid complaining every step at the affront to her dignity. Caged in the back seat, she stewed as Ken made a quick stop at the sheriff's department to drop me off. While family relations between Ken and Cassie hadn't sunk to the level of dysfunction of my own, I was glad enough to escape the confines of the Ford.

Cassie climbed from the back to take shotgun next to her uncle. Before the Explorer pulled out, she rolled down her window and called out to me. "Hey, you want to come for dinner?"

I caught a glimpse of Ken through the open window. He looked ready to implode from the aggravation. Much as I might enjoy adding to his annoyance level, I'd spent too much time with the man already today. I didn't want to fall prey to any old habits that might lead to another bedroom episode.

Ken's gaze locked briefly with mine and I wondered if the same thoughts had flitted through his mind. "Janelle's too busy to come to dinner."

"Uncle Ken can't cook, but if you want to risk it, you're welcome to come." Now I saw the plea in Cassie's eyes. Maybe she hoped my presence during dinner would blunt her uncle's wrath.

She mouthed, "please," and sucker that I am, I couldn't seem to form the word "No." "Sure. Thanks."

As Ken glared at his niece, Cassie tore a sheet of lined paper from one of her spiral notebooks and scribbled their address on it. I didn't recognize the street.

Ken took the sheet from Cassie and added a hastily scrawled map. "It's behind the new development off Patterson Road. We eat between 6.30 and 7.00."

They pulled out with a screech of tires, Ken taking out his anger on the Explorer's suspension. Relieved to be out of that pressure-cooker, I climbed into my Escort and headed over to the motel to check in and grab a shower.

CHAPTER 6

James leaned against the thin pillow he'd propped against the cinderblock wall, Sean snuggled in his lap. The book Mama had given them lay open on the little boy's skinny legs. It had been a present, Mama said, to reward James the first time he'd held the candle all the way to the bottom. He'd read the book so many times now, he didn't need to look at the page to tell Sean the story.

Which was good since even daylight wasn't usually enough to read by. During the day, he did okay if he held the book up toward the window. But times like now, when the sun was on the other side of the house, he could hardly make out the words on the page.

When Mama had come in earlier and lit a candle, James had wondered if he would have to hold it. But Mama had set it on the floor by the mattress. James had almost cried with relief.

James checked the page he was on, the book hard to see in the flickering candlelight. "Then Bunny knocked on Fox's door," James read, "'Where are my carrots?' Bunny asked."

Sean turned the page. The little boy knew the book as well as James. "'Come inside,' Fox said. 'Your carrots are right here.'"

As Sean flipped to the next page, Lydia whimpered from the playpen. James held his breath, hoping the baby would

72

quiet down again. If she got going, she would just cry louder and louder until Mama came.

As Lydia started screaming, James shouted the words of the story over the noise. But Sean covered his ears and hunched over the book, so James got up and went over to the playpen. He patted Lydia on the back like he'd seen his Aunt Marisa do with his cousin. But the baby screeched even harder.

Usually Mama heard the crying and came to check on Lydia. But maybe she wasn't in the house anymore. Maybe she'd already gone out. Except it wasn't completely dark yet. And she hadn't given them their dinner.

Should he go up the stairs and bang on the door? Mama had made it clear they weren't allowed on the stairs. The door at the top was locked, anyway; he heard the deadbolt whenever Mama came or went. Maybe if he broke the no stairs rule for Lydia's sake, Mama wouldn't punish him.

Lydia had started to shriek, the high-pitched noise jolting into silence when she gasped for breath. James knew sometimes babies made themselves sick if they cried too hard. His cousin threw up sometimes.

A flicker of red from the windows caught his eye. Was Mama out there? The window was too high for him to look out. But there were some big white buckets under the stairs. If he turned one upside down, he could probably see.

He dumped out the rags that filled one of the buckets, figuring he could put them back before Mama returned. He set the bucket upside down on the mattress right next to the wall. He had to stand on tiptoes and had to grab the windowsill to pull himself up a bit, but he could see out.

He saw the fire through the vines that crisscrossed the window. It was small, like a campfire, flames licking the air. Mama stood beside it, shadowy in the flickering light.

Mama bent to something at her feet. When she rose again, she held an animal by the scruff of its neck. It looked like a possum or a raccoon; James couldn't tell through the berry vines. The animal wriggled a little bit as Mama lifted it over the fire. It squirmed harder when Mama lowered it closer to the flames. She held it there until the flames nearly reached her hand, then dropped it in the campfire.

James stumbled down from the bucket, feeling ready to puke. He closed his eyes, but he couldn't shut out the image of the animal falling into the fire, the way it struggled. He gagged, his empty stomach knotting even tighter.

He grabbed the bucket and stuffed the rags back inside. Once it was under the stairs, he went to Lydia's playpen and picked up the baby girl. Her sobs were quieter, but she still whined, like that critter must have when Mama held it over the fire. Shutting his eyes again, James paced the floor with the baby, patting her back as he held her close.

CHAPTER 7

When I made the turn off Patterson into the White Oak Village development, I wound my way along Gray Squirrel Lane through a neighborhood filled with the same beige, cookie-cutter stucco houses I'd seen along Highway 50. Kids tossed basketballs into hoops attached to garages while their dads watered postage stamp-sized front lawns. The houses, kids and dads seemed interchangeable and I wondered if a returning commuter ever pulled into the wrong house by mistake.

I passed a few undeveloped micro-lots filled with knee-high brown grass, then Gray Squirrel Lane ended abruptly, the asphalt giving way to gravel. Here was real country living, with black oak and pine shading homes set well back from the road. Based on the spacing of the houses, I calculated the parcels must be five acres, minimum. I wouldn't have thought an SFPD pension would stretch that far.

Ken's place, a two-story farmhouse with a wraparound porch, sat under a massive blue oak with a tire swing hanging from its lowest branch. I tried to imagine wise-ass Cassie using that swing, smiling as her Uncle Ken pushed her. But she would have been eleven by the time she came to live with him, far too worldly to enjoy such a childish pleasure.

I glanced at the car clock before I shut off the engine. 7.10. I was officially late. Once I'd checked into the Gold Rush Inn,

I'd gotten caught up reading the court documents Sheri had emailed me on Pickford's most recent case. When I realized I wouldn't make it to Ken's in time, I considered calling and begging off, but somehow I climbed into the Escort anyway and headed over.

Cassie answered the door sporting an inky black streak in her pale blonde hair. As she led me through the living room, I got a quick glimpse of comfy sofas, dusty knickknacks and books piled everywhere. A few soda cans decorated the coffee table and an afghan sat rumpled on the floor beside a recliner.

"Do you like my hair?" Cassie asked.

It looked as if a reverse skunk had plopped on her head, but I didn't tell her that. "What does your uncle think?"

She nudged me into the kitchen where Ken bent over the open oven door. "He hates it, which is the whole point." She whispered in my ear, "It washes out, but I haven't told him that."

The kitchen was a little worn around the edges, the butcher block island in the middle scarred by years of the attentions of chef's knives, the rustic wood cabinets with dark metal handles stuck in the seventies. Past the breakfast bar, the big trestle table in the dining room with its mismatched chairs had the hallmarks of a yard sale purchase. I guessed that after buying the property, there wasn't much spare change for kitchen remo.

Ken pulled out a broiler pan filled with fat burger patties and set it on the stove. While Ken served up the burgers on buns, Cassie dumped a couple cans of cling peaches in a bowl. A basket of French fries already steamed on the kitchen table.

Aside from blackened edges, the burgers weren't bad. Stuffed with green chilies and jack cheese and paired with a mondo bun, they made for a jaw-stretching mouthful. I slathered mine with salsa and shut my eyes in carnivorous bliss with every bite.

Cassie wolfed hers down in record time, shoving in one last French fry before pushing back from the table. She didn't quite make it to her feet before Ken glared at her. "Cassie–"

The phone rang, freeze-framing the looming showdown between Ken and his niece. When Cassie looked ready to bolt, Ken aimed his index finger at her, cocked like a gun. "Sit. Don't move." Her expression mutinous, Cassie flopped back down.

Just as the answering machine clicked on, Ken grabbed the portable from the breakfast bar. He barked a greeting into the phone, then with an apologetic glance my way, walked off toward the living room, leaving me with a half-eaten burger and a seething teenager.

"Am I supposed to sit here all night?" she huffed.

I took another bite, mumbling out an answer around a mouthful of beef and bun. "Sure he'll be back soon."

She fixed her blue gaze on me, her amped-up righteous indignation fading a bit. "So, did you know my mom?" Her voice broke on the last syllable.

I didn't see how I could avoid that minefield. "She came down to the station once or twice."

Cassie picked at her paper napkin. "She's way prettier than you."

"I think we've established that."

Her hand closed over the napkin, squeezing it into a tight ball. "She's coming back."

Beneath her declaration, I could hear her plea for confirmation. I gave her a non-committal shrug as I munched my way through my burger.

She rolled the napkin between her hands, compressing it even smaller. "Mom's just been waiting for the diabetes to settle down. As soon as I let her know I have my insulin under control, she'll come get me."

The look on Cassie's face told me that even she didn't believe her fairytale. She knew that a mom who never called her daughter, who didn't "stay in touch," wasn't likely to ever want her back. No doubt she'd mentioned her mother to me – a near stranger – in hopes I'd buy into her fantasy so she could convince herself she believed.

That would have been even crueler than leaving Cassie high and dry the way Melinda had. I wouldn't tell Ken's niece what I really thought, that her mother was a worthless excuse for humanity. But I wouldn't join her in her land of denial.

The moment Ken returned, Cassie fell back on her scowling teenager persona again. "How long are you going to keep me chained to this table?"

Ken dropped the phone back on the counter with a clatter. "Did you adjust your insulin?"

Cassie fussed with the box at her waist. "There, it's perfect."

She was up and pushing her chair in when Ken caught her again. "Your homework?"

"If you'll release me from custody, I'll go do it."

He waved her off and she flounced out of the room without clearing her place. "Cassie, your dishes," Ken called after her, but her footsteps already pounded up the stairs.

Ken rubbed a hand across his face. "Are all thirteen year-old girls as mouthy as her?"

"Could be worse," I told him.

"How?" he asked around a mouthful of fries.

"You know how," I said. "You saw enough of it in the City. Sex, drugs, and alcohol. Speaking of which, that McPherson stinks like a distillery."

"Yeah." Ken swirled a cold French fry in ketchup. "He has a cot in his office, sleeps it off there if he's had too much."

"The kids must smell it on his breath," I said. "I certainly did."

"Cassie's mentioned it. She thinks it's pretty gross. Enough that she doesn't seem to have any inclination to drink herself."

Hip-hop music started up, vibrating through the walls, the lyrics a harsh mix of misogyny and homophobia. Ken winced at the volume. "Why is she so pissed at me all the time?"

"You know it isn't about you."

"Her mother. Yeah. Therapist told me that much."

"She still seeing a shrink?" I asked.

He shook his head. "Cassie stopped talking to the woman. Waste of money having her sit there, stone silent."

Stone silent and hemorrhaging inside from the pain. I fidgeted with the fries left on my plate and tried not to think about it. "Who was on the phone?"

Good God, the man was blushing. "Julie Switzer." His gaze riveted on his plate. "She had some paperwork to discuss."

What kind of paperwork would Miss Sweet-as-pie need to mull over with Ken at 7.45 in the evening? I suspected it had nothing to do with police work.

I was dying to know if this was a two-way romance, or unrequited love on Miss Sweet-as-pie's part, but Ken had filled his mouth with a chunk of burger big enough to choke a horse. He didn't look eager to share the details of his conversation with Julie.

I picked up my plate and reached for Cassie's. Ken grabbed for it at the same moment. "I'll get that."

I didn't back away and his hand brushed against mine. As if we were hero and heroine in some sappy romance novel, we locked gazes and leaned in closer. I actually looked down at his mouth and fantasized about kissing him.

Then I came to my senses and backed away, rubbing my wrist against the side of my jeans. I thought about making a joke about wiping away boy cooties, but I was a little afraid my voice would shake if I spoke.

I filled my empty hand with the bowl of peaches, nearly jettisoning the last two lonely slices onto the linoleum. As I followed Ken into the kitchen, I was determined to pretend I hadn't just had a Harlequin moment.

I set the plate and bowl beside the sink. "So," I said, pouncing on a conversational gambit, "no one new after Tara?"

He upended the contents of the fruit bowl into the garbage disposal. "No time. What about you?"

Figuring he wasn't asking about the parade of one-night stands, I racked my brain for a G-rated answer. "Believe it or not, there was one guy, about a year ago."

He slotted plates and bowl into the dishwasher. I had one of those in my tiny kitchen, but it didn't do a very good job with take-out boxes. "What happened?" The silverware clattered as he dropped them in from a height.

"He wanted a family, can you believe it? That wasn't going to happen." He hadn't exactly been someone whose gene pool should have been extended anyway.

Shutting the dishwasher, Ken straightened, leaned his hip against the counter. His blue eyes fixed on me, and I experienced a sudden flashback of the way he'd looked at the moment of climax.

Caught up in sexual fantasy, Ken's question flew at me from left field. "Do you still have the nightmares?"

I let out a half-assed laugh. "Which one? There have been so many."

"Tommy."

I turned away, my skin prickling. "I never even think about Tommy." I stared at the floor, not wanting Ken to see the lie in my face.

"Do you still visit Maynard?"

He meant Maynard Frye, aka, the sickest bastard on the planet. Just because I liked to drop in at San Quentin, satisfy myself that Tommy Phillips's murderer was still under lock and key, didn't mean I had some kind of hang-up about him.

Even still, I didn't want to admit it to Ken. "What business is it of yours?"

Before I figured out what he was doing, he grabbed my hand, pushed up my sleeve. I tried to twist my arm so he wouldn't see the freshest marks, but he held me fast.

"You're still burning yourself."

I tugged my arm free. "A girl's got to have a hobby."

His gaze narrowed on me. "I've never understood. Your father did this to you. Why would you do it to yourself?"

The department shrink had told me that deep down inside, I thought I deserved the punishment. Because of Tommy and all my other failures as a cop. Because I thought my mother wouldn't have died if she'd loved me enough. I never believed his bullshit.

"Have you considered maybe I just like the pain?" I said it lightly, trying to make a joke out of the bald-ass truth. "If you don't care about me, why the hell are you even asking?"

Color rose in his cheeks again and he looked away. "Maybe because I did care once."

No damn way I was following up on that one. I shifted gears to something with a little less emotional baggage. "What do you know about Paul Beck?"

Ten full seconds of silence ticked away before he answered. "He's been here six months. Previously registered in San Diego County."

"What was the charge?"

"Lewd and lascivious with a child under twelve. But as far as I know, he's never been near San Francisco."

"He could have had someone bring him one of the boys. You can arrange just about anything over the internet."

A light bulb went on in Ken's eyes. "The librarian told me Beck surfs the web once or twice a week. Uses the library's internet."

"How close a watch does Big Brother keep on computer users?" I asked.

"They have filtering software so he couldn't access kiddy porn websites."

"Do they censor email?"

"No."

"What about chatrooms?" I asked. "Facebook? MySpace? Lots of ways to contact an underage target."

Wincing, Ken pinched the bridge of his nose. "I'll call the librarian in the morning. See if I can get a record of which sites Beck has been visiting."

The stomp of footsteps on the stairs had me yanking my sleeve down to cover my multitude of sins. Not that I was ashamed, mind you; I just didn't want to give Cassie any ideas.

Ken's niece launched into an elaborate story about a get-together at the electronics store. She insisted she had to go, that every other kid in the universe would be there. Ken played the, "It's a school night" card, Cassie's pleas segued into a high-volume whine and Ken yelled louder. His voice carried to the front door as I slithered through it.

Too much of a coward to stay and listen to their wrangling, I nevertheless marveled over one aspect of Ken's interaction with his niece. He cared about where she went and who she would be with. He'd raised nothing but his voice. A damned novelty in my experience.

The Gold Rush Inn was about a twenty minute drive from Ken's house. There had been a second motel in Greenville once, but it had apparently been converted into a continuation school since I'd left. Exactly the sort of place the Greenville Unified School District would have sent me if they'd had the option back in the day.

If the Gold Rush Inn had been updated in the intervening decades, the changes escaped my notice. There was still the massive statuary of a gold panner holding up a neon sign, half the lettering in "Gold Rush" flickering intermittently. The anonymous 49er had been gilded as if poked by an ersatz

Midas. I say ersatz because the gilding had worn through on Mr Gold Rush's knees, elbows, and the creases of his jacket, revealing the black metal beneath.

There was one surprising upgrade to the property, high speed internet in all the rooms. It cost me ten bucks extra per day, but that was a small price to pay for contact with the outside world.

Room 106, described by the owner as a deluxe accommodation, sat at the far end of the complex, a stone's throw from Highway 50. No worries that my sleep would be disturbed by the country quiet; I'd have the rumble of passing semis rattling the walls of my room all night long. More used to the rowdy screams of partying neighbors than traffic sounds, I wasn't counting on much slumber.

The deluxe bed that I settled on with my laptop was a lumpy queen-size rather than the double in most of the rooms. The television had a working remote – permanently affixed to the nightstand – and the carpet had only unraveled in one or two spots. Clearly, I was living in the lap of luxury.

Once I'd logged into the wireless network, quaintly named The Gold Rush Innternet, I checked email, then brought up my instant message window. A quick scan of which of my "special friends" were online didn't turn up the one I was looking for.

So I fired off an email and waited. A few minutes later, after several games of Spider, my computer mooed and "luvzboyz" came online. An undercover Fresno cop who hung out in chatrooms frequented by slimeballs, he'd made a name for himself nailing child molesters.

A request to go private flashed on my screen. I clicked the link and waited.

What's up, gimpgirl? popped up in my IM box. *Long time no chat.*

Need some info, I typed back. *A Northern California request for one or two boys. Three months ago.*

There was one in Santa Rosa, luvzboyz entered. *One boy, under four. Popped up a month ago. Don't know if the order was filled. Still tracking that one.*

I'm looking for two. I typed in what I knew so far about Enrique and James, then uploaded their pictures. *Might be a Greenville connection.*

After a long pause during which I wondered if he'd logged off, luvzboyz typed, *Nothing about kids in Greenville. Heard about that string of arsons, though. Might have a lead on a firestarter.*

Information like that could be a real gift. Wouldn't help my cause with Enrique and James, but might give me some leverage with Ken. *Be glad for the information.*

Arsonist by the name of Marty Denning relocated there few months ago. Finished his parole, but I had my eye on him for domestic abuse. Emailing further info and CDL. Another pause, then, *Gotta go.*

He closed the private link and a moment later luvzboyz went offline. I checked email a couple times, looking for what luvzboyz had sent, but it must have gotten hung up in the internet ether. Nothing downloaded but Viagra ads and surefire stock tips.

I set aside the computer, feeling more uneasy about Paul Beck by the minute. The thought of what kind of evil he could be doing to Enrique drove me to my feet, sent me prowling across the floor.

I grabbed my car keys. I'd stop by the Hangman's Tavern in town first, then swing by Beck's mobile.

The Hangman's Tavern was pretty dead on a Tuesday night, only three confirmed drunks sitting at the bar and a couple of blousy looking women in a corner booth. Despite California's smoking ban, the place reeked of tobacco, the stench permeating the walls. This wasn't progressive San Francisco where someone lighting up in a public place could be lynched without objection. This was Greenville, a safe haven for tobacco addicts.

The bartender, tall, well-built and better looking than you'd expect in a dive like the Hangman's Tavern, was zoned out on an early season Giants-Padres game. I slid onto a stool and introduced myself, giving him first and last name in hopes he'd do the same.

But Bryan didn't bite, giving me no more than what was engraved on his plastic nametag. I asked if he knew where I could find Paul Beck.

Tall, dark and fairly handsome gave me a sour look. "I have no effing idea. The son-of-a-bitch didn't show up for work two nights ago. I had to pick up the slack."

"What days does he usually work?"

"Saturday through Wednesday. We overlap on the weekends." Bryan gave the bar a swipe with a stained white towel. "Tuesday and Wednesday are supposed to be my days off."

"When did he call in?"

"Hell if I know. Day before yesterday, I guess, since that's when the boss called me." He dumped the remains of two Manhattans and dropped the glasses into a sink of soapy water. "Now my girlfriend's pissed because I promised to take her out for her birthday last night. I'll have to buy her a damned expensive present to make up for it."

My heart bled for his personal problems. "I don't suppose I could take a look at Beck's job application."

Bryan gave me a fishy look. "For that, you'll have to ask the owner. The bastard only waltzes in here once a week, on Fridays."

Before he could launch into another tirade, I thanked Bryan for his time and ambled along the line of barflies. But it was far too late and the bar patrons too far gone for interviews. The first drunk insisted Paul Beck had been there just a moment ago and was probably in the john. The second informed me the man behind the bar *was* Paul and did I need my eyes examined. The third guy, nearly comatose, had sunk into morose silence and refused to answer my questions.

Armed with a tonic and lime from the beleaguered Bryan, I headed for the corner booth. The two fortyish women, their eyes red and their makeup smeared, were engaging in rowdy conversation. That they were still verbal gave me hope they might have some answers for me.

The bleached blonde smiled as I approached, cigarette ash flying as she invited me to sit with them. "I'm Sondra an' this is Liz." Dark-haired Liz waved, then threw back her straight whiskey.

"I'm Janelle." I pulled over a chair and took a long drink of the tonic water. I squeezed my eyes shut and let out a satisfied sigh, as if in reaction to the non-existent gin hitting my bloodstream. "So, are you two regulars here?"

"Oh, no," Sondra told me, shaking her head so hard she tipped to one side. As she righted herself, she sucked in a long hit from a bargain brand cigarette.

"We're jus' celebratin'." Liz got a little stuck on the ending "N", drawing it out in a stutter.

"We don' drink much, Liz an' me," Sondra confided over her beer. "Not like those poor ol' sots." She gestured in the general direction of the bar.

"Have you been here when the other bartender's pouring?" I asked.

Spitting out a shred of tobacco, Sondra squinted through the smoky haze. "Oh. The lil' creep's not here."

Liz pushed out of the booth. "Gotta take a pee." She staggered off.

"Have you ever talked to him?" I asked Sondra.

She took a swig of beer. "Who?"

"Paul Beck."

"Why would I talk to the lil' creep?"

"You know what he did?"

"Ever'body knows." She belched, and hoppy fumes wafted toward me. "Big stink when they sent 'im here."

I poked at my lime with my straws. "Ever seen any kids with him?"

"Don' allow kids in here." She wagged a finger at me. "I allus left mine in the car."

I wanted to break that wagging finger. I didn't know what was worse – abandoning the kids at home to go out drinking like my dear old dad did, or dragging them along with you to shiver in the car.

Sondra had finished her beer and her attention wandered toward the bartender. Before she could slide out of the booth, I blocked her with my chair.

"Did you ever see a kid you didn't know in Beck's car?"

"How would I know which car is his?" She gazed longingly in the direction of the bar.

I moved into her line of sight. "Did you see a boy in any car on a night Paul Beck was working? Maybe three or four years old?"

A moment of clarity in her brown eyes told me she was thinking. "Long time ago. Lil' boy in a car." She edged toward me, looking for escape.

I planted my knee firmly in her way. "How long ago?"

She scuffed the heel of her hand across her forehead. A little ash sifted into her blonde hair. "Can' remember. Got in trouble tha' night."

"What kind of trouble?"

"Cop said I set the dumpster on fire. Tol' him I put out my butt 'fore I threw it in."

If she was too drunk to remember the night, she was likely too out of it to remember if her cigarette was lit before she tossed it. "So you burned up the dumpster."

"It was jus' a li'l fire. Tol' the cop he should check on the kid 'stead of hasslin' me." She stabbed her cigarette in an overflowing ashtray, extinguishing it. "'Cept the kid was gone by then."

Ken could search through arrest reports, find the exact date. "Was Beck working that night?"

"He put out the fire." She tried using her shoulder as a battering ram.

I leaned back out of reach. "Do you remember anything about the car the kid was in?"

But Sondra's patience had run out. She pushed my knee out of the way and squeezed out from the booth. I grabbed her arm to keep her from tipping over. Saw the old burn scar streaking up her inner arm from wrist to elbow.

"How'd this happen?" I asked.

"Acciden'."

"What kind of accident?"

She shrugged. "Fell asleep on the sofa."

With a lit cigarette, no doubt. The woman was a hazard. I would have pressed her further, but she pulled free with surprising strength. She met up with Liz at the bar.

That was likely all I would be getting out of the blonde tonight. But she'd left her purse in the booth, her half-open wallet on top. By angling my head sideways and using a lit match for illumination, I could see her last name on her driver's license. She was a local. If I needed to, I could track her down at a later date.

More anxious than ever to find Paul Beck, I drove over to the mobile home park. There was still no vehicle in the carport, no lights on inside. The mailbox still overflowed with mail. I knocked on the door, more gently than I wanted to avoid rousing the neighbors.

The temptation to employ a little B and E had me fingering the cheap lockset on the doorknob. But despite the ease with which I could pry open the door and the reasonable certainty that Ken wouldn't arrest me, I didn't want to risk my PI license. Likely the most I could expect for my foray into crime would be information that I could more easily extract with the assistance of a search warrant Ken could probably procure.

Returning to the car for a flashlight, I directed it through the ratty curtains into the bedroom, then through the partially open blinds in the living room, which also gave me a view of the kitchen. I saw no signs of a youngster – no toys, no children's clothes lying around. Unless he was squirreled away in a closet, Enrique wasn't here.

I drove back to the motel feeling just as jittery as when I'd left. Once in my room, I settled on the bed with my computer and I updated my database with the sparse bit of intelligence I'd gotten from Bryan and Sondra. I entered Sondra's name and address, adding her phone number after a Yahoo search.

The email from luvzboyz had finally arrived and I considered taking a look at what he'd sent. But since I'd be able to do nothing with the information until morning, I shut down the laptop. A quick pee stop in the bathroom to say hello to the resident cockroaches, some vigorous flossing and brushing and I was ready for bed.

With my mind running a million miles an hour, I expected to toss and turn. But sometimes exhaustion catches up with me and slam-dunks me into slumberland. Instinctive fear almost pulled me back to wakefulness just before I dropped off. But the dream demons had their hold on me and wouldn't let go until they'd taken me to hell.

CHAPTER 8

Sometimes the nightmare plays out exactly as it happened – at least as close to reality as my adrenaline-jacked brain registered at the time. On other occasions, the familiar events morph into a carnival freak show of images, with special appearances by bogeymen from my childhood. Tonight's entertainment leaned more toward the actual than fantasy, although shifting shadows blurred the edges.

I'm twenty-eight years old again, creeping into the Tenderloin district warehouse where Maynard had holed up. The Sig Sauer P229 in my hands got heavier with each step I took until I could barely hold it in position. I knew Maynard was somewhere in the shadows, that he was armed, that Tommy might be with him.

Ken should have been to my left, had been ten years ago. But when I looked for him, he stood nearly out of sight in a far corner of the warehouse. I wanted to signal him to move closer, but I was afraid Maynard would see me. As I peered around the stack of boxes I'd hidden behind, I realized I'd forgotten my vest. Then the boxes vanished, leaving me exposed and vulnerable.

Sometimes, I'm the one who's shot in the nightmare instead of Maynard. The department shrink had told me it was my subconscious attempt to atone for Tommy's death. Personally, I thought that was crap, but either way, it didn't change the fact that I was scared shitless.

In a moment of lucid dreaming, I decided to shoot first. I blasted away indiscriminately into the darkness. Ken never moved, which had been my perception at the time. In reality, he'd covered me, peppering Maynard's position with his Sig until I could get close enough to take the bastard out.

In the erratic way of dreams, I suddenly stood over Maynard, gun trained on him as he bled at my feet. He was still conscious, staring up at me. I knew I had to ask him about Tommy, find out where he'd left the boy. But even though I tried to shout out the question, "Where is he?" I couldn't make any sound. Maynard faded, his eyes slowly closing, a sick grin on his face.

I kicked him, once, twice, to get him to wake up again. As I struck him a third time, I looked at his face in rage... But it wasn't Maynard, it was Tommy lying there, Tommy's blood staining my black boots. Then something wrenched me from the dream and I was falling. Below me, I saw myself, stretched out on the motel bed, Tommy Phillips bending over me.

I jolted awake, gasping, heart hammering in my ears. Reflexively, I looked beside the bed, but of course there was no one there. With cautious dread, I scanned the room, but no sad-eyed boy stood in the corner. Even still, horror still had me in its grip.

In the aftermath of that nightmare, I showed some restraint. I only lit ten matches, eight of them doused in a glass of water while the flame still burned. The other two served their purpose, easing my night terrors with the exquisite pain of expiation.

Julie Switzer scowled at me as I approached the reception desk the next morning. "You lied. You're not a police officer."

I gave her a shit-eating grin. "I never said I was."

Gears twirled in her head as she replayed our conversation. Her pale blue eyes narrowed on me. "Then you tricked me." Her gaze dropped to my chest. "There's coffee on your shirt."

Apparently more offended by my lack of hygiene than the lie, she shamed me into tugging my computer bag strap over the brown stain. As I recalled, it was chicken molé and not coffee, but that was a moot point.

"Is Ken in?" I asked.

"*Sheriff Heinz* is busy," she said huffily.

At that moment, Ken emerged from the direction of his office, hurrying across the lobby. He spotted me. "You'll have to wait in my office. I'll be a while."

Miss Sweet-as-pie looked ready to spit nails at Ken's sanction of my presence in her domain. Pink lips pursed, she took her time arranging the daily log for my signature, then dug through the box of visitor's badges as if searching for an appropriate tag for a miscreant such as myself.

With Miss Sweet-as-pie's stamp of disapproval, I slunk down the hall to Ken's office and opened my laptop on his desk. His computer, with its bouncing Greenville County Sheriff logo screensaver, tempted me, but I heeded my conscience and resisted an exploration of his hard drive. I couldn't get past the password anyway.

I did avail myself of Ken's printer, using my laptop's cable to connect to the network. I printed hardcopies of Marty Denning's driver's license and original arrest report.

When Ken still didn't turn up, I dug out my cell phone to call Sheri. She answered the office phone after a leisurely four rings, mumbling an absent-minded "Watkins Investigations."

"Am I interrupting your morning mocha?" I asked.

"The Chronicle. Some interesting scandals in the mayor's office."

I propped my feet up on Ken's desk. "You do still work for me, right?"

"I'll let you know after I read the comics." The rustle of newspaper carried over the phone. "Three new clients called. I conducted initial interviews and faxed them the contracts. We can finalize when you get back today."

"About that," I said, wincing in advance of Sheri's likely reaction. "I'll need another day."

A few moments of silence ticked away. "Are you making progress?"

I heard the implied question – was there a shred of hope Sheri could dangle out to Mrs Madison. "I'm following leads. Give me contact information on the new clients. I can call them from here."

I typed the names and numbers into the address book on my computer as she rattled them off. Then I spent another half hour touching base with the two women and one man looking for marital closure. I'd just finished typing in the notes when Ken returned, giving me a sour look when he saw my feet on his desk.

He shoved them off, a twinge shooting up my left leg as it dropped on the floor. "You deserted me last night." He dragged over the visitor chair and with his thumb directed my butt into it. "What's that on your shirt?"

I shut my laptop and stuffed it in my bag. "I dropped in at the Hangman's Tavern last night."

He squinted at me, obviously not too thrilled I was poking around on my own. "And?"

"Nothing new about Beck other than he unexpectedly didn't show up for work. But one of the patrons had an interesting story. Sondra. Last name is in my notes."

Ken settled in his chair and propped his feet up where mine had been. "Bleached blonde, brown eyes?" I nodded. "Sondra Willits. Used to be more of a social drinker before she hooked up with that boyfriend of hers."

"You remember something about a dumpster fire a few months ago?"

"Vaguely. I think Alex wrote her up."

"Apparently that same night she saw a kid sitting in a car outside the Hangman's Tavern."

His mouth tightened. "A lot of drunks drag their kids along with them."

"Beck was there that night. I'd like to know if it matches my timeline. Or if Sondra gave a vehicle description when Alex took her report."

He picked up the phone. "Julie, get me Alex's report on that dumpster fire at the Hangman's Tavern. It was about three months ago."

"Did you call the librarian yet this morning?" I asked.

"Leslie gave me a log file listing all the websites Beck visited. He's been on both MySpace and Facebook several times. Used a web mail site. The filtering software keeps a record of attempts to access porn sites, but he apparently kept his nose clean there."

"What about his Facebook and MySpace friends?" I asked.

"I'd need a court order for that."

Which the librarian should have required before handing over the list of Beck's internet usage. But this was Greenville. I couldn't see Leslie the librarian turning down a request from the sheriff. "When was Beck in last?"

"Last time he accessed the library's internet was a couple of weeks ago. Leslie will keep an eye out for him, let me know if he turns up."

I changed course. "How about Marty Denning? You know him?"

"New in town, been here about four or five months."

"You know anything about his arrest record?"

"Domestic violence. He offered that up to me the first time I met him." He took a swig from his coffee cup, then swallowed it with a grimace. "Denning's been keeping out of trouble, far as I know. He works over at Arnie's Automotive."

"Apparently Marty also did time for arson." I offered him the arrest report.

He scanned it. "That, he didn't share with me."

I shrugged. "It's worth following up."

Miss Sweet-as-pie appeared in the door, Alex's report clutched to her chest. Bad enough I was in the sheriff's inner sanctum, even worse that an interloper like me would be privy to confidential information.

When she didn't hand it over, Ken got up and pried the papers from her clenched fingers. "Thanks, Julie."

She lingered in the door a few moments more, a hopeful look on her face. Ken didn't even glance her way. Her love was of the unrequited variety, then. She finally gave up, retreating from his office.

Ken scanned the report. "Sondra set that fire on December 29th."

"That fits the time frame. It could have been Enrique in the car."

"Or it could have been someone else's kid." He paged through. "Sondra mentioned a car to Alex. No real description. Just a dark four-door."

"I don't suppose Paul Beck drives a dark four-door."

"Only vehicle I've seen him drive is a yellow hatchback."

Another damn dead end. Since I wasn't getting anywhere with James and Enrique, I figured I might as well meddle with Ken's investigation. "You want company when you go talk to Marty?" I asked as I packed up my computer. "He might open up to an incendiary kindred spirit."

Ken let me precede him from his office. "I'm headed out to have a chat with Lucy Polovko first."

The name tickled a memory. "Loony Lucy? We used to TP her house on Halloween. She call in a complaint about kids vandalizing her place?"

"Not this time." We climbed into the Explorer and Ken started the engine. "Alex has been checking at the local stores for purchases that might raise a red flag."

"So what did Lucy buy?"

"A half-dozen cans of kerosene. Same as the accelerant on our first two fires."

Greenville County was something of a multi-tiered society. Those whose homes were in or near town had all the modern conveniences – power from PG&E, county sewer lines, water provided by the irrigation district, landline telephones and trash pickup. Propane tank on the property if residents preferred it for heating and cooking. They tended to be county employees or would commute down to Sac for work. Ken and Markowitz fell into that category.

A little farther out, power and phone were still in place, but folks dug wells for water and installed septic tanks for sewer needs. They toted their trash to the dump. A few kept generators on hand in the event power went belly up in the winter. They worked out of their homes, or owned their own businesses. My childhood home fit that niche, although our phone was dicey due to occasional non-payment.

Those hardy souls who were even more isolated dropped off the power grid. There might be one or two high-tech types among them who used solar, but for the most part, they relied on daylight, lanterns and candles for illumination, generators for the few electrically powered appliances they possessed. No landlines, few cell towers. If trash got hauled at all, it might end up dumped on someone else's property. No visible means of employment. Visits to town far and few between. That was Lucy Polovko's world.

Back in my day, we just called her crazy. Now, a psychiatrist would probably diagnose her as schizophrenic with some obsessive compulsive disorder thrown in for good measure. Considering the neuroses I'd collected over the years, I was more inclined to give Lucy a pass than I had as a heartless adolescent.

We passed the back of beyond long before we reached Lucy's place. I marveled at the fortitude of myself and my cohorts in crime, driving all the way out here on Saturday nights just to antagonize the local madwoman.

Just as they had at my father's cabin, blackberries had nearly overwhelmed three sides of Lucy's one-story frame house. She'd kept the front clear, using the space for mountains of newspapers and magazines, barrels full of crushed aluminum cans, and rusted hoes and shovels that had lost their handles. Her wreck of a pickup truck, more Bondo than white paint, was parked off to one side in a carport of berry vines.

Cats were everywhere – curled up on the piles of paper, asleep on the roof of the house, prowling the blackberries for prey. Most of them were feral, scattering as we climbed from the Ford and started toward the house.

I touched Ken's arm and pointed to a circle of ash a distance from the house. A burn pile wasn't remarkable out in the country. With the cooler weather of spring, plenty of folks burned their brush and trash rather than haul it out.

"Has she applied for a burn permit lately?" I asked.

"I'll check. Although a lot of people don't bother with a permit."

"You don't need six cans of kerosene to burn brush."

Ken banged on the door. "Miss Polovko? It's Sheriff Heinz."

No answer. Ken pounded again. "Miss Polovko! I need to talk to you."

I pressed my ear to the door to listen. Nothing from inside. "Truck's here, so she can't have gone far."

I peered inside a window. No curtains, but the overhang of the porch shaded the interior.

Ken moved to the other window, aiming a flashlight through the glass. "Can you see anything?"

"Just more of the same. Junk to the rafters. And cats."

I angled myself to one side, allowing a faint beam of sunlight to penetrate the glass. "That might be the kerosene." I stepped aside to let Ken have a look.

"Looks like three cans." He strafed the interior with his flashlight. "Where's the rest?"

"What are you doing here?"

The imperious demand nearly sent me jumping out of my skin. Lucy Polovko bore down on us from the side of the house, long gray hair unbound and wild, shapeless dress faded from years of use. The top of her head barely came to Ken's chest, but her steps didn't slow as she confronted him. "Who are you? You don't belong here."

"It's Sheriff Heinz, Lucy. Remember, I came out when the Carter boys egged your house?"

She glared up at him. "Did Baba Yaga send you here?"

"I just had a few questions."

"She flew through here last night in her mortar." Hunching, she scanned the sky. "She wants to eat my bones."

Ken glanced over at me, exasperation clear in his face. "Lucy." He put a hand on her shoulder to get her attention. "You bought some kerosene at the SaveMart last week."

She shrugged off his hand, but lucidity flickered in her rheumy gaze. "For my generator. Person's got a right to run a generator."

"Can you show it to me?" Ken asked.

She sidled around him and opened the front door. The reek of cat urine wafted out. I took a breath of clean air before following Ken inside.

Lucy led us along a narrow corridor between ceiling-high piles of boxes, trash cans full of empty cat food cans and miscellaneous household appliances that must have worked at one time. An extension cord ran along the floor. Cats swarmed the interior, plates of kibble interspersed amongst the rubble. Passageways led to the kitchen and what might be the bedrooms, more extension cords snaking out of them. The place was a damn fire trap.

I spotted a door opposite the kitchen, crap piled high against it and blocking access. "Where does that lead?" I asked.

"Basement," Lucy said.

Which would no doubt hold more of the same. She might have started stashing stuff there, then after she ran out of room in the basement, moved on to the rest of the house.

We reached the back door and stepped out into a blackberry cave. A generator sat a few feet from the house, three cans of kerosene and a can of gasoline beside it.

Ken hefted the three cans of kerosene in turn. "These two are full. This one's nearly empty."

"It's in the tank," Lucy said.

Ken looked over the generator, started it up. Surprisingly, considering the state of everything else in and around Lucy's house, it kicked on without a hitch.

Lucy bristled. "You're wasting my kerosene."

Ken shut it off. "You shouldn't be storing flammables in the house, Lucy."

"Have to keep it safe from Baba Yaga. If she gets it, she'll set my bones on fire."

The air left my lungs. "Who's Baba Yaga?"

"The witch," Lucy said, her tone calm and sane. "Her house walks through here on chicken legs. She puts the skulls of her enemies on her picket fence."

"Do you set fires to keep Baba Yaga away?" I asked.

Lucy shook her head vigorously. "Waste of time. Baba Yaga loves fire." Her eyes grew wild. "She would dance while I burned."

That little romp through the mad landscape of Lucy's brain put an end to the interrogation. As if she realized she'd revealed too much, Lucy suddenly clammed up, refusing to answer any more of Ken's questions.

We threaded our way back through the house, Lucy shutting the door on us the moment we stepped outside. I could see her in her living room, spying on us through the dirty glass.

Ken stopped at the old Chevy truck and looked through the open window at the dash. He scribbled something on his notepad.

"Taking the odometer reading?" I asked.

"Just in case." He tucked away the notepad and we climbed into the Explorer.

"What do you think?" I asked as we pulled out.

"She's completely unhinged, but we already knew that. She seems to be using the kerosene for a legitimate purpose."

"You'd better get the fire marshal out before she blows herself and those cats to kingdom come."

"Wasn't so bad the last time I was here." He serpentined down the back roads toward the main highway. "How about we check Paul Beck's place again before we talk to Marty? It's on the way."

"Sure." I didn't mention I'd just been there the night before. What he didn't know couldn't piss him off.

Beck's mobile home was just as unoccupied as it had been last night, the mailbox just as stuffed with junk mail. We nosed around, front and back as we had the day before with the same results.

I saw a curtain twitch on the rear door of the unit next to Beck's. The door clattered, then with slow steps an elderly woman rolled her walker out onto the porch. "Mr Beck isn't home," she called out.

Ken walked around the shrubbery separating the two units. "Do you know where he is..." He glanced at her mailbox. "... Mrs Bertram?"

The old woman crept a little closer to the porch rail. "He might be off visiting his sister. He's mentioned her a time or two."

"Do you know where this sister lives?" Ken asked.

She thought a moment. "I'm afraid not. He might have told me, but my memory isn't what it used to be."

I moved up beside Ken. "Did he say anything about when he'd be back?"

"I don't believe he did," Mrs Bertram said. "He's been gone two... No, three days now."

Squeezing between the photinia and her porch rail, I held up the photos of Enrique and James. "Have you seen either of these two boys with him?"

She took the photos with a frail hand, held them an inch from her nose as she studied them. "My goodness, no. I don't know that I've ever seen company at his house."

Between the size of the hedge between them and Mrs Bertram's failing vision, I wondered if she could see anything at all at Beck's place. "So you've never seen any kids with Mr Beck?"

She shook her head. "He keeps talking about having his nephews come stay with him. He dotes on those two boys."

My flesh crawled at the thought. I hoped Beck's sister was well-informed about her brother's predilections and kept her sons miles away from him.

Ken pulled out a business card. "I'd appreciate a call when Mr Beck returns."

She took the card and peered at the tiny font. I hoped she had a pair of glasses somewhere inside.

We headed back to the Explorer. "I thought you kept tabs on these guys."

"Can't watch them every damn minute of the day."

He was right, but frustration pushed me to goad him anyway. "Beck could have Enrique right now and be doing God knows what with him."

Ken nearly took the door off the Explorer as he wrenched it open. "You don't know if either one of those boys have been anywhere near Greenville."

"I don't." Lifting my left leg in with my hands, I hauled myself into the truck. "But I have no other leads."

My eardrums popped as he slammed the door. "They could both be dead."

Weight settled in my belly. "They probably are."

Ken's cell rang as we pulled out. "Heinz," he snapped into the phone. He listened, his scowl growing darker. "It's nearly eleven o'clock. Why didn't you call before now?" Another pause. "Damn it, Cassie–" He seemed to reel in his anger. "I'll be there in ten."

He clipped the phone back onto his belt. "I have to go home."

Edginess rolled off Ken in waves as we drove into town. "Is Cassie okay?"

"She missed her bus. Again. Took her three damn hours to call and tell me." He barely slowed at a stop sign. "She's missed half her classes."

"Just drop me off at Arnie's. I'll get Denning warmed up for you."

No such luck he'd let me go off on my own. "It'll take twenty minutes, tops."

It took thirty, half of those spent with me bent over my laptop, pretending I couldn't hear Cassie giving her uncle lip and Ken shouting at his niece in return. I'd never been keen to have children of my own. Those fifteen minutes of family disharmony in Ken's Explorer didn't do a damn thing to change my mind.

CHAPTER 9

James lay stretched out on his mattress, wriggling his toes in the beam of sunlight across his feet. He guessed it was close to lunchtime and his stomach rumbled at the thought. It would probably only be the same peanut butter sandwiches and juice that they always had, but sometimes there was an apple or some little carrots to go with it. Once there had even been jelly with the peanut butter.

Dragging his ratty old blanket, Sean returned from the toilet over on the other side of the stairs and snuggled up next to James. The baby sat up in her playpen, her thumb in her mouth, sad brown eyes staring at James. He'd changed her diaper a few minutes ago. The old one sat rolled up on the stairs where Mama had told him to leave it. He was tall for his age, so he could almost put it on the topmost step, right near the door. When Mama brought lunch, she'd take it and leave another clean one.

Sean turned to face him. *"Quiero jugar."* The little boy thought a moment. "Want to play the game."

James had made up a game to play with Sean using a plastic jar full of nails and some of the paper cups Mama brought their juice in. James would hold up his fingers, and tell Sean to put that many nails in the cup. At first, Sean didn't understand what James wanted, but then he figured it out and could count out the nails up to six now.

They only played at night, when Mama went out. James had hidden a candle and matches so he could have light when Mama was gone. He'd found the candle and matches when he'd found the nails, stuck back behind the buckets of rags and cans of kerosene under the stairs. He kept the matches and candle stuffed under his mattress. The nails and paper cups just fit underneath the playpen, in a corner where the baby wouldn't sit on them.

"Tonight," James said. "I promise."

Sean must have been tired, using Spanish that way. At the beginning, when the little boy would mix in Spanish words with English, Mama would scream at him, sometimes slap his face. Once James figured out why Mama was so mad, that she wanted Sean to speak only English, he helped the little boy remember.

James heard the rattle of the lock and quickly stood up as the door opened. "There's the diaper, Mama."

"Thank you, Junior." She went down the two steps to retrieve it, then set a clean one in its place. She placed a cardboard box on the step, too. Their sandwiches and juice would be inside it, along with the baby's bottle. "Mama has to go out."

"But it's daytime." James glanced up at the window; the bright noontime sun still shone there. It was stupid, but for a second he thought maybe that beam of sunlight on his feet had been his imagination. Or maybe Mama had made the night-time come early. "You don't go out during the day."

Mama just stood there, quiet. James wondered if he'd said something wrong, something that Mama didn't like. She'd only slapped him a few times since he'd been here, but he didn't want her to do it again. Or make him hold the candle.

"I just want you all to go to heaven, Junior." Her voice sounded dreamy and distracted. "Like you did before. You and your brothers and sisters."

James felt a tug of fear, like he always did when Mama talked that way. "I'll be good, Mama. I promise."

"I know you will." Now she sounded more normal, almost like his real mama. "Tell Mama you love her."

He hated this the most. She asked him to say it at least once a day. The first time that she'd slapped him, it had been because he wouldn't say it. Because he didn't love her. He only loved his real mama.

But he'd learned to say the words as if he really meant them. It was much better to keep Mama happy. "I love you, Mama." He forced himself to smile.

"And I love you, Junior. Even more than before."

She swung the door shut. He heard the click of the lock, then her footsteps grew softer. He waited, listening to be sure she wasn't coming back.

Then he dumped the rags from two of the buckets and set first one, then another on top of it below the window. He'd figured out he could reach the window standing on both buckets, even though one fit partway into the other. He wanted to look at the window, see if he could open it. He wouldn't be able to fit through, but maybe Sean could.

First James peeked through to watch as Mama headed off away from the house. When he couldn't see her anymore, he set his hands against the window frame and pushed up. It didn't budge at all. He looked at the frame to see if maybe it was stuck with paint. Most of the paint had peeled off, so he knew it couldn't be that.

Hiking himself up a little, he tried to see if there was a lock he'd missed. He had to really twist his neck around to spot the problem. The window had been nailed shut from the outside. He could only see two nails that had bent before being hammered all the way in, but he figured there were more than those two.

James dropped down to the mattress, then put the buckets back under the stairs, each with their pile of rags stuffed inside.

He felt his throat get tight, and he knew if he wasn't careful, he might start to cry. Mama wouldn't like that.

Instead, he got their lunch and the diaper from the stairs where Mama had left them. He gave the baby her bottle and turned the cardboard box upside down to use it as a table for his and Sean's lunches. Once they'd finished eating, he put the box back on the stairs and pulled out the cups and the nails.

"We can play now," he told Sean as he set out the cups and spilled some nails onto the concrete floor. He held up four fingers. "How many is this?"

As Sean dropped four nails into a cup, all James could think of were those others, rusted and bent in the window, locking him in this room forever.

CHAPTER 10

By the time we pulled into Arnie's Automotive, the air in the Ford was as explosive as a primed shotgun. I scanned the open repair bays as Ken angled into a parking slot, looking for a likely ex-con candidate.

I didn't have to search very hard before I spotted the guy in the center bay. He stood under a pickup on a lift, prison tats flexing as he turned a wrench, his scruffy black hair pulled back in a ponytail.

He confirmed the ID when he turned our way. Denning took one look at Ken climbing out of the Explorer, threw his wrench and took off running.

The spectacle of me chasing after a suspect from a cold start isn't a pretty sight. Without my usual stretch and warm-up, I launched into a pitiful, limping crab walk while Ken shot ahead of me after Denning. By the time my muscles had loosened up enough to look more like a human being than a crippled crustacean, Ken had caught up to the ex-con and had him spread-eagled over the hood of the truck he'd been making for.

With speed no longer of the essence, I slowed to a more dignified amble and tried to pretend that pain wasn't screaming along every nerve in my left leg. Having searched Denning's person for weaponry and other contraband, Ken had him upright again, one arm in a compliance hold. With everything hurting from my left hip down my leg to my toes, it took everything in me to keep from taking a swing at Denning.

Ken got into Denning's face. "Why'd you run, Marty?"

Even inches away, the ex-con wouldn't meet Ken's gaze. "You caught me off-guard."

Ken all but whispered into Denning's ear. "Innocent people don't run."

I moved into the ex-con's line of sight. "They say confession is good for the soul, Marty. Maybe you want to get it off your chest."

He gave me an evil look. "Who the fuck are you?"

I stretched my mouth into a smile. "Just trying to give you a little friendly advice."

Denning sneered. "I didn't do nothing. I got nothing to confess."

"Yeah, yeah. Miscarriage of justice." Holding my breath to keep from inhaling the stench of stale perspiration, I took a closer look at his dilated pupils. "You on something, Marty?"

"I'm clean." He said it too fast, with a quick glance to the left. Then, all bravado, he leered at me. "But I'm glad to piss in a cup if you hold it."

Ken torqued Marty's arm a little tighter until the ex-con sucked in a breath. I just kept on smiling. "If I hold it, lover boy, it won't be attached to your body much longer."

He smirked, but kept his trap shut. Ken eased his grip. "If you take off again, I pull out my Glock. Got that?"

Denning nodded and Ken let go. The ex-con shot me another dark look as he rubbed the circulation back into his arm. "If I don't get back to work, Arnie will fire my ass."

Ken tipped his head back toward the repair shop and we strolled on back. Ken twitched a little when Denning retrieved his wrench, but he stepped aside to let Marty resume tinkering with the underbelly of the Ram 1500.

"So what the hell do you want?" Denning asked, ever the charmer.

"Wondering if you've been playing with matches," Ken said.

Marty's grip on the wrench faltered and he nearly dropped it. Then he gave the bolt a hard twist. "That's ancient history. I done my time, finished my parole a year ago."

I grabbed the other end of the wrench. He didn't let go. "It's tough sometimes, quitting," I told him. "Especially when you like it so much. Burning things. Watching the destruction. I bet you still get off on it."

He yanked the wrench away, hefting it like he was going to take a swing at me. I hoped he would, relishing the opportunity to inflict some bodily damage on him in return.

Ken spoiled the fun. "Put it down, Marty." His hand rested on his Glock.

A rattlesnake rendered in black ink coiled around Denning's forearm, its teeth dripping black venom. The snake flexed as the ex-con considered his options. Denning dropped the wrench into his toolbox. "You got something to accuse me of, just say it."

Ken edged in closer. "We've got a string of arsons, Marty. And here you are, with all that ancient history."

He laughed, the twin lightning bolt tattooed on the back of his hand rippling as he worked. "You check my record, Sheriff Heinz. The charge was arson for profit. Who's gonna hire me here in Podunk, California to burn down their shed?"

"Markowitz might have, for the insurance money," I ventured.

"Sounds like a Jew name." The letters "H-A-T-E", tattooed in thick black, tightened on his knuckles. "I don't work with no Jews."

Ken's hand closed over his baton and I suspected he was wishing for an excuse to smack Marty upside the head himself. Instead, he pulled out his notepad. "I need a home address."

"I live out in the back of beyond." Marty dropped his wrench in his tool box and swiped his hands with a greasy rag. "I got a PO box."

"Then directions to your place," Ken told him.

Marty stared at Ken, in silent hatred, for a good thirty seconds. Finally he rattled off a series of twists and turns to a southeast county locale. As familiar as I was with the back roads in Greenville County, I doubted I could have followed the complex route. I suspected the ex-con was making up the directions.

Ken scribbled on his pad. "You live alone?"

Another long delay before Denning answered. "I got a girlfriend."

"Name?"

The response came out of Denning with all the ease of a molar extraction. "Sharon Peele."

"She home?" Ken asked. "In case I want to go out and talk to her?"

Something flickered across Marty's face. Not quite guilt, since this was a man who completely lacked a moral compass. But something that raised my antenna. Ken, his gaze on his notepad, missed it.

"She's visiting her mother," Marty said finally.

If Ken caught the prevarication in Marty's tone, he didn't have a chance to say so. His radio crackled, and he moved off toward where the Explorer was parked. Denning backed out from under the Dodge and activated the lift. The truck lowered to the bay's concrete floor.

I wanted to egg him on a little, see what he might give up, so I asked, "You and your girlfriend enjoy the same hobbies?"

If he was evasive before, now he shut down like the gate to solitary. "What do you mean?"

"Does she like fire, too? Like to burn things?"

His eyes all but goggled out of his head as he stared at me. Then he turned his back. "I got work to do." He swiped his still greasy hands on his jeans, likely the same denims issued to him in prison. I couldn't see his hands shake, but I was damn sure his palms were sweating.

In for a dime, in for a dollar, I figured. I pulled out James's photo and held it in front of Denning's nose. "Have you seen him?"

I saw his reaction as he registered James's ethnicity. I knew what those double lightning bolts on the back of Denning's hand signified, could almost hear the n-word squirming around in the ex-con's warped brain like some toxic worm.

His lip curled in an ugly Elvis parody. "Can't say that I have."

Ken called to me from the Explorer. "We've got a situation."

I stuffed James's picture back in my pocket. As I headed over to Ken, my skin crawled. Marty Denning might hate my guts, but he was watching my butt as I retreated, despite the complete lack of sex appeal in my awkward gait. The thought of his gaze on my body made me sick, which pissed me off so much I longed to sink an elbow into his gut.

It might have been morally righteous, but would just complicate things. I tamped down my fury and resisted the urge to look back as I climbed into the Explorer where Ken waited.

"You get anything else from him?" he asked as he pulled out.

"Those directions to his place have got to be bogus."

Ken nodded as he screamed off up the road. "I'll check around. Ask his boss, or the UPS guy. Someone will know where he really lives."

"Something's going on at his house he doesn't want us to know about. Did you see the look on his face when he mentioned that girlfriend of his?"

Ken shook his head, taking a turn on two wheels.

"What's the hurry?"

Turning toward Highway 50, he hit the lights. "An eight year-old boy fell into the Greenville River."

"What kind of winter have you had?" A drought year meant the river would be running slower, that there'd be a prayer of getting him out.

He glanced across at me, his expression grim. "Plenty of snow and too much rain in March."

There went the prayers. I'd never had much use for them anyway.

I could feel Tommy's accusing stare boring into my shoulder blades from the caged back seat of the Explorer. As if anything that had to do with kids and disasters was my job to fix. I wanted to turn around and yell, It wasn't me that pushed him in, damn it. Go haunt someone else's life.

But I kept my mouth shut and sank into my own private gloom.

The river had been one of my escapes during my early teens, a haven free from my father's attentions. I had a couple of older friends with cars who would drive me out there, just past the Strawberry Canyon turnoff. I didn't mind that my friends used me as cover for their illicit forays into the surrounding woods with their girlfriends. Or that they'd persuaded Mom or Dad they'd be too busy keeping an eye on little Janelle to be engaging in anything nefarious. I was happy as a clam to stay by the river's edge while they found a secluded spot among the trees.

Later, I became one of those girlfriends, losing my unlamented virginity in a prickly bed of pine needles near Strawberry Canyon, with a rock the size of Ohio stabbing my lower back. As Ronny Johnson groaned "Oh, baby, oh baby," in my ear, his breath hot against my neck, I watched a squirrel performing acrobatics in the Ponderosa pine above my head. I remember thinking how funny it would be if the little gray fella crapped on Ronny's head right at the climactic moment.

The turnout Ken pulled into wasn't the same one Ronny had used that day, but it pretty much looked the same. Six miles past Strawberry Canyon, black oaks and incense cedars competed for shoreline space with willows and Himalayan blackberry. Below us, the river roared over boulders, fat with treacherous spring melt.

A couple of cruisers were already there, along with a paramedic truck and a handful of civilian cars. A woman huddled in the back of the paramedic truck in the numb aftermath of hysteria, a blanket around her shoulders.

Kid Deputy – Alex – ambled on over as we climbed from Ken's Explorer. He gave me a once-over, curiosity ablaze in his punk kid face. "Still no sign of a body."

The screech of tires announced the arrival of what had to be the boy's father. He took off at a run for the woman in the paramedic truck, the door to his Subaru still open, the bell dinging out its warning that he'd left his key in the ignition.

"Run me through it again," Ken said, pulling Alex out of earshot of the distraught parents.

"I was on patrol two miles up the highway when the call came in, so I got here pretty quick." Alex flipped open his notebook. "The victim's name is Brandon Thompson. A group of second graders from Greenville Elementary were on their way up to Plover Lake for a field trip. They pulled in to look at the river. They've been studying beavers. I guess they were hoping to spot one."

I took a look down the steep, rocky bank. "How the hell did he get down to the water?"

"His family moved here from Carson City two months ago," Alex said. "The kid hasn't made many friends yet. The girl he'd been buddied with stayed in the car with her friends. The teacher and the boy's mom got to talking and didn't notice Brandon wandering off by himself."

"How do they know he went into the water?" I asked.

"Mom finally went looking for him, was watching when he slipped off a rock and went in. Mom tried to get to him. Would have probably drowned, too, if the teacher and one of the dads hadn't grabbed her before she could jump in after her son. She banged herself up pretty good fighting them."

The image of the boy tumbling into the water was sharp in my mind; from the tightening of Ken's jaw, I imagined it was playing out in his as well. "Did you do a preliminary search?"

"I went far enough downstream to realize I didn't have control of the surroundings. I was about to call OES when you arrived."

"Go ahead, then," Ken said.

Alex pressed the talk button on his radio. "Dispatch, this is Greenville Search and Rescue. We need OES at the turnout at mile marker 23. Tell them we need canine, foot team and swift-water."

Ken eyed the parents clinging to one another, the mother sobbing. "Be right back." He headed over to the paramedic truck, closing the door to the Subaru on the way and silencing the tinny warning bell.

Done with his radio call, Alex pointed his grin at me. "You're still here."

I ignored the implied question of why I was still hanging around. "When I left Greenville, the Office of Emergency Services had about a half-dozen foot search volunteers and two guys mounted." One of whom, my father, was usually drunk when notified of a call-out. Just as well, since he never attended the training anyway. "What have you got now?"

"Greenville OES has fifty-eight foot search, eleven mounted. Only two trained dogs, one experienced, one new. Six guys on the swift-water team. Well, one of those is a girl. A woman, I mean."

The color rose in his baby face as he recognized his political incorrectness. Of course, I didn't give a rat's ass whether he called me woman, girl, broad or dame. It didn't matter as long as he respected me. If he didn't, I'd just whip his Kid Deputy butt.

I moved close enough to the shore to get a better look at the river through the willows. Water crashed into boulders, blue-green turning to creamy white in the river's frantic rush to race down the canyon.

It reminded me of my one whitewater rafting adventure. Got dumped in the drink with the first rapid, smashed my shoulder into a boulder and had to sit there for an hour, shoulder aching, waiting for rescue. Not my idea of a fun afternoon. I didn't want to think about what it might have felt like to Brandon, without a vest, without a helmet.

Ken returned, sober-faced from his no doubt fruitless effort at comfort. "I'll take over coordination while you give Janelle a lift back to her car."

The vicious flow of water mesmerized me. "Any chance in hell he hasn't drowned? That he pulled himself out?"

Ken shook his head. "You know as well as I do the river's damn cold and damn fast with snowmelt. Barring a miracle, an eight year-old boy wouldn't have a chance."

I knew he was right, that this exercise would be less a rescue operation and more recovery. If I left with Kid Deputy, I wouldn't be here when they found that small, still body. I could maintain the fantasy that maybe he was still alive a little longer.

But for some reason, my guilt-o-meter was on overdrive. Maybe because I'd been so impotent so far in the search for James and Enrique. Maybe because I just hadn't burned away enough sins. Or maybe because I was sure I could see Tommy standing beside a willow at the river's edge, his sad, upturned face expectant.

I turned my back on him. "I'd rather stay, help with the search."

Before Ken could respond to my offer of assistance, another arrival in the turnout snagged his attention. "Damn. Channel 9, already. The SAR teams aren't even here yet."

The van parked on the far end of the turnout, then raised the ten-foot antenna on the van's roof. I looked up at the sheer canyon walls on either side of us. "They won't get much signal here."

"Alex, put Janelle on a foot team." Ken started over toward the news van. "I'd better handle these idiots."

Another vehicle pulled in, and men and women in orange search and rescue vests climbed out. I followed Alex over to the SUV. "I knew the way this one would go from the start," Alex told me. "I called these folks myself."

Alex introduced me to the seven foot team members, the four men and three women welcoming and accepting of my addition to their number. Ordinary folks, volunteers supporting the sheriff's department, they likely harbored the same irrational fantasy as me, that Brandon Thompson would be found alive. And just like me, they hoped fiercely they would not be the one to find him dead.

CHAPTER 11

Sergeant Russell, the deputy in charge of the office of emergency services, set up a command post in a larger turnout about a quarter-mile downstream. The remains of a stone and concrete bridge, washed out by time and high water, jutted out on either side of the river, the middle ten feet missing.

The rest of the SAR team trickled in a few at a time, those who lived farthest out in the county reaching the command post last. Swift-water had located a relatively calm stretch of the river another half-mile down from the command post and were setting up shop there. The two dog handlers had gotten the call-out, but since were both out of the county, they wouldn't be able to join the party for another hour.

After a reporter from the Sacramento Bee and two additional news vans showed up, Ken sicced his communications officer on the press and took refuge in the command van with Sergeant Russell. Since crappy reception in the canyon would interfere with communications with dispatch, Ken offered me the option of driving one of the patrol cars to a higher elevation so the team could use the cruiser's radio as a repeater.

Glutton for punishment that I was, I wasn't inclined to sit in the comfort of a cruiser when I could be out hiking the wilderness. One of the other foot team members took the communications job, heading off to the isolated fire road where she'd relay calls between the searchers and dispatch.

Alex teamed me with Charlotte, a tall, mid-fifties woman with a long salt-and-pepper braid and buffed out arms that put mine to shame. She took my hand in a death grip to shake it, smiling with all the enthusiasm of the supremely confident. I had a sneaking suspicion I'd be collapsing at her feet long before she was even winded.

After a quick brief in the command van, we were signed out with a map and our marching orders for the search. Sergeant Russell had paper-clipped a photo of Brandon to the map, although I made it a point to give it the most cursory glance. I didn't want to make him too real in my mind.

Charlotte drove us to our starting point, down to where the swift-water team was setting up. She handed me a life vest. "Swift-water won't let us anywhere near the water without a PFD." She dug in the back seat, producing a helmet. "This too."

"No problem here." If I took a header into that icy river, I wanted something to keep me afloat and protection for the few brain cells I had left.

Our helmets and vests in place, Charlotte and I made our way down the rocky bank to the riverside. "I'll search for items of interest," she told me. "I'd like you to look for footprints and handprints along the river's edge. We'll mark or photograph as needed. Someone should be at the place where the boy was last seen to take us back to my car."

At her direction, I positioned myself behind and to Charlotte's right, keeping my focus in front and to my right, on the rocks and mud closest to the shore. Charlotte scanned in front and to her left, searching the brush at the foot of the steep bank.

It didn't take long to realize that running on pavement in the city was a stroll in the park compared to taking my gimpy leg over shifting riverside rock. I had to take care where I put my feet to avoid disturbing potential clues, any indications that Brandon might have touched shore.

The unfamiliar exercise put an unexpected strain on my left calf. No amount of being a big brave girl and gutting it out allowed me to walk like a normal person would. When my foot slipped sideways between two rocks and torqued my knee, I nearly collapsed in agony. Charlotte couldn't help but hear my colorful exclamation.

She turned and waited while I leaned over, hands on knees, gasping for breath. "Stub your toe?"

I laughed. "Old war injury."

We moved on. She'd slowed her pace imperceptibly. I chose to believe it was to better assess the terrain for clues. "How'd it happen?" she asked.

I briefly considered fabricating a heroic story where I saved the life of a hostage nun. I went with the ordinary truth. "Rookie partner's backup gun fell out while he was getting out of the patrol car. After I'd told him to stay put."

She glanced back at me over her shoulder. "I thought Ken was your partner."

"He'd left the department by then." And I'd be walking on two good legs right now if Ken and I had still been a team. As always, it didn't bear thinking about.

She stopped, bending to more closely examine something wedged between the rocks. She pulled a small orange flag from her backpack and marked the spot. "A candy wrapper. Looks old, but you never know."

She took a photo with her digital, then we moved on. "What are the odds we'll actually find this kid?" I asked her.

"His body will turn up eventually," she said matter-of-factly. "Best case scenario, he washes ashore and foot search finds him or he's wedged under a rock and swift-water locates him. Sometimes it isn't until the end of summer when the water level gets low enough and a hiker gets an unpleasant surprise."

We continued in silence, the shooting pain in my leg retreating to a sullen ache. My powers of observation had always been sharp, but Charlotte's were preternatural. She'd spy out a speck of something from a distance of several feet that I likely would have missed. We each marked and photographed a number of areas of interest, but she had me beat two to one.

As we passed the command post, I heard a dog barking; apparently a canine team had arrived. The antennas of a couple of news vans were visible through the brush and trees on the bank and I wondered if the networks were interrupting the afternoon's soaps with the breaking story.

About a quarter-mile downstream from the place last seen, the river turned especially ugly. The bank on the opposite side rose high and sheer, granite thrusting from the water like a massive wall. Boulders jutted from the river bottom, an impossible obstacle course for a raft, let alone an eight year-old boy.

The roar of water canceled any traffic noise from the highway above us, the sound digging into my ears. "Does anyone live out here?"

"It's all Bureau of Land Management on that side of the river," Charlotte said. "There used to be some old cabins on leased land, but most of those leases have run out by now. BLM hasn't been renewing them."

Up ahead, an oak had ripped its roots from the near bank and fallen in the river. Its base a good three feet in diameter, what was left of the branches reached ten feet into the river.

Charlotte climbed partway up the bank to see if there was a way around. "Be easier to just go over." Charlotte picked her way through the roots to the gnarled trunk. She gave me a hand up, then steadied me as I slid down the other side.

Her hand on a stout branch, Charlotte studied the water where it foamed and crashed through the branches. "A good chance he's down there tangled in the tree. I'll have to contact the swift-water team."

As she made the radio call, I took up her post by the tree. It didn't take much imagination to picture the eight year-old's terror as he struggled to surface, trapped under water. If there was a God, Brandon would have already drowned by then. Better that than be bashed on the boulders just downstream.

As I scanned the length of the tree, my gaze fell on the raw edges of what was left of a broken branch. It looked as if it had struck a rock as the tree fell, then snapped off in the rush of water. It was probably half-way to Jenkins Lake by now where Greenville River spilled the last of its wrath.

Charlotte moved up beside me and gave the water another look. "They'll send the team up this way next."

We resumed our search, just as attentive for clues, but despair burned a hole in my stomach. Tommy always seemed to hover in my mind's eye by the river, recrimination clear in his sad-eyed face. Forgetting I wasn't alone, I muttered an imprecation under my breath of what Tommy could do with his guilt trip. Charlotte's quick look back told me she'd heard. No doubt she was wondering if I'd forgotten to take my medication.

As Tommy's imagined face dissolved in the river's mist, a glint of something shiny caught my eye. I made my careful way over, then crouched to take a better look. A pair of little boy glasses, one of the temple pieces missing, lay half-buried in mud.

"Shit." I backed away, struggling to wipe the memory of that smiling eight year-old face I'd glimpsed in the school photo. As brief a look as I'd given the photo, I remembered the brown hair, brown eyes and Harry Potter glasses.

"What?" Charlotte asked.

I pointed wordlessly at the mud. Charlotte noted the spot with her GPS, then turned away and pressed the button on her radio. "Sergeant Russell, we have an item of interest here."

She took a photo, then stabbed an orange flag into the mud next to the glasses. She had her lips pressed tightly together and her eyes looked suspiciously wet. She wouldn't look at me.

We resumed our slow progress back to the PLS, passed one of the dogs on our way. The black shepherd's handler, a beefy mid-forties guy with a spare tire around his middle, kept up with the enthusiastic canine with surprising agility. The dog had her nose riveted to the ground, and swept from side to side as she followed the scent.

I dragged my sorry self up the bank to the turnout, muttering my favorite four-letter words under my breath with each excruciating cramp of my leg. Still unsettled by the discovery of Brandon's glasses, I didn't see Ken until I'd reached the top. I nearly fell over backwards when he stepped out from between the willows.

I pushed past him. "You scared the crap out of me."

"I've got to get back into town. I can take you to your car now or you can stay and catch a ride with someone else later."

Considering the state of my leg, I wasn't really fit to continue searching. Still, I hated being a wimp.

Charlotte solved my problem for me. "We're pulling back some of the foot search team to give the dogs a chance to work. If you have to go, now would be a good time."

I nearly wept as I climbed into the Explorer and relaxed my leg. It clamored at me as I tried to knead out the knots. I told Ken about Brandon's glasses, about swift-water's plan to investigate under the fallen tree.

We'd nearly reached the exit for Greenville when Ken's radio spat out a call. "Residential structure fire at 9003 Old Ranch Road," the anonymous dispatcher said, followed by a series of tones. "Engines 21, 25, 49, Battalion 7604, Medic 24 and 28 respond. One victim with burns. Another possible victim inside the structure."

"Shit." Ken hit lights and sirens. He gunned the engine, roaring past the Greenville exit.

"Do you know the place?" I asked.

"That's the Double J Cattle operation. If it's Abe or Mary trapped in that shed..." His hands tightened on the wheel as he turned off the highway. "They're both in their seventies and Abe has a heart problem."

The Explorer bumped along a rugged gravel road through pasture dotted with cattle. The rolling hills were still lush green, the oaks dotting the landscape giving the place a picture-postcard look. Except for the column of smoke off in the distance.

"You think this is another arson fire?" I asked.

"That remains to be seen," he said grimly.

"But you think it is."

He didn't answer as an ambulance closed on us from behind. Ken veered off the narrow track as close as he could to the barbed wire lining the road to give the EMT clearance. Once the paramedic had passed us, Ken pulled back onto the track, spitting gravel. We banged into a pothole, and my fillings jiggled in my molars.

One last rise and we drew in sight of the old homestead. The house sprawled on top of the next hill, an authentic ranch style with a front porch that ran its full length. Late afternoon sunshine spilled over an ancient barn, a sprinkling of newer sheds and outbuildings.

Smoke belched from the shed nearest the barn, oily and silky black, a thundercloud demon towering over the structure. Fingers of flame decorated the demon's waist, red gold baubles flung skyward. The hell-born creature expelled embers in all directions, and they floated gracefully from the sky, their brief, searing heat dissipating as they settled on the dirt and green grass surrounding the shed.

It was glorious. It was beautiful. If not for the man trapped inside, the hysterical screams of the seventy-something woman Alex struggled to restrain, I might have begged the firefighters to leave the thing to burn.

Ken parked the Explorer beside Alex's Crown Vic. The three fire engines and the battalion chief's truck were already on scene. Firefighters worked to knock down the fire, inundating the structure with a steady stream of water from 2½-inch hand lines. A firefighter in full rig wielded his ax on whatever blocked the doorway.

A second ambulance pulled in, stopping beside the first. An EMT was working on an Hispanic man at his rig. From the bandages on the Hispanic man's hands, I guessed he'd burned himself, maybe trying to rescue whoever was still inside.

The firefighter disappeared into the smoke and flames. The woman stopped her screaming, maybe letting hope take hold, maybe praying. She extended her hands toward the shed, as if to pull her husband from inside.

It couldn't have been longer than a few seconds, but it seemed forever before the firefighter emerged with Abe over his shoulder. I could see charring across Abe's back, down his left arm. When the firefighter put enough distance between himself and the fire, Alex let the wife go, and she ran screaming toward her husband.

The fire company continued to dump water on the nearly extinguished flames. Alex leaned against his patrol car, shoulders hunched. He'd lost his ready smile. "Any luck with the kid?"

"Found his glasses," I told him.

He nodded as the ramifications sank in. "I knew his mom in high school. Was a couple of years ahead of me."

"You got here fast," I said.

"In the area," Alex said. "On my way to another call."

"How did Abe end up in the feed shed?"

Alex's expression grew grimmer. "He thought one of the ranch hands was inside. Abe saw the smoke and went after him."

I glanced over at the Hispanic man. He stood staring at the other ambulance as the EMTs worked on Abe.

"Apparently he was never in the feed shed at all," Alex said. "His name's Esteban Rodriguez if you want to talk to him."

"Who called 911?" Ken asked.

"Abe's wife, Mary." Alex pointed a thumb back at his cruiser. "Should I head over to that burglary call?"

"Go," Ken told him. "I'll handle this."

With the fire reduced to smoldering charcoal, the battalion chief came around the engine to meet us. His name tag identified him as Peterson. "Rodriguez tried to pull Abe out, burned up his hands pretty good. The paramedic patched him up, but he refused further treatment."

The young Hispanic man paced beside the ambulances, soot covering his T-shirt and jeans.

"How's Abe?" Ken asked.

"Second-degree burns, I'm guessing," Peterson said. "Likely some third-degree as well. Don't know how much smoke his lungs took. All in all, not good for a seventy-six year-old man."

"Damn it," Ken muttered, glaring at the shed. "Do you know what time Abe spotted the fire?"

"Based on what we've been able to piece together, around three o'clock."

Ken's gaze swung toward Peterson. "Are you sure?"

"No, I'm not sure. We haven't even begun the investigation. Mary's in hysterics, and our only other witness *no habla inglés*."

Esteban watched as the EMTs pushed Abe's stretcher into the back of the ambulance then shut the doors. Esteban couldn't have been much older than twenty, young and scared and likely far from home.

Ken still had his teeth sunk in the fire's timeline. "It doesn't fit. It's too late in the day."

We stepped out of the way as the ambulance with Abe inside pulled out. Esteban looked ready to follow it all the way to Greenville Memorial.

"But no flashover this time, thank God," Peterson said, "or Abe would have been charcoal."

"What about the ignition source?" Ken asked.

"If suppression didn't wash it away, we might be able to see if it was another candle," Peterson told him. "From the way it burned, it could have been kerosene as an accelerant."

"Maybe. Could have." Ken shook his head in frustration. "Just get your samples to my DOJ contact ASAP."

I followed Esteban's agitated path. "He doesn't speak any English?"

"*Muy poquito,*" Peterson said. "And I speak even less Spanish."

"A couple of our deputies are fluent." Ken handed me his notebook and a pen. "See what you can find out in the meantime."

Two years of high-school Spanish hadn't made me an expert, but my time with SFPD had given me ample opportunity to practice. I was beyond rusty now, more capable of ordering *pollo molé* and *cerveza* than conducting a cogent conversation.

I wandered over to the young man, in my mind cobbling together a few Spanish phrases from my limited lexicon. I motioned toward the burned out shed. "*¿Qué pasó?*"

He rattled out a torrent of Spanish words, overflowing my capacity to understand. I waved my hand to stop him. "*Mas despacio, por favor. No entiendo.*"

He took a breath, then recited his story more slowly. I still didn't catch every word, but with some judicious interruptions and requests for clarifications, I managed to patch together a story, scribbling it as fast as I could in Ken's notebook.

"*¿Todo lo demás?*" Anything else? I asked when Esteban had finished.

He thought a moment, swiping sweaty soot from his forehead with the back of his hand. "*Anoche. Oí los perros ladrando.*" I heard the dogs barking.

"*¿Cuándo?*" I asked. When?

"*A las cinco o cinco y media,*" he said. "*Momentos antes de amanecer.*"

Just before dawn. "*¿Viste alguien?*" Did you see anyone?

He shook his head and the motion nearly knocked him off his feet. I steadied him, urging him over to a rock outcropping to sit. I cadged a bottle of water from the EMT and stood over Esteban as he downed it.

I remembered the photos in my back pocket. "*Una otra cosa.*"

"*¿Sí?*" His eyes shut, he swayed slightly, empty water bottle clutched in his hand.

I pulled out Enrique's picture. "*¿Conoces este niño?*"

He took the photo in a shaking hand. "*Quizá...*" His brow furrowed. "*Lo he visto en alguna parte, pero no recuerdo...*" I've seen him somewhere, but I don't remember...

His brown eyes lit with recognition, and hope sparked inside me. "*Es el nieto de Señora Lopez. Yo trabajaba para ella tres, cuatro meses pasado. Ella tenía lo mismo en su casa.*" Mrs Lopez had the same photograph.

Excitement prickled up my spine; maybe he knew where she'd moved. "*¿Sabes dónde vive ella ahora?*"

"*No, no sé.*" He slumped tiredly.

My enthusiasm deflated. "*¿Pero, estuvo lo mismo fotografía? ¿Exactamente? ¿Estas seguro?*" Was he sure it was the same photograph.

"*Sí. Seguro. El venía a vivir con ella.*"

So she had a recent photograph of her grandson and was expecting him to come live with her. "*¿Viste el niño?*"

He shook his head. He'd never seen Enrique. I got Esteban another bottle of water, then let him be, thanking him for his time.

So, had Enrique arrived in Greenville? Had Mrs Lopez taken her with him when she left? The boy could be safe, for all I knew, in his grandmother's care.

I caught up with Ken at the Explorer. He waved off the notebook when I held it out to him. "Tell me as we drive."

As we bumped our way back along the gravel road, I flipped open the notebook. "Abe asked Esteban to check the shed for some kind of horse supplement. Twenty minutes later, Abe goes outside and sees the smoke. Esteban is nowhere in sight, so Abe enters the structure, thinking his ranch hand's inside."

"Damn lucky Abe told Mary to call 911 before he went in."

Lucky if Abe survived. Ken knew as well as I did how badly burned the man had been.

"So where was Esteban?" Ken asked.

"He'd gotten distracted along the way. A calf got itself caught in barbed wire, and Esteban went over to cut it loose. He was on the other side of the barn and didn't see the smoke. Then he heard Abe yelling." I tapped the notebook on my knee. "You said the timeline didn't fit, that it was too late."

He jammed on the brakes as a deer leapt across the road. "The other fires started at ten, eleven in the morning. We've never had one so late."

"How many fires are we talking here?"

He grimaced. "Counting this one, seven in the last three months. All with traces of candle wax left behind."

"Pretty low tech ignition source."

"Provides a time delay for the fire. We haven't got trace results back on all seven blazes, but from the first few, it looks as if the candle was set in kerosene-soaked rags piled on the floor."

"Regarding your late start." I flipped a page on the notebook. "Esteban heard the dogs barking around five or five-thirty this morning. Just before dawn."

"Five-thirty's not so early on a ranch. The dogs could have been barking at one of the other hands."

"Dogs wouldn't bark at someone they knew," I pointed out. "Could have been your arsonist getting a late start. If the fire was set around five, it would match the timeline of your previous arsons."

"I suppose." He grabbed his cell phone from his belt and dialed. Phone wedged between shoulder and ear, he dodged potholes on the rutted road as he talked. "Yeah, Pat. Ken Heinz here. Any word on Abe?" He listened, his expression growing darker. "Damn it. Keep me posted, okay?"

"Well?" I asked.

"He had some kind of heart episode on his way in."

"Heart attack?"

"Cardiac ischemia, whatever the hell that is." We reached the highway, the Explorer sliding to a stop. "This shouldn't have happened. We should have had these arsons nailed down before now."

"You're sure they're all the same person? Not just local kids getting their kicks setting fires?"

"Kids would want to watch the fire. That's the big thrill, watching the flames, seeing the destruction first hand." He turned to me. "But these fires have eight, ten hour time delays. They're set in the middle of the night to start in the daylight hours."

"Maybe they come back later." Even as I made the suggestion, it didn't make sense. Why come back during daylight when the chance of getting caught was so much greater? "No witnesses at all?"

He waited for a semi to pass, then pulled out onto the highway. "Folks aren't awake at three in the morning, generally. The perp's quiet." He accelerated to pass a slow-moving RV. "When are you heading back to the city?"

"Tomorrow. I have a few cases close to resolution and three new clients waiting."

"What about the two boys?"

Culpability draped itself, shawl-like, around my shoulders. "I've done what I could." Which was piss-poor little. "I'll take a look at Paul Beck's place one last time before I leave."

Rather than grapple with guilt over my failure to find the boys, I surrendered to my fire compulsion. My brain redirected itself to the scraps of information I'd learned about Ken's arsons. A notion had crept into my mind, a dangerous proposal. I tried to keep my mouth shut, to keep from opening that Pandora's box, but I've always had crappy impulse control.

"I could give you a hand before I leave," I said. "With your arsons."

He flicked a glance at me as he slowed to exit the highway. "Yeah?" There wasn't a wealth of encouragement in the tone.

Still, I plowed on. "I could come over to your place tonight with my computer. Run ProSpy against what we know. You bring the incident reports and we can brainstorm, see what we come up with."

Say no, say no, say no, say no! my better judgment screamed as a long beat of silence passed. "You think that's a good idea, Janelle?"

It was a lousy idea; we'd be tempting fate. But I chose to sidestep the main issue. "You don't want my help?"

His jaw flexed. "Cassie's not home tonight."

"Where is she?" Not that it mattered. Without the scowling teen there as a buffer, Ken and I would be skirting perilous territory.

"Spending the night at a friend's house," he said as he pulled into the sheriff's office parking lot. "A birthday slumber party."

"Don't you think we can behave like adults?"

"That's what I'm afraid of." His hands strangled the wheel. "I suppose you'd expect dinner, too."

"I'll pick up takeout. Burgers and fries from Emil's."

"I eat there too much as it is." He shut off the engine. "Hell, I'll cook. Give me a couple of hours."

I bid my farewells and headed off to the motel. It was time I checked in with Sheri, although she'd probably already left the office. I'd have to call her cell.

As I lugged my computer inside, I tried to ignore the palpitating dance of my heart. It would be wrong in so many ways if I indulged in some bedroom athletics with Ken again, but that didn't stop my overactive imagination from considering the possibilities. That we'd be alone at his place only made the temptation harder to resist.

I'd be an idiot to give in. But then, I was always stupid enough to play with fire.

CHAPTER 12

It took Mama longer than usual to get down to the river. Daylight disoriented her, piles of dry brush on either side of the deer trail distracting her. When she went at night, by moonlight or the dim beam of a flashlight with dying batteries, she could focus on the path ahead. With the sunshine pouring down, the brush in clear view, Mama had to fight to keep her mind off the lighter in her jacket pocket.

She should have waited until tonight. She always waited until dark to cleanse herself at the river. Then she would be ready for the purification that would come later.

But she hadn't expected to find the creature yesterday, trapped at the river's edge, half-drowned in the water. Her first impulse had been to set it free, let it go to live or die. But when she shone the flashlight on it, the eyes glowed red. Fear coursed through her as she recognized Satan inside the creature. She had no choice then but to burn it, even though it would delay the night's ritual.

Afterward, she'd performed her fire sacrament with a new purpose, knowing she had pleased God. That sense of righteousness had persisted in the morning, consuming her, taking her by the throat so tightly she could barely breathe with the memory of it. She understood God wanted another sacrifice and since she wasn't yet ready for the ultimate act, she would have to find another instrument to demonstrate her devotion.

Still, she should have waited until nighttime. But with the passion upon her, she couldn't sit still contemplating it. What if Satan crawled from his carnal domain and inside another creature, then used that innocent being to commit foul, filthy deeds? If she waited, lost her opportunity to intervene, she would never be able to expiate that sin.

The trees thinned around her, giving way to a wide sloping expanse of granite and shale. She was still out of sight of the river and more importantly, the highway on the other side. The trees and thick brush that grew alongside the river screened the highway. At the speed most drivers went, they were unlikely to spot her, even as exposed as she was.

At least here temptation wouldn't prickle along her fingers and the lighter would stay in her pocket. Not only was there nothing to burn, the sheer granite face and slippery shale made for unreliable footing. If she didn't maintain her focus, she could twist an ankle, or worse, could tumble down the rocky slopes. There would be nothing to stop her fall until the creek near the bottom.

Mama breathed easier as she reached the narrow stream that bordered the next stand of trees. The creek dropped into a ten-foot waterfall to her left, but above the fall two or three large stones gave her a path across. Stepping carefully on the dry tops of the stepping stones, she hurried under the cover of trees again.

She could hear the river now. Over its muted roar, Satan whispered in her ear, telling her the same lies he always did. That the necessity to keep his evil self at bay wasn't what drove her to perform her nightly rituals. It was the fire itself, her own selfish need to burn. Why not stop now amongst the trees, pull out the lighter and set that glorious flame to the pine needles at her feet or to the rotted log across her path? The fire was what she really wanted, not Satan's sacrifice.

She didn't listen, just kept walking, certainty of her righteousness growing. Satan was near, lurking at the river.

Only she could stand between his putrescence and an ignorant world. Between human sin and the glory of God.

As she reached the last cluster of trees before the slope opened up again, her compulsive sense of purpose made her careless. She nearly marched right out into the open, stopping herself just in time as a car whipped by on the highway.

Mama forced herself to wait, to search the shore for intruders before she allowed herself to start down the rocky bank. Although not as precarious as the granite, the hillside still required caution. So eager and anxious was she to reach the water, she didn't react quickly enough when a rock shifted under her foot. Going down on one knee, she scraped her hand on a broken tree branch. She found a wadded up rag in the pocket of her jacket and wiped the blood on it as she continued on.

When she reached the quiet cove where she'd found the creature last night her heart sank in disappointment. There was something tangled there, something draped over the submerged tree that had lodged there. But it was only a bundle of trash, not anything she could sacrifice to God. Her trip down here had been wasted.

But when she drew closer to get a better look, elation filled her, making her almost dizzy with happiness. Beyond all hope, the Lord had blessed her again. It was her son that lay slumped across the tree branch, Thomas miraculously returned to her, just as Lydia and Sean and Junior had been.

Despite the rapture filling her soul, Mama knew she had to be careful. She took off her running shoes and rolled up her pant legs. She avoided the mud where she might leave a footprint, stepping on the rocks instead.

The water curled gently in the protected cove, lapping nearly to her knees. Even as it numbed her feet, strange, treacherous thoughts filled her mind. What if she lay down here beside Thomas, let the river envelope her from head to toe? Release the last of her breath, let the chill soak to her bones, quench the fire that scorched her soul. Find peace.

Mama stood over the tree branch, the longing to sleep beside Thomas overpowering. She could pull him down with her, finish the river's job, take them both to heaven not with fire but with ice.

But she couldn't leave God's work undone. She couldn't leave her other children behind. It would be selfish to depart from the evil of this world, to go on to paradise without them.

She bent to pick up Thomas's slight body, his wet T-shirt and jeans soaking into her jacket. One of his feet snagged in a vee of the tree branch, catching his shoe. The sneaker floated off, spinning, until the fierce rush of the river carried it away.

Thomas close to her chest, Mama returned to where she'd left her shoes. It didn't seem wise to walk home barefoot, so she set her boy down to put her shoes back on.

Thomas's lips were so blue, his thin arms and legs so cold. Bruises colored his swollen right wrist and the hand was twisted at an odd angle. One of the fingers on that hand was bent to the side.

Mama quickly took off her jacket, grateful it was big enough to enclose her boy in its warmth. Once she had him wrapped, she eased him over her shoulder and climbed from rock to rock up the hill.

She was winded when she reached the trees and had to stop to catch her breath. As she leaned against a tall cedar, she looked down at the river again. Her heart raced when she saw the man on the other side. He was behind a screen of willows, head bent down, arms at his sides. When she realized the man was relieving himself, she turned away, cheeks hot with mortification.

Mama took a tighter grip on Thomas as she crossed the creek. Behind the cover of a manzanita, she eased Thomas down, then gathered enough dry twigs to make a cleansing offering.

She stuffed the twigs between two rocks, far enough from the manzanita to avoid a spark igniting the highly flammable red branches. Once the flame died down, she packed dirt over the embers.

Thomas in her arms again, ready to make her way back up the bare granite, she considered the possibility that the man might have seen her after all. She had to be sure no one could track her home. She had to keep her children safe.

Slipping off her shoes again, she tucked them into the jacket pockets and stepped back into the creek. Luckily, its course was gentle upstream of the waterfall. She could walk through the shallow water for quite some distance before the going would be impossible to navigate.

Once she left the creek and returned to the safety of the trees, Mama contemplated the way the man on the other side of the river had fouled the earth. The careless sins of man always astonished her. The surrogate fire she'd set on this side wasn't sufficient. Someday she would have to make her way across the river and burn away the man's stain.

If only she could burn the man himself.

CHAPTER 13

Voicemail picked up when I called the office from the motel. Sheri didn't answer her cell, either, although at this time of day, she was probably riding BART. The subway shielded cell phone signals, making it one of the few places in San Francisco where every other person wasn't jabbering away on their Nokia.

While I waited for her to return my call, I got a head start on the night's work by setting up a database in ProSpy for Ken's arsons. I'd made a concerted effort to steer clear of arson investigation, worried I might end up like John Orr, the fire investigator serial arsonist that Wambaugh wrote about.

I created data fields for everything I thought might be of interest in arson fires: date of the fire, likely time the fire was set, time of ignition, type of structure, the ignition source, accelerant. Ken could clue me in later on anything I might have missed.

With the database constructed, I entered what I knew about the most recent fire, then considered propagating that data for the other six. But as Ken had reminded me, I shouldn't make assumptions about anything. The theory should suit the facts, rather than vice versa. I'd wait until Ken and I looked over the incident reports.

With only seven fires to process, ProSpy wouldn't be able to tell us anything more about the data than what we already knew. I'd need to link the ProSpy engine to a backend database. Thanks to a fire investigator I knew in the Bay Area, I had access to CAIRS, a statewide data program that mandates reporting by all fire departments in the state. ProSpy would provide a search engine capability for CAIRS.

I switched to the boys' database and entered the pittance I'd learned for the day. The fact that Mrs Lopez kept a recent picture of her grandson, that she'd expected him to come live with her soon, at least partially balanced the other side of the equation that Mrs Martinez had supplied. I just couldn't yet provide confirmation that Enrique was safe.

My telephone chimed out the melody to "Light My Fire," a ring tone I'd downloaded last night after I'd finished playing with matches. "Private Number," on the display told me it was probably Sheri; she kept Caller ID blocked on her cell, the by-product of being the daughter of a judge.

"Get any work done today?" I asked her in lieu of a hello.

"Finished my Contracts paper. Thanks for asking."

I told her the slim pickings I'd harvested on Enrique. "Made progress on your Lopez calls?"

"I've made my way through the first hundred or so."

"Go ahead and do an internet search on Mrs Lopez," I told her. "I already checked the freebie search sites. So you can skip Yahoo, Google and BRB and go straight to Argali and Intelius."

"You have a phone number?" Sheri asked.

"Just the last-known address I gave you before. No forwarding. We're guessing she used a PO Box for her mail, maybe in Sac."

"A driver's license?" Sheri prodded.

"No record of one. No California ID card either. The woman lived off the grid."

"An illegal?" Sheri asked.

"Maybe. I'll ask Ken. Anything else?"

"Yeah," Sheri said. "Some guy named Rodney called. From the Arco in Emeryville."

An image of pimples and greasy hair sprang to mind. "Where James was last seen. What'd he have to say?"

"After he finished hitting on me, he told me the owner of the Arco finally got a copy of the police report from that day."

Sheri liked to take her own sweet time to get to the point. She seemed to think confusion was good for the soul. "And they filed a police report because...?"

"Someone set a fire in the women's restroom the night James disappeared. Police told the owner it was vandals, probably kids, low priority crime. Owner was having insurance problems, finally requested a copy of the report."

Chill fingers danced up my spine. A fire. Set at the same location James disappeared. If it had been in the men's room, I might have conjectured that James had done it himself, acting out. But I couldn't see a twelve year-old boy going into the women's room, no matter how angry he was.

A dim memory bubbled through my brain cells, but wouldn't surface. Something about fire. I set the notion aside for the moment.

"Email me a copy of that police report," I told Sheri. "Any other calls?"

"Benjamin. Called around three."

Guilt tugged at me. The nine year-old lived across the street from me. With his mother working graveyard, he slept at my place sometimes.

Damn. I should have let him know I'd be gone a couple days. "I'll call him back."

A brief silence ensued. I waited Sheri out.

"So," she said finally. "How does he look?"

"Who?"

"Don't play dumb, Janelle."

I considered fabricating a pot belly and bald spot, but tamped down the urge. "He looks okay."

"Just okay?"

"More gray."

"Distinguished," she said.

And yet, on a woman, a few silver hairs turned her into a hag. "You want to hook up with him? I'll give him your number."

"Just sleep with him, Janelle. It'll do you some good." She disconnected before I could muster a response.

Stewing over Sheri's relationship advice, I dialed Benjamin. He answered in the middle of the first ring. Likely his mom was still asleep.

"Hey, Benjamin."

"Janelle," he said softly. "I wanted to let you know I'm keeping an eye on your place."

"You're not going over there by yourself, are you?"

"I have to make sure no one's messing with your stuff while you're gone."

"You can watch out from home." Last thing I wanted was Benjamin getting hurt trying to thwart a break-in at my apartment. "You see anything, you call 911, okay? No playing cop."

He agreed reluctantly, then spent the next quarter hour regaling me with the minutia of his life, the B on his math test, the mystery meat the cafeteria had served that day, how he'd accidentally smacked his best friend in the face with a tether ball and gave him a bloody nose. He might lead a less than ideal life with his father dead and his mother working all night and asleep all day. But his childhood was a paradise compared to what mine had been. His boyish chatter never failed to put a smile on my face.

Once I hung up with Benjamin, I still had another twenty minutes before I had to leave for Ken's. I stretched out on the bed and shut my eyes. As exhausted as I was with the previous restless night, I knew I wouldn't sleep, but if I let my thoughts percolate, I might be able to put a few pieces of the puzzle together. Maybe that fragment of memory would coalesce.

Regarding Enrique, there were a couple of possibilities: he'd either arrived safely at his grandmother's or he hadn't. If he had, all was well; if he hadn't, he could be anywhere on God's green earth. Either way, Greenville was a dead end as far as Enrique was concerned.

James, on the other hand, might still be here somewhere, with the mysterious scruffy guy and a woman with a baby. But in nearly lily-white Greenville, a black eleven year-old boy should have been such an oddity that someone would have noted his presence. That Ken, who despite his insular tendencies seemed to keep a close eye on his adopted hometown, had never seen James didn't seem likely. If he was here, he'd stayed below the radar. Or been kept there by scruffy guy.

I'd have to just start asking around, flash James's picture and see what I came up with. Ken wouldn't like me tromping all over his turf, but he had his own hands full with the arsons. He couldn't follow me around everywhere.

I'd give it one more day. I'd check out of the motel in the morning, take a look at Beck's place, then do some interviews around town. If I came up empty, I'd at least be able to tell Mrs Madison I'd made the effort. She'd have to be satisfied with that.

I did doze off, drifting just into the leading edge of sleep, vague dream images tangling with my thoughts of James and Enrique. Flame and water swirled and mixed, twisting together like an elemental braid. Smoke and steam clouded my mind, drowned consciousness. I saw Brandon Thompson's face, his mouth moving as if he were trying to impart an urgent secret. Then the image vanished into darker dreams.

••••

When my eyes snapped open, a sense of doom sent me groping under the pillow for a gun I no longer owned. My heart hammering a million beats a minute, I nearly fell off the bed when the motel phone ran. I fumbled with the receiver, mumbled a greeting.

"Did you change your mind?" Ken asked.

I squeezed my eyes shut, trying to reorder my sleep-muddied thoughts into something resembling sense. A glance at the clock told me it was nearly eight, long after I'd intended to be at Ken's. "Overslept. Why didn't you call my cell?"

"You slept right through it. I was about to send Marylou in there to see if you were still alive."

"Be there in twenty minutes," I told Ken, then rolled out of bed.

I made it in seventeen, gunning the Escort down the gravel road leading to his house, fishtailing and kicking up dust. He was waiting for me on the front porch, arms crossed, expression somber as I climbed from the car. He was wearing well-worn jeans and a T-shirt advertising a local bluegrass festival. He'd showered, his still damp hair slicked back.

"How's Abe?" I asked as I hitched up the stairs.

"Doesn't look good." He opened the screen door for me, then followed me inside.

He'd tidied the living room. No more soda cans, the books were neatly piled, and the afghan was folded over the back of the recliner. He might have even knocked some dust off the knickknacks. A spooky thought, that he'd cleaned up for me.

I entered the kitchen, spotted the towering stack of incident report folders on the trestle table. Ken spared me a glance over his shoulder, then pulled a casserole out of the microwave and set it on the counter. "I had to reheat it. It'll probably taste like hell."

He plopped a generous spoonful of a cheesy chicken and rice concoction on each of two plates, then served up some broccoli that was sadly past its prime. We sat on opposite sides of the trestle table, Ken's attention focused on his plate as he inhaled dried-up casserole and soggy broccoli.

He watched me as I finished my own plate, his gaze intense and troubled. I avoided direct eye contact, the electricity zinging between us palpable and perilous. In that moment, he looked so damn vulnerable, I had to squelch the idiot impulse to step around the table and put my arms around him.

Last bite finished, I pushed my plate away, then leaned well back as he cleared the table. As he washed dishes, I booted up my laptop and double-clicked on ProSpy.

"Any word on the Thompson kid?" I asked as the ProSpy welcome screen displayed.

"One of the foot team dug one of his sneakers out of the mud. No sign of his body, though." Ken set a rinsed water glass in the drainer. "Divers couldn't locate him under that snag where you found the glasses."

I clicked on Ken's arson database. "What about the dogs?"

"They went haring off up the bank and we thought by some miracle the boy had dragged himself out of the river." He shut off the water. "Then they hit a creek and lost whatever scent they were tracking."

"Couldn't pick it up on the other side?"

"They crossed and took off up the creek for quite a ways, then gave up." He dried his hands on a kitchen towel. "It's shale and granite beyond the creek. Tough for a dog to track. In any case, it didn't seem to be the boy's scent they were going after. Letting them sniff Brandon's jacket just confused them."

"Could it have been one of the other searchers they were picking up on? Someone out there before the dogs showed up?"

"Entirely possible. Someone had set a fire on the far side of the creek. Maybe that messed them up."

A fire. The memory twinged inside me again. A fire at the Arco station the day James disappeared. A fire near where the Thompson boy fell in the river.

Ken must have noticed my glassy-eyed stare. "What?"

I told him what I'd learned from Sheri. "My brain is trying to tell me something."

"Two fires don't make much of a pattern." He dried his hands on a kitchen towel, the motions of tendon and muscle riveting.

A tendril of heat burst into flame inside me. My heart hammered in my ears as I imagined what those hands might feel like on my skin. Skimming along my hips, my belly, between my legs.

Squeezing my eyes shut, I dug my thumb into my brow to the point of pain. I needed a distraction damn quick. "Maybe if we work on your problem."

"Want a beer?"

I wanted him to stop radiating testosterone. The way it was rolling off him, he was either going to wrap that kitchen towel around my throat or spread-eagle me on the table and rip off my clothes a la *Body Heat*.

I ignored the shiver spiking along my spine, the catch in my breathing, and focused on the beer. "What have you got?"

"Bud," he answered succinctly.

As my grandmother would say, I could piss stronger than that. "Anything else?"

A ghost of a smile curved his mouth. "Bud Light."

Crazed laughter wasn't really called for in that moment. "A Bud's fine."

He brought the beers, setting a can beside my laptop before downing half of his. "So how do we do this?"

On the table works, I mused. Move the napkin holder and the salt and pepper shakers, lose the bottle of barbecue sauce. I shook off the image of Ken clearing the table with a sweep of his arm.

He leaned over to check the screen. "This is what you used to use for your profiling."

"Similar. It's got a few more bells and whistles, but it's basically the same software."

He dropped into a chair next to me. "What do you want to know?"

"You tell me everything about the arson fires. I enter the data and the program puts it together."

"And out pops a suspect."

"Not quite so easy." I edged my chair away from his a scosh. "First tell me about possible motives."

"For arson? You've got six basically." He held up one finger. "Profit."

"That was a high-ticket car that burned at the Markowitz's."

"The rest of the structures have been like Abe's shed. No insurance value." He unfolded another finger. "Then there's vandalism."

"Still possible."

"Except the targets don't make sense. Vandals are usually kids. They'll set fire to a trash can at school, maybe an abandoned building or car."

"Profit, vandalism," I prompted.

A third finger went up. "Crime concealment."

"Doesn't fit. What are the odds so many different people have something illegal to hide?"

"Right. Same problem with revenge. Unlikely someone had an axe to grind with all these different folks." He held up four fingers. "Then there's extremism. Using fire as a form of social protest or terrorism."

"If that was the case with your fires, some wacko group would be taking responsibility."

"No one has. Excitement is number six. Thrill seeking. Need for attention. Sometimes there's a sexual component."

That froze my brain in its tracks. Hearing the word "sexual" from Ken's mouth brought me back around to the naughty thoughts I'd been entertaining. A tangible energy lingered in the air between us.

I remembered it all, the way his legs felt sliding between mine, his tongue in my mouth. His groan as he climaxed.

Those memories were a damn slippery slope. I shook them off. "You think it's number six, then? Excitement?"

His gaze fixed on me, he swirled the can of Bud. "Doesn't make sense they wouldn't stay to watch the fire."

"What if they *are* coming back? Hiding somewhere we can't see them?"

"Maybe at Markowitz's place where the tree cover is dense. But where would someone hide at the Double J? It's all open country. And why not just watch it burn when it's set? Why use a delay at all?"

"Then we're out of options."

He took a sip of beer. "There is irrational fire setting."

"Meaning?"

"It's motiveless. Or at least it seems that way to you or me. To a perpetrator with a mental disorder, his reasons for setting a fire are completely rational."

"Then by process of elimination..."

He nodded. "We've ruled out everything it couldn't be. We can start with the theory of an irrational fire-setter. See where the facts take us."

"You've already given this some thought, though."

"Yeah. I already got to this point."

He didn't seem very happy with it. I couldn't blame him. Even I, who could easily fall into the excitement category if I let my obsessions take complete control, felt uneasy at the irrationality of these fires.

I scooted back up to the table and my computer. "Let's get into the details."

Ken moved his chair slightly closer to mine. As if I was a magnet and he couldn't resist the pull. "They've all been structure fires. Some brush burned incidental to the main blaze."

"What kind of structures?" I floated my hands over the keyboard.

"Sheds, barns, a chicken coop. A garage."

"I'll need them in date order."

He pulled several folders off the stack and flipped through them as he checked dates. "The first was an old chicken coop on January 16th. Then two sheds, one on February 9th, the other on the 27th. The first barn was on March 5th followed by another shed on March 15th. The second barn burned on March 22nd. The garage was yesterday, the fourth shed today."

As he reeled them off, I entered the dates and structure types in the appropriate data fields. I angled the laptop toward Ken. "These are the fields I have so far. Anything I should add?"

He glanced at the input screen. "Area of origin, point of origin, type of fuel, maybe some kind of checkbox for flashover."

I gave myself a mental palm-slap to the forehead for forgetting it. Flashover happened when a contained fire, like in the sheds, the barns and the garage preheats the room like you'd preheat an oven. When the fuel all reaches ignition temperature at once and the entire space is consumed by flame in an instant, that's flashover.

I right-clicked to select the field creation menu and added the additional fields. Then I switched back to data entry mode. "So flashover occurred in how many of your arsons?"

"All but one of the first five. The chicken coop was such a wreck, it wasn't truly a confined space."

I clicked the checkboxes on the appropriate entries. "No flashover in the one today, according to the fire captain."

"No windows in the shed, just big vents along the roof. Abe introduced oxygen by entering and leaving the door open, but with the venting, the fire still wasn't energetic enough to form a sufficient hot gas layer required for flashover. Since Mary called 911 the moment she and Abe saw the smoke, suppression started sooner than with the other fires."

With flashover temps in the neighborhood of one thousand degrees, not only would Abe not have survived, there wouldn't be much left of him to ID. "Any evidence left of ignition source?"

"Even with flashover, the investigators found candle wax left behind at the first six fires. It helped that the candles were set on the floor."

"And kerosene was confirmed as the accelerant in the first two fires?" I asked.

"Those are the only two I have official results from. Investigators are pretty certain they'll find the same in the others as well, based on the fire behavior."

"You told me, no assumptions."

"Right. Except..." He dragged over the rest of the folders. "These are reports of arsons in the area over the last five years. We average a half-dozen or so a year. Most burn brush or forest, idiots get a kick out of throwing matches out a car window or kids start fires out in the woods. Like I mentioned before, we've had some trash can fires at the high school. When there have been incendiary structure fires, the homeowner's always been involved – insurance fraud, that kind of thing."

"Excitement, vandalism and profit motives."

"Right." He stabbed a finger at the other stack. "Eight in three months is unprecedented. They all seem to have been set during the night because there's been no sign of an intruder within at least an hour or two of when the blaze starts. Candles as ignition source, kerosene-soaked rags, the areas of origin on the floor away from windows or doors. We've seen the same patterns of clean burn in all of them."

With clean burn, the accelerant creates such an intense fire, the soot gets burned away. A fire so hot it would burn away all my sins.

I flexed my shoulders to throw off the notion. "Flashover could have burned away the accelerant too."

"In some cases it did."

"Then theoretically, those could have been accidental fires," I suggested, playing devil's advocate.

"The structures all had plenty of fuel – hay in the feed shed, old lumber out at Sadie's place – but the owners tell me there were no flammables stored inside."

Which meant less likelihood of an accidental source. "Electrical short?"

"None of the sheds were wired," Ken reminded me.

"And the electrical in the garage was brand new and to code." Somehow Ken had moved his chair closer; I edged mine away. "Let's go through them one at a time, make sure we have everything."

He read through one folder after another, pulling out the data I needed to enter into the fields we'd set up. I filled a few empty holes.

I eyed the ignition source field. "I'm still having trouble with the idea of an arsonist using a candle. It seems so old school."

Ken tossed the last folder back on the table and leaned back in his chair. His arm brushed against mine, an electrical shock of awareness jolting through me. Just like that, the memories came tumbling back, reaching inside with hot intensity.

Ken flicked a glance at me. He knew what I was feeling. "Since he's not sticking around to watch it, I'd say our arsonist isn't as interested in the fire itself as much as its end result."

"Destruction of whatever he's burning," I suggested, wishing I could destroy the sensations rocketing around inside me. "Although that doesn't explain why."

"If it is an unbalanced individual, his reasons probably won't make much sense to us."

Ken was so close, I could feel the warmth of his skin. "Any connection between the victims?" I asked.

He took another swig of Bud. "Nothing we've been able to find."

"The program might be able to make some correlations." And kick my brain onto a less dangerous path. I returned to field creation mode and added several columns to the database. "Let's go through it all again, but with our focus on the victims."

Rising from his chair, Ken laid out the eight folders along the table for easy reference. "The chicken coop was on BLM land along the river, nearly all that was left of a defunct ranch that used to lease the property. The first shed was northeast about ten miles as the crow flies at Sadie Parker's place. The second was southeast of Sadie's, nearly three miles away. A contractor put in the shed to store supplies while he built a client's house."

His hands propped on the table, he checked the next folder. "First barn was farther south and east, at a ranch on the north side of the river. The Westfields bought the place a few years ago and built their house and a second barn on the property, but only the older barn was burned. The McKays owned the third shed; it's a good five miles west of the Westfields'."

He moved to the last three folders. "Second barn was on a parcel that's up for sale nearly at the south edge of the county. Elvin Hughes caretakes it. He lives in an old modular on the property. The garage you saw yourself."

I shook out a cramp in my hand, then resumed typing. "Markowitz's place is what... maybe two miles north of town?"

"Something like that. He bought the place last year and had the garage built in the last month. Abe and Mary's place is south again, a bit west of Markowitz's property."

"Sadie's been in Greenville since dirt was invented, so I'm guessing she's well acquainted with Abe and Mary. What about the others?"

"Markowitz likely doesn't know anyone since he's so new here and a horse's ass to boot. The Westfields are more sociable, but they haven't been here long either. Their kids are young, so they usually interact with other young couples. The contractor's from out of town. The McKays are from the Bay Area and Mr McKay is only here on the weekends. No one knows them very well."

"So other than Sadie and Abe, the people involved don't know each other." My fingers ached, tension tightening my arms from wrist to elbow. "Anything else?"

He sank back in his chair. "They were all fairly isolated locations. Other than the garage, they were all old structures. Other than the chicken coop, someone was in residence when the fire was set."

"Occupations?" I asked, taking a stab in the dark.

"Sadie still publishes the Greenville Gazette, believe it or not."

"Good God, she's got to be nearly ninety. Still a muckraker?" She used to take great delight in skewering the town council whenever possible.

"I nearly lost the election when I turned down her invitation to coffee and cookies."

"What does she think of you now?"

"I hang the Moon." His smile just about stopped my heart.

"Managed to develop a little charm since you left SF?" I laced my query with as much sarcasm as I could muster.

He ignored the jab. "Mr Westfield runs a computer consulting business out of a home office, his wife is a stay-at-home mom. The McKays, I have no idea. Markowitz commutes down to his law office in Sac."

I entered everything, even though it might turn out to be useless garbage. "Let's see what ProSpy makes of this mess."

One hand on my chair, Ken looked over my shoulder, his breath warming the back of my neck. "How's Darren been doing? Staying out of jail?"

Darren had created ProSpy as a sixteen year-old genius twerp. "He's a hotshot senior scientist of some cutting edge tech company."

Ken must have straightened his fingers because I could sense them stretching toward the nape of my neck. "I don't remember the program looking this good."

I tried to build a mental wall between us, shutting out his touch. "He keeps me updated. It's light years ahead of what I used to run. Does a better job of isolating connections between disparate data elements." I wasn't entirely sure what I was talking about, but I figured it would impress the hell out of Ken.

"Could I get that in backwoods country sheriff terms?"

"Think of it like a jigsaw puzzle." I turned toward him, despite my better judgment, edging nearer. "You pick up a piece, consider the color, the shape, look at the options for where it fits in the picture. Or you have a piece missing, so you visualize it in your mind as you search."

"Haven't played with puzzles since I was a kid, but okay." His fingers grazed the curve of my ear. "It's a jigsaw puzzle."

I should have shrugged him off again, but it was late and I was tired. And wanting him, inside and out. "I treat the arsons like a puzzle, but instead of shape and color forming the picture, I use the common elements we come up with."

"And the program does the rest." His knee pressed against my leg.

I pressed back. "The program organizes the elements optimally. I still have to rank the results to eliminate superfluencies. Pieces that come from a different puzzle, parts that don't fit."

Damn him, he got closer, his mouth brushing against my hair. Breathing became a real issue. "I tweak the data... put the brown pieces in one corner, the reds in another... The program makes correlations a manual search might not..."

He kissed my cheek, then the corner of my mouth. My libido was reporting for duty, every nerve in my body standing at attention. I didn't want to think about that little girl inside me, always aching for affection.

I turned toward him, my hands curling around his shoulders, my mouth ready for tongue-wrestling. I summoned up a modicum of self-control.

"Back off, Ken," I said with little conviction.

"I lied to you, Janelle." His voice rumbled in my ear. "I do care. Never stopped."

"I'm not good for you."

"You think I don't know that? I wish to hell you'd never come here."

The honest truth of his declaration hurt more than I wanted to admit. "My bed's already too crowded with monsters, Ken. There's no room for you in there."

He stroked my hair. "But there's no one to stop us, Janelle. Tara's gone. You have no one in your life."

I was ready to melt against him. Instead, I grabbed his wrist to pull it away. We stared at each other, gazes locked, temptation digging in its claws. "Don't."

One more tantalizing moment sizzled between us, then he shoved back his chair and grabbed his empty beer can. Slapped it into a can crusher in the kitchen. The sound of him pulverizing the defenseless aluminum jolted me. I could relate, though, since I wanted to pitch my laptop across the room.

When he returned to the trestle table with another Bud, he positioned his chair a good foot away from mine. So he wouldn't go blind trying to read the screen, I angled the laptop toward him and shifted my own chair out of his way.

I could tell myself it was all for the best. Entangling myself in Ken's life again would be like jumping in front of an armed perp and daring him to take his best shot.

Even still, deep inside I knew that was one bullet I would have been glad to take.

CHAPTER 14

The computer beeped as ProSpy completed its processing, and a message flashed telling me the results were ready. Now it was time for the real number crunching part. Using the criteria ProSpy had spit out, I had to search against the California All Incident Reporting System database.

"You use CAIRS?" Ken asked as I double-clicked the appropriate icon.

"I have access to the arson module through a friend." The less said about that the better since my use of CAIRS wasn't entirely kosher. I'd called in a favor when the cheating husband of one of my clients had tried to destroy marital assets by burning them.

A dialogue box popped up on the screen, whining about the lack of a connection. "What do you use for internet out here?"

"Satellite and wireless network. I'll set it up for you." He scooted closer to the table, reaching for the keyboard.

I imagined an invisible keep away barrier around Ken pushing me back in my chair. While he tapped away at the computer, I took my half-empty beer into the kitchen and emptied it into the sink. I wondered if he had any hard liquor in the house, considered searching through the cupboards. Instead I took a glass from the dish drainer and filled it with water.

The glass lifted to hide my face, I surreptitiously spied on Ken. Physically, he was everything a woman could have wanted in one boffo package. But it wasn't raging hormones that had me feeling restless and agitated. It was the connection that still threaded itself between us, first woven when our professional partnership began, strengthened each day the trust between us grew. Seemingly shattered the day Tara discovered us.

"We have internet," Ken said.

I set aside the empty glass, then returned to the computer and started up ProSpy's search and match function. Too edgy to sit while waiting for the results, I wandered around the dining room, nosing through a bookshelf full of well-thumbed paperbacks. The mysteries and thrillers didn't surprise me; the classics did. *Grapes of Wrath. Huckleberry Finn. Heart of Darkness*.

I turned to find him staring at me. He didn't drop his gaze when I caught him. I had some trouble breathing.

Would you have left her for me? For a moment, I was terrified that I might have spoken it out loud. I don't know where it came from, knew damn well I didn't want to hear the answer.

Saved by the computer. With a beep, it displayed the first 20 of 586 matches to the data we'd entered.

Ken broke his eye-lock on me and adjusted the screen for a better look. "Those can't all be my arsonist."

Maintaining a safety zone, I returned to the table and scrolled through the hits. "I still have to massage the data. Eliminate the most obvious mismatches. Overlapping dates too far separated by distance, solved cases where the perp is incarcerated and therefore couldn't have set your fires."

ProSpy included a feature that allowed me to list terms that would filter the results, both adding to and deleting items from the results. I entered the appropriate terms and ran the filter against the first set of data. "I threw in questionable cases, fires not definitively ruled intentional."

ProSpy hummed along, the little hour-glass turning end over end. My better judgment seemed to have evaporated. Ken and I had drawn closer together, like flames reaching across a backfire. Maybe I should have followed Sheri's advice, gotten Ken out of my system. Not that that was likely to happen.

Another beep from ProSpy and 21 matches displayed on the screen. I scrolled through and made a quick assessment. "Six of the eight Greenville fires. Seven in Mojave. The rest all over the state."

"Not all over the state." Ken drew a finger down the list. "Two in Bakersfield. Three in Visalia. Two in Fresno, one in Modesto."

The light bulb clicked on. "They're all along State Route 99."

"Can you map them?" Ken asked.

"Alas, no map function in ProSpy. I'll have to do it the hard way, with Google Maps."

"I'll get a printer. And a map of the state."

I grabbed the addresses one by one and pasted them into Google Maps. Once we'd connected Ken's color printer, we ran off hard copies of each location. Using Post-it flags, we marked the spots on the California map, including the incident date and sequence number.

"There's a year's gap between the first one here and the last one in Modesto."

"Maybe the guy was incarcerated?" Ken suggested.

"Maybe." I looked through the list of results again to confirm the dates and realized we'd missed one. I clicked to page two of the results. "Huh. An outlier. Something that fits... But doesn't."

Ken looked at where I pointed on the screen. "What is it?"

"We didn't map this one. Near Victorville, in San Bernardino County. A year and a half ago. A month before the first Mojave fire."

"But that's a house fire."

"Right. Every other arson on the list involved outbuildings, sheds, barns. No occupied structures."

Ken clicked on the details link and read the report. "This was ruled accidental. Why did the program pull it up?"

"Same accelerant. They found traces of kerosene." I scanned the report for other common elements. "There was flashover."

"How did it start?"

"The investigators determined the kerosene had been stored too close to a gas water heater in the service porch." I stared at the screen. "This seems familiar. I must have read about it at the time."

"A house fire in Victorville? Maybe two column inches on page nineteen in the Chronicle."

"Yeah. It reminds me of..." Thoughts bubbled up to the surface. "The Nguyen's Laundromat," I murmured.

"Sounds like the title of a Vietnamese art film."

I laughed, too dead tired to resist the sick humor. "Place around the corner from me. Burned down a few months ago. The Nguyens stored kerosene in a storage room near a gas water heater. Fire investigators determined that someone – vandals, kids likely – had broken in overnight, made a mess with the kerosene. Some malfunction in the water heater started the fire."

Another spark of inspiration struggled to ignite. I shut my eyes and willed it to consciousness. The fire at the Arco. The fire at the river. A fire in the dumpster at the Hangman's Tavern. And...

Ruth Martinez's words came back to me. When the landlord checked on Enrique's apartment. *Vandals had set fire to the sofa.*

"Oh, my God," I whispered.

"What?"

"Fires and missing kids."

"You've lost me."

"Someone set a fire at Enrique's place around the time he went missing. Someone set a fire at the service station where James disappeared. Brandon went into the water and vanished – and someone set a fire."

Ken narrowed his gaze. "Except vandals set the fire at Enrique's. Likely the same at the service station. The fire by the river is the only one that connects to the others in Greenville County."

I scrubbed at my face, shoulders sagging in exhaustion. "You're right. The fires in the Bay Area have nothing to do with yours."

But if there were a connection, no matter how slim, between my missing boys and fire, wouldn't it be a worthwhile avenue to follow? It was dangerous territory, and I'd damn well have to keep my mind on finding the boys rather than catering to my hell-born obsession. But it would be worth the struggle if fire was the key to break the logjam in discovering James's and Enrique's whereabouts.

I groped for my phone, intending to call Sheri's cell. Luckily, I squinted at the time on the display before I dialed. It was nearly midnight.

I called the office instead, leaving a message. "Sheri, do a search cross-correlating that missing eight month-old with fires. Dumpster, structure, whatever." I disconnected, slumping in my chair. "Damn, I'm tired."

I scrubbed at my face. My eyes closed, I tensed at the first feather light touch of Ken's fingers in my hair. When he brushed along the curve of my ear, I ordered myself to move away, but just sat there, frozen, slave to emotions that should have been dead.

"Why don't you stay the night?" he said softly.

I let myself enjoy the forbidden a moment more, then pushed back my chair. Since I was doing such a lousy job fending off Ken's advances on my womanhood, I needed my own personal IED to keep him away.

I shoved up my T-shirt's long sleeves and thrust my arms out to him, exposing the decorations dotting my skin. "You know I didn't do all these myself."

His gaze flicked down to the staccato pattern reaching from an inch above my wrist to the bunched up sleeve. "Your father–"

"Not just him, either."

He might have seen where I was going, because he took my hand and tried to tug the sleeve back down. I pulled out of reach. "Listen to me, Ken."

He looked away. "It doesn't matter."

"It does." I turned his face toward mine. "I'm a sick puppy, Ken. You knew that three years ago when we stomped on your marriage vows. Let's just say I've gotten a little more twisted since you left."

"I don't want to hear this." He started to rise.

I grabbed his arm and yanked him back into his chair. "Sometimes, I ask a guy to do it. A cigarette, a hot match head. Right before we do the deed. Sometimes that's the only way I can get off."

The horror in his face drove a spike into my stomach. As god-awful as what I'd told him was, it was the truth, although I hadn't done it in a good long while.

"You do that now?" he asked, his voice so low I could barely hear him.

I could have told him the rest of the story, that I'd grown some self-respect and avoided intimacy altogether, but knowing how noble Ken was, that would take us back to square one. "Would you burn me?" I whispered, bile rising in my throat. "If I asked you, would you take a match–"

"You know damned well I wouldn't." He jumped to his feet and stalked off toward the kitchen.

I pulled my sleeves back down, my hands shaking. "You still want me to stay?"

He stopped, took a breath, then turned back toward me. "You can sleep in Cassie's room."

I ought to head back to the motel, take a cold shower, go for a run. Set my room on fire. Anything but stay in Ken Heinz's house.

But I seemed to have lost all judgment between Ken's first touch and my loathsome confession. "Sure," I said calmly, as if I hadn't just ripped open my soul. "Thanks."

After I'd shut down and packed away my computer, I dutifully followed Ken upstairs to Cassie's room. Her decorating scheme was pink and posters, completely at odds with the Cassie I'd met.

"Those boy bands are a little out of date." I pointed to the largest poster that hung over the bed. "That kid's been in and out of rehab the past two years. This one just announced he's gay."

"She's been bugging me to repaint."

"Let me guess, black? With a glow-in-the-dark pentagram on the ceiling?"

His mouth curved in a faint smile. "Something like that."

Together we remade the narrow twin bed with fresh sheets. "I put clean towels in Cassie's bathroom. Next door over. I'm at the end of the hall."

"Hoping for a *tête à tête* during the night?"

He walked out without further comment. I waited until I heard his bedroom door shut, then found the bathroom. A T-shirt lay across the two haphazardly folded towels, a faded Greenville County Fair logo on it.

I stripped and showered, then threw on Ken's castoff shirt. It hung to mid-thigh, but the short sleeves didn't provide much coverage to my arms. No one to see the scars but me and God.

I gave my tighty-whities a quick wash in the sink, then hung them over the shower rod. I carried the rest of my clothes back to the bedroom and dumped them in a pile by the door.

I hadn't spent the night in a chaste twin bed like Cassie's since my first year in the dorm at SFSU. As I slipped under the covers and rested my wet head of hair against the pillow, I wondered if it had crossed Ken's mind that maybe my sins would rub off on the flowered sheets. I wasn't so sure myself that the darkness of my soul might not leak out during the night.

My nightmare *du jour* was a reworked version of my flashback the day before at the old homestead. Daddy on the sofa, his cigarette hanging from his mouth. Him yelling for a beer, me, dutifully toddling off to what passed for a kitchen in our house to fish one out of the cooler. My careful passage back, eyes fixed on the floor and the obstacle course of crap Daddy had left there.

I tripped, stumbled, spilled the beer. Daddy grabbed my arm, plucked the cigarette from his mouth. He lowered the tip to my arm. The familiar nightmare barely raised my heart rate.

Until I looked up at Daddy and saw his wicked face morphing, changing into Tommy Phillips's. Tommy pressed the glowing cigarette to my skin, grinning and wild-eyed, the sweet boy transformed into an avenging evil.

I must have screamed; next thing I knew I was bolt upright in bed and Ken was barging into Cassie's room, lit by moonlight, bare-chested in boxers. For a moment, I didn't know him, my addled brain turning him into my monster of a father. I screamed again, then felt like a right idiot when I came to my senses.

I struggled to breathe. "Sorry. I thought you..."

He stood over the bed. "Are you okay?"

"Yeah. Just a dream. Just..." Now my heart hammered, almost too loud for me to think. I looked up at him, at that acre of bare chest and the main attraction under boxer shorts at eye level. I considered how nice it would be to have someone else to hold the nightmares at bay for once.

And I caved. I scooted over, pulled back the sheets. "Just stay with me," I told him.

He didn't move. "Janelle..."

"Nothing else. Just sleep with me."

Another hesitation, then he crawled into bed beside me. The moment his skin hit mine I realized the insanity of "just sleep." I ignored the warmth that crept inside me and its whispered suggestions. Not to mention Ken's little buddy at full attention against my hip.

I don't know how long we were both awake. I do know we didn't move an inch all that time.

I snapped to consciousness at 6am and discovered my mouth smashed up against his shoulder and Ken's hand cupped tight as a barnacle over my left breast. I managed to dislodge his fingers without waking him, pretended I didn't feel his morning hard-on when I disengaged my leg from between his. I snagged my clothes and hobbled from the room, expectation that he'd catch me sneaking out knotting tension between my shoulders.

I dressed, then coped with a nasty case of bedhead before creeping downstairs. Ken scared the crap out of me when he popped out of the kitchen, still bare-chested, although he'd had the decency to pull on a pair of jeans.

"Just starting the coffee," he mumbled as he passed me. He cleared me by inches, our mutual keep-away vibes colliding between us.

I was shoving my feet into my Nikes, hoping to make a speedy escape, when my calf locked up. Huffing like a woman in labor, I hopped to a chair in the dining room and fumbled into it.

As I tried to massage the tortured muscle, my cell chimed out its Jim Morrison tune. It was barely 6.30am, so Sheri's chipper hello surprised me.

Phone wedged against my ear, I bent to tie my shoes. "Don't tell me, aliens have landed in San Francisco."

"Old news," Sheri said. "They've been here for years."

Finished with my laces, I tried again to stretch out my left calf. It didn't. "You're quitting law school to become a rabbi."

"Are you interested in what I've dug up on Pickford and Beck or would you rather keep busting my chops?"

Abandoning the effort to recover my useless leg, I found a pad of paper in my computer bag. "You got my message from last night?" She assured me she had. "Okay, what have you got on our friendly neighborhood SOs?"

"I emailed you Beck's arrest records and some additional info on Pickford. Pickford was into pretty standard stuff, if you can call that sicko stuff standard. He's been everyone's favorite neighbor or soccer coach, always glad to give extra special attention to any kid that needs it."

"I picked up that much from the court records you sent before. Was it just boys? Or girls too?" I asked. "And what ages?"

"Boys exclusively. The youngest was seven, the oldest ten. He drops them when they hit puberty."

I tapped my pen on the pad. "Doesn't quite fit either Enrique or James."

"Speaking of which..."

"You know as much as I do." I wasn't about to mention my latest theory to her. It sounded even more preposterous in the light of day.

"I just thought when you left that message–"

"Just a wild hare. Probably won't pan out." I gave my leg another try, wincing as invisible demons used my calf for target practice with a white-hot poker.

"I've told Mrs Madison there's nothing new," Sheri said. "But if you could call her–"

"And say what? That I know bupkis about where her son might be?"

I propped my foot up on the trestle table, hoping to give myself more leverage. I couldn't hold back a wussy little whimper.

"What's wrong?" Sheri asked.

"Leg," I told her, knowing I would need no further explanation. "What about Beck?"

"That's more interesting. He's a collector."

"Child porn on the computer?" I gasped as I leaned forward.

"No evidence of that. He collected *things*."

Ken entered the kitchen, decked out in his uniform, and headed straight for the coffee pot. He glanced over at me, scowled at my foot on the table, then pulled two mugs from their hooks above the Mr Coffee. He clunked a mug in front of me, the cup of brew doctored perfectly with a scoop of creamer and two sugars.

He stood over me, sipping his coffee as I finished up with Sheri. When I set down the phone to suck up some caffeine, he stared at my foot as if it would levitate from vision power alone.

"It's dead meat this morning," I told him. "Apparently Paul Beck is a collector."

Ken pulled up a chair opposite me. "Porn?" he asked, taking my foot into his lap. He slipped off the shoe and sock, then pushed my jeans up to my knee. He pressed his thumbs into either side of my calf.

I shook my head, gritting my teeth to keep from moaning in agony. "Trophies and souvenirs. A boy's sock. A candy bar wrapper. One kid's retainer."

"Yuck." He dug deeper, hitting the mother lode of pain.

"Pictures the boys drew. A pencil." At his questioning look, I added, "It had the kid's teeth marks on it."

Ken grimaced in disgust. "So, if we could take a look at his place..."

"We might find some kind of indication that Enrique's been there." I sighed as his prodding fingers released a knot.

"Not James?"

"He's too old." I sagged in my chair as the last of the pain subsided. "He liked having lots of kids around. Invite them over for video game parties, that sort of thing. His favorites he'd have over for special, private games."

He kept rubbing my leg, his hands warm against my skin. "But did any of those kids disappear?"

"No."

My foot rested alongside the placket of his khaki trousers. Just an inch to the left and I'd see just how much he was enjoying the massage session.

He stroked from knee to ankle. "About last night..."

I tried to pull my leg free, but he held on tight. "We should go back to Beck's place today," I said, trying to launch the conversation in another direction. "Can you get a warrant?"

"Probably," he said. "I know it's none of my business..."

Another play for freedom, but he had me in a death grip now. "Pickford knew something about Enrique. It might be worth another visit to him."

He leaned toward me. "Janelle–"

"Uncle Ken?"

I hadn't heard the front door open. Obviously Ken hadn't either, which was why he was caught flat-footed, so to speak, when Cassie suddenly made an appearance in the dining room.

"Charlie horse," I told her as I slipped free, grateful my leg would support me now.

Ken pushed to his feet, hands in his pockets. "I thought you were staying at the Hamptons all day."

Cassie's avid gaze ping-ponged from Ken to me and back. "My insulin cartridge ran out. Mr Hampton dropped me off on his way to work so I could get a fresh set."

Turning away from Cassie on the pretext of grabbing his coffee, Ken slurped down half the cup. "Are you going back?"

"I'd like to. Can you take me?"

"Sure." He sidled around his niece into the kitchen. "Get your set. I'll meet you outside."

Cassie gave me another look, then left the room. Ken dumped his coffee in the sink, then pulled keys from his pocket. He started to take one off the ring. "Finish your coffee. Lock up when you're done."

"Hell, no. I'm getting out of here before she comes back." I slid the mug across the breakfast bar. "Her wheels are turning fast enough as it is."

I slung my computer over my shoulder and made a beeline through the kitchen. Ken followed me into the living room. Cassie had left the front door open, maybe had tiptoed up the porch steps as well after seeing my car cozied up to Ken's Explorer.

Ken pushed the screen door open. "I'll call you when I have the warrant."

I ducked under his arm, flapping my hand in a farewell wave. Cassie appeared as I started up my car. She was grinning now, no doubt thoroughly enjoying Ken's discomfort at the situation.

I had to back up around Ken's truck to get myself pointed down the driveway, so I spotted Cassie's smirk as she and Ken headed out to the Explorer. I rolled down my window a few inches as I pulled around and heard Ken's heated defense to whatever Cassie had asked him. "Not any of your damn business," and, "Nothing's going on," filtered over to me as I took my time shifting into drive. When he caught me listening, Ken speared me with the evil eye before he climbed in the Explorer.

Facing his wife, Tara, after she discovered our affair had probably been a cakewalk compared to being busted by his thirteen year-old niece. I ought to have a little sympathy for him.

I really shouldn't have laughed as I pulled out of his drive.

CHAPTER 15

I made a quick pit stop at the Gold Rush Inn to freshen up and change into another of my thrift store castoffs, then headed over to Beck's place. He wasn't home, although the mailbox had been emptied. Mrs Bertram didn't answer, which worried me; as old as she was, she could have died in her sleep.

I flagged down an elderly couple on a power walk through the mobile home park. "Janelle Watkins. I'm a private investigator." I put out my hand to shake.

The woman's grip nearly brought me to my knees. "Raelene. My husband, George."

"Any idea where Mrs Bertram is?" I asked, trying to rub some circulation back into my fingers.

They walked in place, arms pumping. "Grandson picks her up early on Saturdays," George told me, barely out of breath. "Spends the day with her."

I flashed my dog-eared photos of Enrique and James. "Have you seen either of these kids around here?"

"This is an adults-only park." Raelene sneered in the general direction of Beck's mobile home. "Which is why they sent *him* here to live. Believe me, if I saw anyone under the age of eighteen with him, I'd be on the phone to the sheriff's office."

"Has Beck been home? I noticed his mail is gone."

"I haven't seen him," Raelene said, fingertips against her wrist, eyes fixed on her watch.

169

"Do you know where he might have gone?"

Raelene lifted her knees higher as she marched. "I overheard him tell the manager he was going to visit his sister up in Santa Rosa."

Santa Rosa. Where my Fresno undercover buddy, luvzboyz, had told me a young boy had been requested on the internet. I didn't like the coincidence. If Beck was up there, he might well be up to no good.

"Have you ever met his sister?" I asked.

"Never. I spend as little time in that man's presence as I can." Raelene snagged George's arm. "Got to keep our heart-rate up." Off they went.

I could see two possibilities, both of them ugly. Either the sister did exist and Beck used his visits with her to either get close to his nephews or some other young boys in Santa Rosa without being under Ken's nose. Or there was no sister at all. He'd mentioned her to Mrs Bertram and the manager just to give him cover for his trips to Santa Rosa. He could be president of the local Man-Boy Love association up there and Ken would be none the wiser.

I climbed back into the Escort, unsettled by Paul Beck's continued absence. Even though it would be the most outrageous quirk of fate if Beck was in Santa Rosa picking up the young boy luvzboyz mentioned and even more bizarre if that boy happened to be Enrique, I still wouldn't be satisfied until I could talk to the molester. If he didn't turn up today and I left as planned, I'd likely never get the chance to grill him.

Cranking on the engine, I eyed the car clock. Not quite nine. If I intended to go home later today, I had to check out of the Gold Rush Inn by eleven. I knew I ought to do that now, before I started my interviews. Then I could take off when I either ran out of time or ran out of townspeople to harass.

But I drove right past the Gold Rush Inn, hunching a little as I passed under the glowering 49er. He probably still didn't forgive me for painting a certain part of his anatomy pink back in junior high.

Over the years, Emil's Café probably would have spent more time shut down due to health violations than it would have serving hash browns and burgers if Emil's brother, Constantin, hadn't worked for the county health inspector. I'd actually worked at Emil's the summer I'd turned fifteen and quickly adopted a "don't ask, don't tell" approach to what those cockroaches were doing in the dry stores room.

When I entered the time warp of Emil's, I was astounded that so little had changed in the twenty years since I'd left. The same cast iron skillets and copper bottom pots hung on the walls, although the inch of dust that had always coated them was gone. The gothic-looking, wrought-iron chandeliers still lit the place, but the cobwebs that had given Emil's a year-round Halloween ambiance had been cleared out.

The cast of characters had changed, too. I didn't recognize the twentyish blonde balancing four plates as she threaded her way through the tables, or the late-twenties, dark-haired guy working the kitchen. The cook had Emil's hawk nose and eye squint, so I suspected the family still owned the place.

I sat at the counter and plucked a menu from its holder behind the napkin dispenser. Same old grease-larded breakfasts, but they had added a spinach and cream cheese omelet.

The waitress headed back my way with a twenty and a food ticket. "Give me a minute, hon," she said before ringing up the sale.

The waitress – her nametag read Diana – slapped a plastic glass of ice water in front of me. "Coffee?"

"Sure."

She set down a mug – clean, I noticed – and filled it with coffee. The cook caught my eye and smiled as he slid two filled plates on the pass-through and dinged the bell. A big improvement from Emil, who was convinced everyone he encountered was ready to either cheat him or stab him in the back.

"Give me just another sec." Diana grabbed the steaming plates.

While I waited, I dumped two sugar packets and three creamers into my coffee. "Is Emil still around?" I asked when Diana returned.

"Passed away," she told me. "That's his grandson. Andros and I just took over the place six months ago."

"I bussed tables here back in high school. Hasn't changed much."

She looked around. "Yeah, the decorating scheme is hideous. I'm working on Andros to update but I haven't gotten past the nostalgia factor yet."

I laid the boys' photos on the counter. "Any chance you've seen either of these kids?"

She studied them a moment, then picked up James's picture for a closer look. "My husband might have seen this boy. Andros? Come take a look at this."

He pushed through the swinging doors and took the photo Diana held out to him. "Who's this?"

"Could be that kid you saw," Diana said. "Remember the nutcase guy?"

"Yeah. Right." Andros tapped the photo. "Could be him."

"When was this?"

"We started closing early about four months ago," Diana said. "I think it was about a month after that. Late December? Not long after Christmas." She caught sight of a customer holding up his coffee mug. She grabbed the pot and headed off for a refill.

"Emil's used to stay open until ten," Andros told me. "Once Diana had the baby, we started closing at eight instead."

Diana returned and started another pot of coffee. "I was nursing the baby in one of the booths and this guy pounded on the door, all frantic. Scared me half to death."

"What did he look like?" I asked.

"Creepy looking," Diana said. "Big full beard, eyes a little crazy looking. Andros saw the kid with him."

"In the car," Andros said. "I unlocked the door to see what the guy wanted, and he had his car parked out front."

"What kind of car?"

"A Volvo 240 sedan," Andros said. "Probably early 80s."

"Why so sure of the make?"

"Same as my first car," he said, smiling. "A hand-me-down from my granddad."

I could easily imagine the thrifty Emil driving such a sensible car. "What color?"

"Dark. Navy blue or black." His brow furrowed as he tried to bring back the memory. "There was a decal on the windshield, a parking pass for CCSF. It stuck in my mind because I took some hospitality classes there before we took over the café."

CCSF. City College of San Francisco. The Airport Campus was on the other side of McLaren Park from me. "So you saw James in the car."

"He was in the front seat. A woman was sitting in the back. I thought it was a little weird that the kid was black and the guy and his wife were both white."

"But it could have been him?" I asked, pointing to James's photo.

He glanced at the picture again. "Looks about the right age. He wasn't smiling when I saw him. Looked a little scared."

A customer yelled for Diana and she hurried away. I took the photo back from Andros. "Have you seen him since?"

He shook his head. "I should have done something. I had a feeling something wasn't right."

"You couldn't have known. I'm sure you had other things on your mind." I appreciated the fact that Andros had a conscience. "Do you know what the guy was so frantic about?"

"He needed some baby aspirin. You know how it is around here, small town like this rolls up their sidewalks early. Nothing was open and I guess their baby had a fever."

"Did you see a baby?"

"The woman might have been holding one. She had something in her arms. But she never got out of the car."

I thanked him, turned to go, then spun back. "That night, was there a fire anywhere nearby? In a trash can or dumpster?"

I saw the surprise in his face. "One of the trash cans across the street. We saw it smoldering as we were heading for home. I had a gallon jug of water in the trunk and poured that on it. I figured it was kids, or a smoker who didn't put out their butt."

With another thank you, I left. Apparently, James had been here in Greenville, with the same man that Emma at McDonald's had seen him with. Sounded as if the baby was with them as well. And based on timeline, that might have been their dark sedan at the Hangman's Tavern later that night when the dumpster burned. No way of knowing if James or the baby were still here, but the McD's girl had heard them ask about Greenville, which implied this was their final destination.

A hand on the door to the Escort, my gaze strayed over to Greenville Electronics, directly across Main Street from Emil's. McPherson had said the shop had sent someone over to Mrs Lopez's house to install a new television and Blu-Ray. It hadn't occurred to me at the time to ask who'd done the installation. If the guy was still local, maybe he could give me some insight into where Mrs Lopez might have moved. And if I got another look at the invoice, maybe I could make out whether there was a phone number at the bottom.

I hitched my way over to the electronics store, my left leg surprisingly supple after Ken's morning massage. I wondered if I could wrangle another session from him before I headed home.

The electronics store's front door was locked. A CLOSED sign hung from a placard listing the hours, nine to six. I peered inside, looking for some indication Rich McPherson was in residence. Although the lights were on, no one was home. I knocked on the door; maybe the guy was in the office or crouched out of sight behind the counter. No luck.

As I crossed the street again, I heard my cell phone trilling out the last notes of a call through the open window of the Escort. Caller ID didn't display the number.

About thirty seconds later, the phone beeped, telling me I had a voice message. I pressed the retrieve message button and punched in my access code.

It was Ken. "Janelle – get over to the SaveMart. Rich McPherson just spotted Lucy Polovko there with a little Hispanic boy. It could be Enrique."

I disconnected and tossed the phone to the seat, then cranked on the engine. As I backed out into Main Street, I nearly creamed someone pulling into the parking space beside me. My tires squealed as I jetted off toward the highway, trying to form a mental map of where the SaveMart was with respect to Greenville. It was no more than twenty minutes away, a few miles down Highway 50.

A sprawling department store-cum-supermarket, the SaveMart was huge by Greenville standards. Built long before big box stores had begun to dominate small towns across the nation, SaveMart had been the bane of Greenville's mom and pops and the guilty pleasure of its citizens.

The two decades since I'd seen it last hadn't been kind to the SaveMart. As I pulled into the near-empty parking lot, I could see the place looked worn out – a window broken and boarded up, trash overflowing the bins, weeds creeping through cracks in the asphalt parking lot.

Ken's Explorer was parked beside Lucy's old truck. A pickup with a cheapo blue paint job was positioned behind Lucy's vehicle, blocking it from leaving. McPherson stood beside his Chevy, hand wrapped around the stub of a broken radio antenna, looking jittery as a cat.

I'd seen it before in citizens taking police matters into their own hands. They couldn't handle the adrenaline rush.

"You need me to stay?" he asked, looking ready to jump out of his skin.

"Go on back to the shop," Ken told him. "The fewer the civilians, the better."

Ken and I headed toward the store. "Rich was getting ready to open up when he saw Lucy drive by. He spotted the little boy in the car. Rich got in his truck and followed Lucy, called me as he drove."

"Called you and not 911?"

"He's got my cell since Cassie hangs out so much at the store." He pushed open the door for me. "The deputy that works this zone is at least an hour away on a domestic abuse call. On top of that, we've got an Amber Alert this morning. A little boy taken from his bedroom. A witness saw a man driving away from the scene."

That put a fist to my gut. "You're sure Lucy is still in here?"

"I called ahead and made sure they had employees on both doors." He pointed a thumb at the young girl in a SaveMart shirt fidgeting by the entrance. "She hasn't left."

"What about the bathroom?" I glanced over in the direction of the women's room.

"They've been locked." Ken motioned me past the registers. "You take this end of the aisles. I'll take the other."

Out of habit, I patted my hip where my Sig Sauer would have been. Nothing there but the box of matches stuffed in my jeans pocket. I wouldn't need a weapon; the idea of Lucy with a gun was laughable. Even still, knowing how unbalanced she was, I missed having a sidearm handy.

Ken and I kept pace as we passed the pharmaceutical aisle, then personal products and hair care, then paper products. I thought we might get a hit on the candy aisle, but there were only a couple women browsing the Junior Mints and Tootsie Rolls. They looked up in surprise when they saw the sheriff and my own skinny self eyeing them in passing.

We hit pay dirt on the toy aisle. Lucy held the boy in her arms, snuggled up against her chest. Dressed in striped shirt and denim overalls, a ball cap on his head, the boy looked the right age to be Enrique, but I couldn't see his face clearly.

Lucy stood pondering a display of dolls. Beyond the creepiness factor of Loony Lucy holding that sweet innocence so close, the thought of her buying a doll for the boy seemed wrong.

My leg took that opportunity to suddenly cramp, the instant pain throwing me off-balance and into a display of cheapo video games. The noise of the plastic handhelds falling to the floor alerted Lucy to my presence. Sudden paranoia twisted her face and she turned away from me as if seeking escape. Ken was already there.

"Lucy, let go of the boy," Ken said, his voice soft and calm.

Lucy clutched the kid tighter. "You won't take my baby girl."

Baby girl? I crept up the aisle, trying to get a closer look. The boy had his face buried in Lucy's neck. "His folks are pretty worried about him. How about you put him down?"

Looking from me to Ken, Lucy just shook her head. "She might get lost again."

Ken closed in from the other side. "You see anything in her hands, Janelle?" he asked.

"Nothing." The smelly, ragged dress Lucy wore could have hidden any number of deadly weapons, but the madwoman didn't seem inclined to let go of her prize to reach in her pockets.

Ken got near enough to take Lucy's arm. "No one wants to take your baby girl. We just need to check her over real quick. Make sure she's okay."

Sudden tears filled Lucy's eyes. "My baby girl's not sick again, is she?"

I put a hand on Lucy's shoulder, cringing at the odor wafting from her. "She might be. How about if you let us take a look?"

Reluctantly, Lucy relinquished her hold, letting the boy slide to the floor. I picked him up the moment he was on his feet, finally getting a good look at his face.

Not Enrique. Disappointment tied a knot in my stomach.

Ken pulled Lucy's hands behind her back and cuffed her. She went completely apeshit, screaming at the top of her lungs as Ken muscled her down the aisle. I followed with the boy.

"Is it Enrique?" Ken shouted over Lucy's indignation.

"Must be your Amber Alert," I yelled back. "But I thought witnesses saw a man."

Ken sidestepped an attempted head butt by Lucy. "They must have been mistaken."

I followed with the boy. "What's your name?" I asked him.

He yawned. "Norberto."

"Norberto, what?"

He shrugged. Too young to know his last name, or too shy to tell me.

I bought a Three Musketeers bar at the checkout counter and unwrapped it for Noberto. A little chocolate would go a long way toward making things better.

By the time I got outside, Ken had shoehorned Lucy into the back of the Explorer. She'd gone nearly catatonic at that point, rocking in the restraint cage, mouth open, eyes wide. I took Norberto over to my car, keeping him out of sight of Lucy. Ken came over as I set him in the front seat.

"I'd heard stories that Lucy was married once," Ken said. "Maybe she had a little girl."

"But after all this time, why would she suddenly go looking for a kid to snatch? And how'd she manage to take him anyway?" I winced as Norberto smeared a chocolate-coated hand on my cloth seat.

"Mom had left Norberto playing in his room while she cleaned up from breakfast. There was a slit in the bedroom window screen. Lucy must have cut the screen, then talked the kid into coming over to the window. When he got close enough, she just reached in and grabbed him."

I found a stack of napkins in the glove box and made a vain attempt to tidy up the little boy's hands. "Considering Lucy's state of mind, can you picture her reasoning all that out?"

"No. And I checked her odometer just now. Not enough change since yesterday's reading to account for a trip to the boy's house and a trip here." Ken glanced over at the madwoman in the back of the Explorer. "It makes no sense. But she had the boy."

"Mom on her way?" Norberto smiled up at me, chocolate from ear to ear.

"One of my Spanish-speaking deputies is bringing her over." Ken turned back to me. "I appreciate you letting him sit in your car. Lucy's riled up enough as it is."

"No problem." Other than the handprint in chocolate on my car window. "You going to search Lucy's place?"

Ken's distaste was obvious. "Have to. A couple of my deputies are on their way down there now. Warrants are in progress."

"I suppose it's possible she's got something incriminating stashed away somewhere. Who knows what's in that basement of hers." Ken's deputies would deserve hazard pay for excavating through it. "Speaking of warrants, you have the one for Beck's place yet?"

"It's waiting for me. Once we're done here, I can pick it up on the way, meet you over there."

"That works. I really ought to stop at the motel to check out." At least that had been the plan when I'd woken up that morning.

"Heading back today?" I couldn't tell from the pinched look around Ken's mouth if he was happy with my departure or not.

"James was here, Ken. I showed his picture to Andros at Emil's Café. Andros saw him. And told me someone set a fire nearby around the same time."

I expected Ken to vent about me nosing around his town. Instead he asked, "Then, are you staying or going?"

I swiped the smeared chocolate on my window with my thumb. "Even if he was here, he may be dead by now." I imagined myself telling that to Mrs Madison, imagined her pain.

"Then go on home." He walked off toward the Explorer, leaving me to my cowardly indecision.

Mrs Vallejo arrived a few minutes later, jumping from the patrol car the moment it stopped beside mine. Norberto screamed out, "Mama!" then burst into tears as his mother snatched him up. Whatever melted mess was still on the kid's face and hands transferred to Mrs Vallejo's white shirt. I doubted the woman minded at all.

CHAPTER 16

Huddled on his mattress, James held the baby in his arms, Sean beside him. Thomas, the boy Mama had brought yesterday, lay on Sean's bed, still and quiet under his blankets. He was older than Sean, but younger than James. Mama had told James that Thomas was his brother, like Sean. Like baby Lydia was his sister.

Mama had gone out in the daytime yesterday, had come back with Thomas, then had been gone all morning. Daddy had brought them breakfast instead of Mama. James had been surprised to see him since Daddy almost never came into the basement. James had been even more surprised when Daddy had slipped and called him by his real name instead of calling him Junior like Mama did.

It was nearly lunchtime. He wondered if Daddy would bring their peanut butter sandwiches and juice instead of Mama. It would be nice to hear himself called by his real name again.

When the door lock rattled, James got up and set the baby in the playpen. She whimpered a little and James thought maybe she'd start crying. But it seemed like she'd given up, just like Sean had. Like James almost had.

It was Mama at the door. He thought she'd set the tray down like she always did and take the dirty diaper. But although she picked up the diaper and tossed it through the open door, she kept on going down the stairs. She walked right past him into

181

the room with the tray and set it down on the floor between the mattresses.

And she'd left the door open.

James stared at that open door, at the stairs leading up to it. He was between the stairs and Mama. She was busy with something on the tray; from the steam, James thought it might be hot soup. She turned to Thomas, the steaming bowl in her hands, her back to James.

He sidled toward the stairs, keeping his eyes on Mama every inch. Sean looked over at him and he willed the little boy to keep quiet, prayed Mama wouldn't check to see what Sean was looking at.

He reached the bottom of the stairs. Placed his foot carefully, quietly on the first one. Stepped up to the next, the next. Mama still hadn't noticed.

He made it halfway up, lifted a cautious foot to the next step. Didn't lift high enough. His toe caught on the wooden step and he stumbled, falling face first on the stairs and barking his shin on the edge.

Of course Mama heard the noise. She spilled the soup when she set it down in a hurry, came running toward him. He tried to make it up the rest of the stairs, thought maybe he could shut the door and lock her in. But Mama caught his leg before he could completely get to his feet. He banged his shin again, hard enough this time that he'd probably cut it through his jeans.

She half-dragged him down the stairs, across the floor to his mattress. Threw him down so hard, he accidentally hit Sean in the face with his elbow. His hand on his cheek, Sean started crying. James tried to tell the little boy he was sorry, but Mama kept slapping him on the face so he couldn't talk.

She stood over him, her rage terrifying. "Maybe you won't go to heaven when I send the others! Maybe you'll go to the other place where the fire never stops burning!"

Mama grabbed his shirt and made him sit up. She took a candle from the pocket of her jeans and broke off a short piece, then stuffed it into his hands.

She pulled her lighter from another pocket and struck a flame. For a moment, she stared at the fire as if she wanted to climb inside it. Then she lit the candle and knelt before him, watching it burn.

CHAPTER 17

On my way to Beck's, I took a side trip back into town to have a chat with Rich McPherson. I found him in his store, still a little hyped-up over the morning's excitement. He jumped at the beep of the opening door, dropping a handful of phone cards he'd been hooking on a display.

He bent to gather them up. "Everything turn out okay with the little boy?"

"He's with his mama, safe and sound." I gave him a pat on the back, relieved at the absence of booze breath. "Good job. Sheriff owes you a medal."

He hung the last of the cards on the counter display, then grabbed the empty box. "What can I do for you?"

"I'd like to take another look at that invoice for Mrs Lopez's TV."

Fingers wrapped tight around the box in his hands, he stared at me. "I might not have it anymore. I cleared out a bunch of the old invoices after you were here."

"You threw them away?"

The box started to collapse under his grip. "I don't know. I'm not even sure if I did anything at all with it."

I wondered what had happened to Mr Helpful of two days ago. "Take a look, see if it's still there."

"The truth is, the owner of the store, Mr Templeton, didn't like me showing you the invoice in the first place. He says that information is private." He continued to mangle the box. "I'm sorry."

"Any chance I could talk to Mr Templeton about that?"

"He's an out-of-towner. Even I have a hard time reaching him." He set the crushed box down on the counter. "What was it you were looking for? Maybe I could check the invoice myself and see if the information is there. I don't think Mr Templeton would mind that."

McPherson hadn't struck me as the "company man" type, but maybe Templeton had busted his chops when he'd found out Rich had been showing the store's business files to overly nosy private investigators. "I just wanted to know who installed the equipment Mrs Lopez bought."

He went behind the counter and opened the file drawer. When he pulled out the invoice, he held it close, like a poker player protecting his cards. "Oh," he said, the single syllable rich with meaning. He looked over at me. "It was Chuck Pickford."

"What lamebrain hires a child molester to go into people's homes as an installer?"

McPherson stuffed the invoice back into the filing cabinet. "He's Mr Templeton's brother-in-law. He only lasted a week. Too many customers complained."

I thanked Rich and left. On my way to Beck's, I passed the Gold Rush Inn again, but figured I didn't have the time to stop. Ken probably had turned over booking Lucy to one of his deputies, and might already be at the mobile home park.

I'd definitely have to have another conversation with Pickford before I left. I couldn't see Mrs Lopez confiding her deepest secrets to him, but maybe he'd seen something that would give me a clue as to where to look next.

Ken was parked out in front of Beck's mobile when I got there, waiting inside his Explorer. He was typing into his onboard computer with the same henpeck he'd used back at

SFPD, but he'd gotten surprisingly fast with the two-fingered approach.

He picked the warrant up from the seat and slung a digital camera around his neck. "The facility manager gave me the key."

Ken knocked first, even though there was still no car in the driveway. "Paul Beck! Open up. I have a warrant to search your premises."

As expected, no answer. Digging a couple of pairs of latex gloves from his pocket, Ken unlocked the door and pushed it open. The cloying smell of over-ripe garbage wafted out as we stepped inside. It didn't have the familiar stench of a rotting body, but a thrill jetted down my spine at the thought that maybe Beck hadn't answered because he'd offed himself in his bedroom.

No such luck. Beck was just a lousy housekeeper. He'd left a half-filled bag of trash in the kitchen and nature had taken its course over the few days he'd been gone.

Although dirty dishes littered the kitchen counter, he kept his living room neat. Not much in the way of furnishings – a thrift store sofa and coffee table, an easy chair with stuffing coming loose, a VCR and old 19-inch television. A few magazines on the table – *Newsweek*, *People*, *Better Homes & Gardens* for God's sake – nothing that raised red flags.

Gloved up, Ken snapped some pictures, then rifled through the video tapes. "They all have commercial labels. No porn. No kiddy movies."

I perused the pile of books on the floor beside the sofa. "He could have recorded over them."

"True. I'll take them in to be sure." He started stacking the tapes on the coffee table.

"Books are all thrillers, mysteries. A Sudoku magazine. A book of baby names. That's creepy." I set it on the coffee table. "A newsletter from the Holy Rock Baptist church." I slipped it out from the pages of the hardcover Beck had stuffed it in.

"Maybe he's got religion," Ken suggested with a straight face.

"Or maybe that's a good place to meet kids."

I lifted the sofa cushions and found a couple of well-chewed pencils, several pennies and a cough drop. Then I stretched out on the floor and checked under the sofa. Nothing but dust bunnies.

"Ready for the bedroom?" Ken asked.

I levered myself up and followed Ken down the hall. The double bed looked as thrift store as the living room suite, its chenille spread threadbare. The mini-blinds over the window were bent and, based on the tangled cord, were stuck halfway up. The lamp on the battered nightstand alongside the bed was missing its shade.

On a hunch, I lifted the side of the bedspread and bent down to take a look under the bed. I found a shoebox tucked up alongside the nightstand. "Can I borrow that camera?"

I photographed the bed with its upturned bedspread, then the box in place. Using Ken's flashlight to extend my reach, I slid the box out, then set it on the bed.

I stepped back, musing that it would be nice if the box contained a stash of baseball cards, or Beck's stamp collection. Wishful thinking.

Ken tipped off the lid, took a couple of pictures, then removed the items one by one and laid them on the bed. They really didn't look like much – a couple of boys' socks, a video game case, a bookmark, a small plastic weapon from some action figure. But knowing what those odds and ends represented to Beck gave me the heebie-jeebies.

"You think this stuff is recent?" I asked as Ken photographed Beck's collection.

"The video game is for a Super Nintendo console. Those haven't been out for a long time." When I gave him a look, he shrugged. "I found one used at a yard sale. Cassie read me the riot act when I tried to give it to her."

"Then maybe these are old souvenirs."

Footsteps in the living room brought Ken to attention. He stepped between me and the bedroom door, had his hand on his Glock .22 when Paul Beck appeared in the doorway.

Beck gave us an innocent, puzzled look. "What's going on?" His gaze fell on the bits and pieces we'd laid out on the bed. His eyes widened.

"You want to tell me about this, Mr Beck?" Ken asked.

He swallowed hard, his Adam's apple working. "I found them."

"Where?" I asked. "In some little boy's bedroom?"

Beck shook his head. "Just around. The socks at the Laundromat, the video case in the trash. I'm allowed to pick through the garbage if I want."

Ken gave him a nudge. "Let's talk about this in the living room, Mr Beck." We trooped out of the bedroom.

"Does your parole officer know what you keep under your bed?" I asked.

Beck suddenly found his toes fascinating. I stepped into his line of sight. "How do you think the parents would feel knowing you're using their kids' castoffs for inspiration on lonely nights? It's not a long step toward using the kids themselves."

Beck turned away. "I've been chemically castrated. Even if I wanted to, I couldn't."

I moved to get in his face again. "If you wanted to, you'd find a way."

I saw the guilt in his eyes. A powerful need had driven him to collect those childish odds and ends. He knew I saw it, too.

Ken elbowed me aside. "Where have you been, Mr Beck?"

"At my sister's place," Beck said. "In Santa Rosa."

"Have you been messing with those boys?" Ken asked.

"No!" Beck whined. "My sister knows better. She sends them off to her ex when I'm there."

"Why so spur of the moment, Beck?" I asked. "You up and left with hardly a word to anyone."

"Our father died last week," Beck said, getting all misty eyed. "My sister and I are settling his affairs."

I had a sneaking suspicion it was dear old dad who made Beck the man he was. I still found it difficult to generate any sympathy for him.

Ken pulled out his pad and a pen. "Write down your sister's phone number. I need to talk with her."

All woebegone, Beck took the pad. "You won't tell her about my box?"

"Write down the damn number," Ken growled.

Beck wrote the number in neat digits and handed the pad back to Ken. Ken stepped outside to make the call. The metal shell of Beck's mobile home made cell reception impossible.

I tipped my head toward the bedroom. "All that crap in the box probably violates your parole."

His lower lip trembled like a remorseful little boy's. "Please. Can't you just take it, throw it away?"

"Help me out here," I said, implying we'd scratch each other's backs. I showed Beck James's and Enrique's photos. "Have you seen these two around?"

He looked at them sidelong, as if the temptation to stray would be too strong viewing them straight on. "No."

I stuck them back in his field of view. "You sure?"

He gave the two pictures another quick once-over. Recognition lit in his face. He gave me a wary look as if he was afraid I was trying to trick him.

"Maybe..." He reached for James's photo.

Remembering Pickford's sick delight at touching the picture of Enrique, I held James's slightly out of reach. "What?"

Beck shook his head. "Probably not the same kid."

"Tell me anyway," I pressed.

He glanced down at James's photo again, then up at me. "I was fly fishing on the river late one afternoon. Fishing helps me think. Keeps my mind off... You know, things."

I tamped down my impatience. "So while you were communing with nature, what did you see?"

"I saw someone running through the trees on the other side of the river. It was such a quick glimpse, I thought I was seeing things. But then I heard someone yelling for him to stop."

"Did he look like this kid?"

"I told you, I just saw him a couple of seconds. But it could have been a black kid."

A chill trickled down my spine. "When was this?"

"About the time I started working at the Hangman's Tavern. So it would have had to be three or four months ago."

It fit the damn time frame. "Where on the river?"

He shrugged. "Maybe ten miles out of town. A quarter mile or so past the big turnout with the washed out stone bridge. There's a tree down in the river upstream of there. A good spot for fishing."

"An oak tree? Pulled up by the roots, maybe three feet or so in diameter?"

His head bobbed in agreement. "That's the one."

The same tree where I found Brandon's glasses. Maybe. Or maybe Beck was making up the whole thing to make me happy. "So the kid's running, people are screaming at him, it didn't cross your mind to do anything about it?"

"When it comes to kids, I try to mind my own business. Keeps me out of trouble."

I could see his point, but if it *was* James running for his life, it made me sick that Beck had done nothing. "You work at Hangman's Tavern."

"His gaze grew wary. "You won't tell my boss–"

"You get your parole revoked, it won't matter," I told him. "Back at the end of December, do you remember a man with a heavy beard and long hair coming into the bar?"

He stared at me blankly a moment, then recognition lit his face. "The night Sondra set the dumpster on fire? The guy said his kid was sick and he needed baby aspirin."

"Did you see the baby? Or some other kids in the car?"

He shook his head. "I told you, I stay away from kids."

"Yeah, yeah, keeps you out of trouble." But he'd confirmed for me that James's kidnapper had been at the bar.

Ken's boot steps on the stairs signaled his return. "His story checks out." He ducked into the bedroom and returned with Beck's treasure box. "I'll be talking to your parole officer."

As we were about to walk out, another thought struck me. "If you heard anything about that boy in Santa Rosa, you'd tell the sheriff, wouldn't you, Paul?"

His eyes grew to saucer size. "I, uh... I don't..." Beck didn't do innocence well.

"I'm sure your parole doesn't allow you to surf the internet," I reminded him, "but we know you've been down to the library. I'm betting you know about the request for a boy in Santa Rosa." I could see from his reaction he knew exactly what I was talking about. "Has that request been fulfilled?"

"N-n-no." His Adam's apple bounced.

Ken approached Beck, closing the distance between them to inches. "Stay off the computer, Mr Beck. Next time the librarian sees you on it, she'll call me."

Having scared the crap out of Beck, Ken walked with me to my Escort. "Sister said he was there the last three days."

"How do you know she's not lying for him?"

"She referred to him several times as 'my creepy pervert brother.'" He opened the car door for me.

"He confirmed he saw the shaggy-haired guy at the tavern. He also gave me a story about seeing a kid out in the woods," I told Ken. "Close to where Brandon went in, but on the other side of the river."

"There's maybe a half-dozen houses out there on a couple thousand acres of BLM land. What the hell would James be doing in such a remote location?"

"Someone took him there." Likely to kill him. I couldn't think of any other reason.

I swung into the Escort, my leg twinging. "You can't drive out there, take a look? It sounds like it's the same place where the fire was set, the one that threw the dogs off."

He looked at me as if I was a loon. "I could if there were roads to drive on and the manpower to search. Or I could ask Sergeant Russell to deploy a mounted SAR team. But you want to be the one to articulate to him what your basis is for that wild-ass goose chase?"

He was right, but it didn't make me any happier about it. I had one iffy witness of questionable character telling me that *maybe* he saw someone and *maybe* it was the kid I was looking for.

"Besides," Ken said, "I thought you were leaving."

Truly, I had all the data I needed. Any further investigation I could do from home in my spare time. If I came up with any solid leads, I could let Ken know.

I shoved my key in the ignition. "I will, as soon as I talk to Pickford again. Turns out he installed Mrs Lopez's television."

"I'll follow you," Ken said, swinging the door shut so I couldn't argue.

I pulled out of the mobile home park, Ken on my tail, Tommy occupying my imagination. His sorrowful mug kept me company all the way to Pickford's place.

Knowing I had to face the stairs again leading up to Grandpa Chuck's, I made Ken wait for me while I did some calf stretches, my hands against the hood of the Explorer like a perp about to be searched. Ken took in every unsightly grimace and whimper of pain, never once offering up his services as a masseur. Obviously there was a cruel streak buried somewhere deep inside him.

My exertions put me in a nasty mood by the time I dragged myself up to the third floor. Pickford's grandpa smile when he answered the door polished up my crappy disposition. His opening remark, "Good to see you again, Sheriff. Miss," added the finishing touch.

I stiff-armed him backward into his living room, taking great satisfaction in the way he stumbled over an ottoman and fell on his butt. The son of a bitch just gave me a mournful smile, as if he didn't understand why anyone would be pissed at him. Coming up beside me, Ken didn't say a word about my rough handling.

I wrenched Pickford to his feet and shoved him down onto the ottoman. "Let's talk about Mrs Lopez."

He gave me a soulful look. "There's no need to be rough. I'm glad to tell you what I know."

"You installed her television and Blu-Ray. Did you see the boy there?"

He shook his head, brow furrowed. "What boy?"

Ken stepped in, a friendly hand on Pickford's shoulder. "The Hispanic boy in the photo she showed you the other day."

As if he'd only just remembered, Pickford's face lit with recognition. "I do remember now. The little boy that's missing."

I leaned over, level with his face. "Where is he? Have you got him somewhere?"

"No!" His eyes widened, just a trace of fear flickering through them. "I never actually saw the boy. I only saw his picture."

Disappointment nibbled at me. "At Mrs Lopez's?"

He nodded. "She had it up on the wall. Alongside a few baby pictures."

"Any sign that the boy was there?" Ken asked. "Toys strewn around? Kids' books on the table, anything like that?"

"Not that I saw." He locked his fingers together and rocked forward and back. "I was just there to do a job. I only noticed the pictures because they were on the wall above where I put the TV."

Yeah, right. His wandering gaze likely zeroed right in on Enrique's picture. "I bet you asked about him."

"I was just trying to be friendly." Chuck smiled, blue eyes all but twinkling. I wanted to rip away his kind facade, expose the evil behind it. "She was glad for the opportunity to talk about her grandson. She said he was three years old and he'd be coming to live with her soon so her daughter could get back on her feet."

"Did she say when he'd be coming?" I asked.

Rubbing his chin, he made a show of trying to remember. "I don't recall her mentioning when. Soon was all she said. She showed me the room she had set aside for him."

Ken dug his fingers in a little deeper. "You had no business going into his bedroom."

Pickford tried to wriggle out of Ken's grip. "I told you. I was only being friendly. She offered to show me."

No doubt after he dropped a few hints. I bet you have a nice room all ready for him, Mrs Lopez. The thought of him sniffing around the little boy's room made me want to lop his head right off his shoulders.

Swallowing back my disgust, I got nose to nose with him. "I'm thinking Enrique *was* there. Maybe you were so friendly that day, Mrs Lopez invited you to come back. Maybe you even got to babysit the little tyke."

"No. I'm telling you I never saw him."

"And while you were alone with Enrique, you did what you do best. You showed him how much you really liked him. Didn't you, Grandpa?"

"Damn it, I never saw the boy. He wasn't living there yet."

I wasn't even sure what I was driving at, what I was hoping to get from Pickford. But I kept at him. "I bet you were disappointed, seeing all those pictures, hearing Mrs Lopez talk about her sweet little grandson. You were just aching to get your hands on him, weren't you?" Remembering Beck's stash, inspiration struck. "You took a souvenir instead, didn't you? What did you take home that day, Grandpa?"

Now his blue eyes nearly goggled right out of his head. "What do you mean?" He choked out the words.

I angled a glance up at Ken. "Where is it, Pickford? Where'd you hide it so the sheriff couldn't find it?"

He squirmed against Ken's tight hold as if the miniscule fragment of guilt that he still harbored inside had broken loose and was worming its way through his body. His gaze shifted away from mine. "I wasn't hiding it. I was just keeping it safe."

Ken moved his face into Pickford's line of sight. "Where is it?"

His mouth got a mean set to it. "I'll have to show you."

Ken released Chuck and backed away. Pickford led us into the bathroom. A claw foot tub had been crammed into the tiny room, its enamel surface chipped and pitted with rust. The toilet lid was up, its yellow contents stinking. The slimeball couldn't even flush his own toilet.

Some baby blue fabric had been glued in a ruffle to the rim of the sink, concealing the plumbing beneath it. Pickford went to his knees and pulled back the drape where it split in front.

"I looked in there," Ken said.

His head half under the sink, Pickford reached around behind it, into the space between the back of the sink and the wall. When he emerged, he held a plastic zipper bag with a photo folded inside.

Ken took the zipper bag by a corner and led the way out. "Flush the damn toilet, Pickford."

In the living room, Ken held up the bag. The photo had been folded so that only the boy in the picture was visible. Pulling out Enrique's photo, I compared it to the one year-old in the bag. Same eyes and carefree grin. When Ken turned over the bag, I could see what Pickford had folded out of sight – Mrs Lopez and her daughter. I recognized Felicia's photo from the folder Mrs Martinez had given me.

Proof that Enrique's grandmother had indeed lived here in Greenville. If Pickford could be believed – and I couldn't see any reason for him to lie about it – the boy had been on his way here.

Ken planted a hand on Pickford's shoulder again. "I'm taking you in."

Pickford turned those grandpa eyes on Ken. "It was just a photo. I still have the frame. I'll give it back to you."

"What do the terms of your probation say about pictures of unrelated children in your possession?" Ken asked, giving Pickford's shoulder a shake.

Pickford flapped his mouth a couple times in indignant silence, then clamped it shut. Ken marched him from the apartment.

We tramped back down the stairs, Pickford whining and moaning and groaning as we went. While Ken packed Chuck away in the Explorer, I returned to my Escort. Bending over the hood, I stretched again in a vain attempt to remove the twelve-inch hunting knife someone had shoved up into my leg.

As Ken approached, I gave up on the effort. "Enrique's probably safe and sound with his grandmother."

"Maybe."

I jammed my fingers into my hair, trying to remember if I'd brushed it that morning. "And James is just a runaway. If he's not dead already, he'll make his way home someday."

"Could be."

I tried to cling to the fairy tale. "There's no crime in me choosing to believe that."

"Right," Ken agreed.

I took a stab in the dark. "You wouldn't happen to know if anyone in town owns an early 80s Volvo sedan?"

Ken's gaze narrowed at the off the wall question. "Have a hankering to own a Volvo?"

"That's the kind of car Andros at the café thinks he saw James in."

Ken gave it some thought. "I see Volvos around here all the time, but mostly late model. I can't say I've noticed one that old."

"Damn." I rubbed my temples where a throbbing beat in time to the ache in my leg. "I'm going to lose three new clients if I don't get back. They'll get tired of waiting and find another private investigator."

"Then go home," Ken said.

He wasn't even going to try to talk me out of it? I opened my car door. "See you around." I sat abruptly, my left leg too wracked with pain for a graceful descent.

Ken blocked me from shutting the door. "Stay one more night. You can get an early start in the morning."

I peered up at him. "Stay with you?"

"At the hotel, in your car… I don't give a damn." He looked away, maybe to search for some patience. "There's a benefit dance tonight at the community center for the Thompsons. To raise funeral expenses."

"Have they found a body?" I would have thought he'd tell me if they had.

"Not yet. But he's dead. Drowned. That's a near certainty."

If I stayed, I could evaluate the data I'd gathered so far, see what ProSpy could tell me. Investigate the fire connection further. "You know I can't dance."

"Then come and watch me make a fool of myself."

That notion held some appeal. Also, with everyone in town likely attending, maybe the owner of the Volvo would show up. "I could stay another night. Today's shot anyway."

"I'll pick you up at eight." He let go of the door and walked to his Explorer.

I felt a little suckered, not so much by Ken as by my own demons. Bad enough that guilt at the lousy results in the search for James and Enrique goaded me into staying. The irresistible compulsion to follow the trail of arson had its hooks in me as well.

The impulse to save the boys was a human enough inclination – I'd let their identities bore into me too deep to easily let go of them. But I trod on thin ice by giving in to my fascination with fire.

At least Tommy, lurking as usual in the back of my mind, wasn't snickering at me. That would have been enough to shatter the camel's back.

CHAPTER 18

Before I returned to the Gold Rush Inn, I detoured back to the SaveMart and spent an excruciating twenty minutes wandering its women's clothing section. I could have freshened up the previous day's T-shirt in the bathroom sink, but I wasn't sure it would dry in the five or so hours before Ken picked me up. So I opted to buy something new instead, a near life-altering decision since I loathed shopping for clothes.

I found a long-sleeved polo shirt in a color that didn't completely suck, then splurged on a new bra and underwear. Fantasies of Ken stripping them off me drifted into my mind like a scene from a damn romance novel. I almost put the clothes back, dithering over whether my scummy current shirt would do. I decided even my personal hygiene hadn't sunk that low.

At the checkout, I dropped my pile on the conveyer behind a box of tampons and tin of chew. I was digging in my wallet for plastic when a familiar voice snagged my attention. Marty Denning glowered down at a bone-thin bag of nerves with long, scraggly black hair, midriff-baring tank top and size zero jeans.

"I gave you the cash yesterday," Marty hissed. "Have you spent it all already?"

So the girlfriend wasn't a lie. Under Marty's dark glare, she plowed into her cavernous purse. Pawing with both hands, she muttered to herself as if to summon the missing money. Her brown eyes, wide with fear, seemed to fill her face. Considering the exemplary character Denning had displayed at Arnie's, a bruise or two on Sharon's cheek wouldn't have surprised me. But other than a healed sore, her too-pale skin was unmarked.

She pulled her hands free of her purse, holding them out in an awkward shrug. Exasperated, Marty looked past her, scowling as he recognized me. But I only spared him a glance. What I saw on Sharon's hands was far more interesting – burn marks on her knuckles, on her wrists, on her fingertips.

Denning figured out where I was looking. He snatched Sharon's hands down, pulling her behind him. Then he dug in his back pocket for his wallet.

They zipped out of the store in record time, leaving me with a host of tantalizing questions. Was Denning's girlfriend playing with matches, too? Had their mutual attraction to fire drawn them together? It certainly wasn't Marty's charm. On my way back to the Gold Rush Inn, I made a mental note to mention the condition of Sharon's hands to Ken.

I'd planned to utilize my time until eight by running my ProSpy data against other child abduction cases online, try to find any others with links to fire. But thanks to construction up the road, the motel's internet connection was down. So I spent an antsy two hours updating the database I'd set up for James and Enrique, checking on my connection status about every two seconds. My addiction to flame and self-abuse had some strong competition in my compulsion to check email.

When I finally had internet, I came up empty on cases similar to Enrique's and James's. There wasn't much involving an age spread as wide as a four year-old and an eleven year-old, certainly not with different ethnicities. There were no cases with bearded suspects accompanied by a woman. And although there were cases where the victims themselves were burned, none where fires were set nearby.

Those abductions that came close, where one boy disappeared, not two disparate boys like James and Enrique, did not end well. In all cases, the child was found dead, sexually assaulted either pre- or post-mortem. Not a scenario I wanted to ponder for James or Enrique.

I snapped the heads off two boxes of matches as I worked, then set the heads on fire in the bathroom sink. As I breathed in the beguiling scent of sulfur, racking my brains for another approach that might bear fruit, my mind circled back to Ken's arsons. Not that they related to James and Enrique, but I was tired of the futility of finding the boys. Ken's mystery might only be a distraction, but maybe pondering it would loosen up a few brain cells. Or feed my fire fix.

Rather than do any hard thinking, I let my thoughts flow freeform as I showered. A series of fires with similar MO threading their way up Highway 99. Three, possibly four kids missing, fires set at various locations where they'd been spotted. An irrational, motiveless fire-setter.

Drying myself off, I changed into my new duds, pulling on the least disreputable of the two pair of jeans I'd brought with me and headed out for a bite to eat. Emil's Café was jumping, no doubt catering to the pre-dance crowd. I got a chicken fried steak and Coke to go, then slunk out with my white plastic bag.

Another check of email as I wolfed down my food, then a whimsical Google of "bearded man." Some goofy stuff came up – political blogs, a webpage on Mayan culture, another on Hungarian fairy tales. When I added "abduction," I got more crazy stuff – a story of a purported UFO abduction – but a few child abduction cases involving a bearded man. None of them recent, most far from California.

I channel-flipped a while, checking my watch every few minutes. When Ken finally knocked, I'd become absorbed in a Discovery channel show on Mesopotamian agriculture.

He gave me a quick once-over. "You bought a new shirt."

"Is it that obvious?"

"It is when you leave part of the tag on." He reached behind me and gave a tug, then showed me the plastic tether I'd neglected to remove.

I could still feel where his thumb had brushed against the back of my neck. "I can't even dress myself properly."

The two of us alone in that room together brought to mind too many potential activities, so I scooted past him and waited for him to exit before locking up. He had the good sense not to open the car door for me, letting me climb into the Explorer on my own. I wasn't about to think of our getting together as a date.

"What did you find out from Lucy?" I asked, hoping to defuse the tension.

"A crazy story. She heard the kid crying, went out to find him on her porch. Couldn't stop him from crying, so took him down to SaveMart to buy him a doll."

"Except it was her supposed daughter she thought she was buying the doll for."

"Yeah," Ken said. "Lucy swears she never went to the Vallejo's house. Her pickup truck is similar to the one the witnesses saw, but the mileage to and from doesn't match the odometer."

"It's a pretty generic truck," I pointed out. "You really think she took that boy from his house?"

"How'd she get hold of him if she didn't?"

I had no answer to that. I told him about Sharon Peele's burns, and he agreed it was worth a conversation with her. He still hadn't tracked down Marty's actual address – Arnie only had a PO Box and Denning didn't exactly have a host of friends in town who might know the location.

The parking lot of the community center off Main Street was packed with cars. I could hear the music blasting from inside the moment I opened my door. Teens and tweens swarmed the wide lawn in the front of the building, boys and girls eyeing each other, considering the possibilities. Cassie sat with a cluster of her friends on a tree swing that had been set up under a massive blue oak.

Just inside, a shrine of sorts to Brandon Thompson had been set up. His mother and father hovered nearby, mom's eyes red but dry, dad looking lost. Photographs and memorabilia of Brandon's short life, from baby photos and a soft, knit blanket, to soccer pictures and well-worn shin guards surrounded a basket filled with checks and cash. I dropped a ten into the basket.

The band was live and raucous, bluegrass with a sprinkle of rock. The musicians ranged from early thirties down to one young man who looked barely out of his teens. An enthusiastic crowd gyrated on the dance floor, couples whirling past me at light speed.

Ken leaned close to shout in my ear. "That's Brandon's oldest brother on fiddle. The one on the left."

That explained how they'd been able to muster such an accomplished band on such short notice. Watching the dancers, Ken's foot tapping in time with the music, I had an uneasy suspicion he was about to ask me out on the floor. He'd turned to me, put out his hand when rescue arrived in the form of Miss Sweet-as-pie.

"They're playing Levi Jackson Rag next, Sheriff," she informed him. "I'm looking for a partner."

She gazed up at him dreamily, then gave me a narrow-eyed glare behind his back. I gave her a friendly smile. "Have at it."

Ken mouthed Save me! as she dragged him out on the dance floor. I ignored him, dodging the gyrating bodies searching for sanctuary. Flip-down chairs were installed along the walls that flanked the stage and a table with munchies and punch was set up beside Brandon's shrine. The chairs were mostly occupied by the older, blue-haired set who probably wouldn't appreciate a young, spry thing such as myself in their company. So I scooped up a handful of chips and found a corner beside the snacks table where I could hide.

I found McPherson there, swaying slightly, sipping punch from a red Solo cup. I guessed that the bulge in his jacket pocket was his friend, Mr Gin Bottle.

I raised my voice so he could hear. "Can you explain the small town appeal to me? Is it that everyone knows your business... but pretends they don't when it's convenient? That they love to sit in judgment and sniff out your dirtiest laundry? Or just that you can't get a decent cup of coffee anywhere within fifty miles?"

Whatever high he'd experienced from saving Norberto had come crashing down. He looked at me blearily, as if I'd intended he take my questions seriously. "Can hide inna small town if you want to." He slurred the words only slightly.

"You can hide in the city," I pointed out.

He shook his head, then took a healthy swallow of the boozy punch. "People're everywhere. Watching you. Here, you can fall inna river an' no one will ever find you."

He stared morosely down at his cup. Had the alcohol put him in such a damned gloomy mood, or was something else eating at him?

"We found the kid Lucy took," I reminded him.

I thought he'd smile at that, him being the hero, but he only looked more morose. "What 'bout those two boys? Ones you been looking for?" he asked.

"Still missing."

He took another sip. "Too bad."

Ken and Miss Sweet-as-pie do-si-do'ed or sashayed or whatever dancers do past me, the admin glowing as she gazed adoringly up at him. When the dance ended and the band launched into a polka, he put out a hand toward me, begging again for rescue. Cold-hearted bitch that I am, I backed out of reach and left him to Miss Sweet-as-pie's tender mercies.

Rich gripped his cup so hard, a little of it sloshed on his hand. "D'you got kids?"

I thought of Benjamin. "No, I don't. How about you?"

He shook his head slowly, his gaze fixed on something across the dance floor. A woman was shaking an angry finger at her five year-old son. The boy said something to her and she gave him a swat on the butt.

Victim of abuse that I was, I generally had two responses to that sort of thing – instant knee-jerk fear, or blinding anger, depending on whether it was the child me or adult me that stood up inside. More adult than child tonight, I wanted to walk over and give that mother a shake.

McPherson looked mildly horrified at the woman's treatment of the boy, and I wondered if he was a member of my club. "Your parents hit you like that?"

He shook his head. "Din't believe in phys'cal pun-ish-ment." The last word came out in three carefully enunciated syllables.

He tipped up the cup, gulping down the last of it, then made his unsteady way to the punch bowl. He served some more up, only half of it landing in the cup. He must have trusted me, or else he was too far gone to care because he turned back toward me, coming close enough so my body would shield him from view of the room. Then he reached inside his jacket for the bottle and topped off the punch cup.

Tucking the gin away again, he drank deep. The band's fiddle player launched into a long riff and the dancers spun past us in a whirl of skirts and cowboy hats knocked askew.

McPherson stared at the little boy who was now screaming his head off. Rich's eyes were red and he blinked slowly as he struggled to focus. "More'n seven," he muttered.

"Seven what?" I asked.

"Jus' the ones we count."

What the hell? I peered at the swaying McPherson. "I'm not following you."

He took another slug of his drink. "T'others're way worse."

While I wrestled with McPherson's drunken non sequitur, Ken snaked his way toward me through the crowd. I could see Miss Sweet-as-pie on tiptoes trying to locate him through the press of bodies.

"Have a heart," he said, grabbing my hand, "or she'll have her hooks in me all night."

I tried to break Ken's hold and nearly jabbed an elbow into McPherson. Rich gave me one more bleary, alcohol-infused look, then wandered off toward the exit.

"I don't think he's okay on his own," I said to Ken.

"Jim!" Ken called out to a lanky teen behind the snack table. "Make sure Mr McPherson gets to his store." Jim loped after Rich.

"Dance with me," Ken said. "Save me."

"You know you want her, Ken," I said, grinning. "Just surrender to it."

He looked over his shoulder. Miss Sweet-as-pie was closing in on him. "You only have to follow. I'll go slow."

Ken all but yanked me onto the dance floor as the musicians started up a slow, plaintive melody, a cowboy cry-in-your-beer kind of song. One hand on my waist, the other locked with mine, his restraint was as secure as any compliance hold. Miss Sweet-as-pie huffed on the sidelines, a woman scorned.

After I'd stomped his toes four times in the first twenty seconds, Ken pulled me in a little closer. "It's a waltz. One-two-three, one-two-three. Anybody can do it."

"Anyone with a pair of functioning legs," I muttered. Pain shot up my left calf every other step, transforming the count to one-stab-three, stab-two-stab.

He grabbed me tighter around the waist. "Just hang on. I'll hold you up."

I dug my fingertips into his shoulder. As we waltzed past the munchies table a third time, I spotted McPherson still there, still holding that same crumbling pile of chips.

Ken put his mouth next to my ear. "What were you and Rich talking about?"

"I'm not exactly sure. Small town life, raising children. Seemed like there was a rain cloud hovering over him tonight."

"I don't know the whole story, but scuttlebutt around town is that his kids all died in some kind of accident."

That tickled a brain cell somewhere deep inside, but I couldn't wrap my thinking processes around it. Besides, the pain in my leg did ease with use and I was actually beginning to enjoy myself. Not that I'd ever tell Ken that. I let him haul me around on the floor, his toes still in peril from my klutziness, my palm dampened by the sweat soaking through the back of his shirt.

When the music changed to a faster rhythm, he pulled me closer, turned me faster, until heat radiated off both our bodies. It was like sex, fully-clothed in public, and I wondered why I'd never tried dancing before.

Miss Sweet-as-pie had hooked up with Alex, the two of them cheek to cheek as they spun through the crowd in some kind of intricate dance. She kept an eye on Ken and me, no doubt looking for her opening. Out of breath and slathered in sweat, I was ready for a break by the time the band jump-started yet another fast-moving dance. But Ken kept an iron grip on me to prevent Miss Sweet-as-pie from cutting in.

When he finally let me stagger off the floor, he was right behind me, following me outside. All that physical contact had my libido sitting up and clamoring for attention, the spring breeze tantalizing rather than cooling me. When Ken tugged me into the shadows beside the community center, I didn't resist. When he kissed me, I was ready to pull him right down my throat.

After a few minutes of hot and heavy, Ken pulled back, gasping a little as he stared down at me. I read the question in his eyes.

"Yeah." I groped for oxygen. "Let's go."

We kept a couple of feet of space between us as we walked toward the Explorer. Ken smiled and waved at a few Greenvillians along the way, then did open the car door for me. A weak, girlie part of me appreciated the gesture.

I saw Cassie still lingering under the oak tree with her friends. "What about your niece?"

"She's staying with a friend again," he said as he pulled out of the parking lot. "Over at the Clarks'." He glanced over at me. "I made sure she had her insulin squared away."

I could almost hear the mood music playing in the background. We traveled in silence, edgy energy bristling between us. The first time we'd had sex, we'd been at his place mulling over a case. His wife had been out of town and we'd let ourselves get carried away.

Tonight wasn't happenstance. Tonight I could pull the plug at any time. At least until I was naked with him between the sheets. Naked and exposed, every scar revealed.

That thought was almost enough to stop me cold as we stepped into his house. Except this wasn't some low-life I'd picked up in a bar on Market Street. This was Ken, a man who knew every dark corner of my damaged soul.

He should have torn off my clothes, should have had me, right there on the living room floor. Taken me quick and hot, so I could pretend it was just a one-night stand like all those others had been. So I could keep my grip on the truth I'd nurtured inside for so many years – that I was degraded and bad, deserving of the worst a man could offer up.

Instead, he kissed me up the stairs, down the hall to his bedroom. His mouth lingered on mine with each step, feathering along my cheek, my throat. Breathing into my hair.

When he undressed me, he took his time, pulling off my jeans, skimming my shirt up and over my head. His palms hesitated over the worst of the burn scars, the ones he remembered and the ones that were new to him. Not a word spoken as he unhooked my bra, saw the circle of healed desecration around my right nipple.

I fought back tears more than once. Shook with the effort of it as he turned away to pull a condom from the nightstand. Squeezed my eyes shut so tight as he nuzzled my neck, I thought I'd never open them again.

Climax caught me by surprise, wrenched from me by Ken's touch. After years of finding pleasure only with a lit match, it didn't seem possible to achieve it through tenderness. While I lay there, overwhelmed, staring up at him, he came, sending me over the edge again.

He didn't let go. Just fell asleep still inside me. I lay there, the man so tightly wrapped around me I could scarcely breathe, and finally let the tears go. They slipped into my hair, my ears, dripping onto the pillow.

I don't know what terrified me more, that I'd rediscovered what had made our lovemaking so profound or that this man was the only one on the face of the planet who could make me feel that way.

I'd seen the look in his eyes when he came. He was hoping for possibilities in our reunion that I couldn't possibly allow to happen. I was beyond damaged goods, a reality I'd never been able to get through to him.

A few minutes later, he finally relaxed enough that I could ease him from my body and wriggle free. I found my clothes, pulling them on as I went. I was halfway to the door when I remembered I didn't have my car.

I dithered for a moment, then spotted Ken's cell on a table by the door. With barely a whit of shame, I thumbed through his address book until I found Alex's number. I called him on my own cell.

He answered after one ring. "Deputy Farrell."

I could hear the music in the background. Apparently the benefit dance was still going strong. "It's Janelle. I need a favor, Alex. No questions asked."

I wasn't sure the young squirt would have the necessary discretion, but he said, "Whatever you need."

"Pick me up at the sheriff's place. I'll be outside."

To his credit, he didn't say a word. With only the slightest hesitation, he said, "I'll be there in twenty."

Quiet as a thief, I crept outside and stood in a chill drizzle waiting for Alex. It struck me as I shivered in the cool wet that the nearest box of matches was back in my room. I didn't even care.

CHAPTER 19

As dawn faded the blackness of the dark basement to gray, Mama sat on the top step of the stairs and watched her children sleeping. Junior lay sprawled on his stomach, his arms stretched above his head. Sean snuggled up beside his brother. Sean should have been sleeping in his own bed, but the boy worshipped his older brother. Just like before, he'd wake during the night and go find Junior.

Baby Lydia dozed lightly, faint whimpers telling Mama she'd be awake soon. Thomas slept just as deeply as he had since Mama had first brought him home. She'd tried to rouse him enough to tip a little water past his lips, to spill some broth into his mouth, but he just lay limp in her arms.

Junior shifted onto his side, tucking his arms close to his chest. Her oldest boy's behavior lately troubled her. He'd never been like this before; rebellious, disobedient, prideful and angry. Something had changed in the time between before and now. It was almost as if he wasn't her son anymore.

That notion set off a burning anxiety in the pit of Mama's stomach. When she'd found baby Lydia, she'd been sure it was the Lord's way of sending her a message, that Mama was worthy, that He approved of the rituals she'd performed in His name. Then Sean had come back to her and her fount of blessings overflowed. Then Junior's return so soon after.

Maybe Junior had been touched by the devil during his time away. Maybe that was the wrongness she sensed in him. She knew there was goodness in him still, but at times the evil seemed to crowd that out, forcing him into dark deeds.

She needed Angela so desperately. Her oldest had just dipped a toe into womanhood when she'd gone away. She'd always lived up to the name Mama had given her, virtuous and pure-hearted. If Angela was here, she would drive the taint from Junior's soul and restore Mama's oldest boy to her.

If Angela was here, Mama could finish it. The last ritual, the final purification. Instead of destroying them one by one as she had been, she could burn away all the sins festering around her, threatening to pull her into Satan's grasp. With one last candle, she could light a final cleansing conflagration.

Bring me Angela, Lord, Mama prayed. *Before I lose Junior entirely. Before the world's wickedness pulls us both into the pit.*

She waited for the glow inside her, the heat that told her the Lord had heard her entreaty. But as dawn spread its faint hope into the corners of the basement, Mama only felt colder.

Time was running out; Mama could feel its imperative looming over her. If the Lord didn't intend to return Angela to her, would there be another sign she should watch for? How would she know when the time had arrived?

Do it now, Satan whispered in her ear. *Why wait?*

Even as a thrill of anticipation shivered down her spine, Mama resisted. *Not by Satan's command, Lord*, Mama vowed, *only by yours.*

Only by yours.

CHAPTER 20

I was deep in a damn good dream, an X-rated fantasy involving me and a Keanu Reeves lookalike, when the room phone interrupted me. Brain only half-engaged, I pressed the phone to my ear and drifted off again. Ken shouting my name in my ear jostled me back into semi-awareness.

"Yeah, what?" I muttered as I struggled into an upright position.

"You left," he said, the accusation clear in his tone.

I scrubbed at my gritty eyes, forcing the guilt away. "Tell me that's not why you called."

"There was another fire. A shed again."

I swung my legs over the side of the bed. "Anybody hurt?"

"Homeowner was able to get water on it before it got too far. Fire unit finished up the job."

"That's good." I tentatively stretched out my left leg. "Unless you caught the arsonist, I'm guessing that's not why you called either."

"A guy named Dave Sanders is on his way into the Sheriff's office. He saw something interesting down at the river the other day."

My calf contracted with a painful good morning greeting. "Was he on the SAR team?" I couldn't remember anyone named Sanders, but maybe he'd arrived when I was out searching with Charlotte.

"He's a copier repairman. On his way to a service call over in Carson City, he stopped by the river."

I tried to massage loose the muscle in my leg the way Ken had. Apparently I didn't have the touch. "Could we cut to the chase here?" I said, the pain making me impatient.

"Dave Sanders might have seen someone pull Brandon Thompson's body from the river."

My whiny calf took second place to that astonishing news. "Where?"

"Don't know yet. I'll ask him when he gets here."

I squinted at the bedside clock – 9.30. "I'll be there as soon as I can." I hung up to avoid an argument. I figured he wouldn't have called me if he hadn't intended to invite me to the party.

Hopping on one foot, I retrieved my overnight laundry from the shower curtain rod and dressed. By the time I pulled on shoes and socks, I could hitch along on my left leg without screaming in agony. It would stiffen up again on the drive into town, but hopefully it would be serviceable enough to crab walk me into the building.

Except when I crossed the still damp parking lot of the sheriff's office, the front door was locked up tight. No Miss Sweet-as-pie on a Sunday. I had no choice but to call Ken's cell and hope he'd be willing to let me in.

Before I could dial, he poked his head out of a doorway down the hall and spotted me. He glared at me, disappeared inside for several moments, then reappeared, glowering down the hall toward me. His neat slacks, dress shirt and tie made my nearly clean T-shirt and three-day jeans feel even grungier.

He opened the door. "Can you keep your mouth shut? Let me run this?"

I drew a zipper across my lips. He squinted at me suspiciously, then led me down the hall to the briefing room. A balding guy in his late thirties sat at the table spooning creamer into a paper cup of java.

After the intros, Ken nodded at Sanders. "Start at the beginning again."

"I was driving over to Carson City on Friday. Client had a C5180 that needed servicing." He sipped his coffee. "I pulled off the highway to take a..." His gaze flicked over to me. "...to take a break. You know, stretch my legs. I took a little walk, you know, to look at the river."

"Where was this?" Ken asked.

"I'd probably have to show you. Maybe five miles past Strawberry Canyon?"

Right in the ballpark of where Brandon had gone in the river. I shifted in my chair, feeling like a five year-old with the answer to the teacher's question. But I kept my mouth shut.

"What did you see?" Ken asked.

"A woman climbing down the bank over on the far side."

I couldn't help myself. "A woman? Are you sure?"

"I was too far away to make out the face, but it was definitely female." He slurped up some more coffee.

When I took a breath, Ken put up a warning finger. "Was she white?" he asked. "Black? Hispanic?"

"White for sure," Dave said. "Dark hair. She was wearing jeans and a big, baggy jacket."

"When did you see the boy?" Ken asked.

"When she got down to the river. I saw her bend over to look at something. I didn't know what it was at the time."

Again, my inner five year-old got the upper hand. "How could you not recognize a body?"

Ken grabbed my wrist, digging in his fingers. "What did you think it was?"

Dave shrugged. "I was so far away, it just looked like a bundle of something. Old clothes maybe."

Lips pressed together, I cast a pleading look at Ken. He scowled, but nodded my way. "As fast as the river was running," I asked, "how do you suppose the body ended up there?"

"I know that spot," Dave said. "I've stopped there quite a bit to... stretch my legs. There's a sheltered cove on the other side. I've seen dead raccoons, possums wash up. They get snagged in the deadfall."

"What happened next?" Ken asked.

"She stepped into the water and picked up the kid. Wrapped him in that jacket of hers, then started back up the hill. She might have seen me... She stopped at the top and looked back across the river."

I squeezed in another contribution to the interview. "Did you see anything else up the hill where she took the kid?" I left the query open-ended.

Sanders's brow furrowed as he considered. "Yeah, actually. As I pulled away. I thought I saw smoke through the trees."

Ken and I exchanged a look then he asked the next obvious question. "Why did you take two days to report this?"

"I had a job to get to. It wasn't until I saw it in the Sacramento Bee that I put it all together."

"You have time now to take us out there?" Ken asked.

Dave checked his watch. "I've already missed the morning Bible reading at Holy Rock. My wife will give me hell."

"It would be a big help, Mr Sanders," Ken said.

"Can I take my own car? Then I can still make the tail end of services and lunch at Emil's after."

Ken pulled in behind Dave's red Honda and we headed toward the highway. I prodded my leg with my thumbs, trying to dig out a knot. "Why would this woman take a body from the river, then not report it?"

"Folks living on that side of the river don't come to town very often. They keep to themselves." Ken followed Sanders onto Highway 50. "She might not be in a big hurry to bring in a body."

"Still, it's been two days."

Silence ticked away as Ken whipped around the highway curves. "Why'd you leave?"

"Did you want to try for round two?" I asked, to annoy him, to deflect the need for a real answer.

He flexed his hands on the steering wheel, all male ego and wounded pride. "Don't tell me you didn't enjoy it. Without any damn matches."

That he understood the significance of what we'd done just made things worse. I told him softly, "It didn't change anything, Ken."

"I thought I might have mattered to you, just a little bit. My mistake."

He mattered too damn much. But if I let him in, let him tear down carefully constructed walls, all the ugliness would gush out, destroy us both.

I couldn't let that happen. "I've always disappointed you, Ken. I don't know why you thought this would be any different."

I saw him shutting down, as if a mask obscured his face. Then silence settled between us, heavy and suffocating.

The turnout Dave led us to was four and a half miles east of Strawberry Canyon, according to Ken's odometer. "A mile and a half from where Brandon went in," I noted. "The dogs searched here?"

"They did." Ken's tone was neutral and distant. "Lost the scent past the creek on the granite and shale."

"Where that fire was set."

"Yeah."

As we followed Sanders through the willows shielding the river from the highway, moisture from the night's drizzle soaked through the sleeve of my T-shirt. "This wet won't make tracking easy if you send the dogs out again."

We caught up with Dave where he had stopped at the top of the bank. "I was in there." He pointed to his private outhouse within a thick screen of willows. "She was over there." He gestured across the river.

Boulders had tumbled down into the river sometime in the past, creating a sheltered cove. A downed tree added another protective arm. Bank, rocks and tree surrounded the quietly swirling stretch of water on three sides.

"She slung him over her shoulder and zigzagged up the hillside," Sanders told us, tracing out a path with his finger. "Kind of took the easiest path up, then hit the trees about at that big pine."

The boulders almost stair-stepped up the rocky bank. I could imagine the woman climbing with the boy's body in a fireman carry. He was slight for his age, only about fifty pounds according to the SAR briefing. Even with Brandon over her shoulder, it would have been hard work getting him to the top.

Sanders fidgeted, checking his watch. "Okay if I go now? As it is, I'll barely make the fellowship."

"Sure," Ken told him. "We'll call you if we need you again."

After Sanders left, I contemplated the steep rocky hill. "That's a hell of a schlep to the top carrying dead weight. Why would she have bothered taking the boy's body all that way? Why not just call the sheriff and let you take care of it?"

"Don't know. Unless..." He hesitated. "No."

But I picked up on his audacious train of thought. "Unless Brandon wasn't dead."

Ken shook his head. "If he was alive, don't you think the woman would call 911? Because the boy's sure as hell going to be in sad shape after that ride down the river."

"But why take him at all if he's dead?" I pressed, unwilling to give up the possibility that Brandon wasn't.

"Maybe she just didn't want a coyote or mountain lion to make a meal out of his body."

My stomach clenched at the ugly picture. "You won't wait for her to call, will you? You'll bring out search and rescue again?"

"Yeah. One of the CSIs as well, see if we can find any footprints or trace."

"After last night's drizzle, not much hope of that."

Back at the Explorer, Ken called Sergeant Russell and requested one of the dog teams. The CSI on duty was thirty minutes away at the high school. Ken read him the GPS coordinates from the unit on his Explorer.

"Still planning to go back today?" Ken asked as we pulled onto Highway 50.

"I should. Less traffic getting into the Bay Area on a Sunday."

"Don't want to wait and see what the dogs find?"

"If it's going to be a dead body, then no, I don't." I stared at the trees across the river, listened to the thrum of the tires on the pavement, watched a squirrel skirting the highway via a power line.

I did a double-take when I saw the smoke. "Turn around," I told Ken. "There's something burning back there."

Ken veered into a turnout, then waited with ill-concealed impatience for a minivan towing a fifth wheel to get out of his way. "Where?" he asked, gaze on the thick cover of pines and cedars.

At first I thought I'd been mistaken, then I spotted the puff of gray. "There."

Ken gunned the Explorer past the spot. "There's a bridge another half mile ahead." He got on the radio, called central dispatch for fire and backup.

We roared over the bridge and up a pitted dirt road. "It could just be someone burning brush."

"You said there weren't many houses over here. Who would be burning brush?"

"There are a few old BLM cabins." At a blind curve, he yanked the wheel left to avoid a boulder. "Homeless folks hole up in there sometimes."

Ken tried to accelerate, but the terrain we covered could only charitably be described as navigable. The Explorer jounced and groaned into potholes and over rocks littering the road. The trail of smoke, now visible, now concealed by the trees, beckoned us on.

One more teeth-jarring concussion over the rise and we reached a clearing with a rundown shack of a cabin. My heart sank when I first spotted the fire – it looked exactly like a pile of brush being disposed of by a thrifty homeowner. Except the homeowner in question was ex-con arsonist Marty Denning, and the moment he spotted us, he took off on his signature run.

Ken wrenched the Explorer around into Marty's path. When the ex-con bolted around the Ford, Ken jumped from the vehicle, shouting the de rigueur, "Police! Stop!" and took off after him. As luck would have it, Marty caught his foot on a tree branch and did a face plant in the pine needles. Ken caught up and cuffed him, then all but dragged him back toward the cabin.

Meanwhile, I slid from the Explorer and registered for the first time the musky sweet stench that mingled with the smell of burning gasoline. Good thing I'd had nothing but coffee that morning, because it wasn't just brush Marty was burning. At least the ex-con's unconventional fuel was too large to be James or Enrique. The waifish Sharon, I guessed.

Ken and the squirming Marty joined me beside the roaring blaze. Ken's jaw worked as he perused what was left of the charred corpse amongst the brush.

"Who is it?" he asked Marty.

Marty wouldn't look at Ken. "Girlfriend," he confirmed.

I stepped into his line of sight. "Was she dead before you set her on fire?"

Improbably, my question had offended Marty. "I wouldn't do that."

"Then you killed her first?" Ken asked.

Marty shrugged. "She OD'ed last night."

"And you didn't bother to call 911?" Ken asked. "Notify the sheriff's office?"

Marty's shifty gaze strayed to the ramshackle cabin. Now I saw the telltale signs – industrial sized buckets piled alongside a mountain of discarded cans and bottles. I couldn't read the labels from that distance, but I knew what they were. Acetone. Toluene. Lye. Drain cleaner.

I could see Ken having his own light bulb moment. He clamped an unfriendly hand on Marty's shoulder. "You're cooking meth in that cabin, aren't you?"

Denning offered up a preposterous defense. "It was Sharon's idea."

Ken looked as if he'd like to shove Marty into the fire. As far as I, his only witness, was concerned, he could have done it with a clear conscience. We could have crafted a plausible story of Marty kicking over the can of gasoline, dousing himself and accidentally stumbling into the flames.

Alas, the scream of approaching sirens eliminated that appealing option. The fire was extinguished within twenty minutes. Ken turned Marty over to a deputy then had to wait for the arrival of Hazmat and drug enforcement before we could head back to town. The whole way, the stench of flambéed Sharon hovered in the Explorer, permeating our skin, our clothes.

As we passed down Main Street, the parking lot of Holy Rock was still full of cars and people. Ken stopped to let a parishioner exit the lot and I spied Dave's red Honda next to an old clunker of a sedan. As I contemplated whether Sanders had arrived in time to preserve marital bliss, I focused on the ancient black sedan, its windshield bright with glare.

It was a Volvo. A CCSF decal gleamed in the noon sunshine.

Ken stepped on the gas. "Stop," I said, putting a hand on his arm. He pulled into a parking space vacated by a churchgoer.

"Give me a minute," I tossed off as I slid from the Explorer. I limped through the parking lot as fast as I could, hoping to catch the driver of the Volvo before they left.

Luck was on my side. An old lady had caught up with whoever sat behind the wheel to chat while the idling Volvo spewed gas fumes. The long-winded old biddy beside the car went on and on about how some in the congregation weren't picking up the slack at church fundraisers as I tried not to inhale the exhaust that curled around the car.

She finally hobbled off with her walker just as Ken arrived. He hovered over my shoulder. "What are you up to?"

Before I could come up with a reasonable response, someone called out to him, drawing him away. Unencumbered, I stepped up to the driver's window.

It took a moment to recognize the vaguely familiar face of the elderly woman behind the wheel. Sadie Parker. She had about a million more wrinkles creasing her weathered skin than the last time I'd seen her, but she hadn't lost her crafty wariness.

She peered up at me suspiciously. My face hadn't changed that much and Sadie was a sharp old lady. "Janelle Watkins," she said finally.

I'd been too intimidated by Sadie twenty plus years ago to commit the kind of idiot petty crimes I'd pulled on many other Greenville notables, so I could smile at her with a clear conscience. "How are you, Mrs Parker?"

Her eyes narrowed. "I still haven't forgotten that pumpkin."

Good God, what a memory. That one little Halloween prank had slipped my mind. "Sorry about that, Mrs Parker. I had a question about your car."

"You want to buy it? It's a piece of crap."

"Have you had the car a long time?"

"A few months," she said. She patted her sparse white hair where a wisp had escaped her tight bun. "Traded my great-grandson's truck for it."

My heart went from pit-a-pat to light speed in an instant. "Who traded with you?"

"A bushy-bearded fellow. Glenn... can't remember his last name. Started with a C." She waved out the window at the pastor. "Truck was a worse piece of junk than this, but he didn't care. He saw it parked one morning at the church, for sale or trade sign in the window. Called me up and we made the trade."

"You still have the paperwork for the car?"

"Sent the pink slip in to DMV when I transferred ownership. Threw away the old registration slip when I got the one with my name on it."

Trust Sadie to be efficient. "What kind of truck was it?"

"An old Chevrolet. Supposed to be white, but had so much Bondo on it, you'd think it was gray. Great-grandson thought he would fix it up. Then Ben went into the army and gave the truck to me."

Every other pickup in the Greenville area was a Chevy, more than one patched together with Bondo. Had I seen a white one covered in Bondo? "You wouldn't remember the year and model, would you?"

"I can do better than that." She leaned over and opened the glove box. "I found the truck registration in a desk drawer a week after the trade. I hung onto it in case Glenn turned up in town. Haven't seen him since." She gave me the registration slip. "I guess it doesn't matter since he's transferred it by now."

With my prize in hand, I stepped away and let her back excruciatingly slowly from her parking spot. Ken was on the other side of the now nearly empty lot, his cell phone pressed to his ear.

I scanned the registration slip. It listed Ben Waring as the owner of a 1985 Chevy S10. I could use the license number or VIN to locate the current owner. After all the ritual beating of my head against brick walls, this one was almost too easy.

Ken's expression as he tucked away his cell phone derailed me for the moment from my request for a check of ownership.

He started toward the Explorer, waving at me to fall in beside him.

"Something happen to Cassie?" I asked.

"Cassie's fine. She talked Rich McPherson into opening the store on a Sunday so she and a bunch of her friends could have some kind of video game competition." He climbed into the Explorer and waited until I got inside. "How committed are you to going home today?"

"Don't be a putz. Tell me what's going on."

He handed me his cell. "Take a look at the last number called."

Tamping down my irritation, I checked the call log. A Sacramento area code with a 306 prefix. The 306 sparked a memory – I'd seen it on Enrique's grandmother's invoice. "Is that Mrs Lopez's number?"

"It is," he said smugly. "I just spoke with her. I'm on my way there now. Unless you'd rather I take you back to your car."

I gave him a sweet smile. "I could go see her on my way out of town, if you'd give me the address."

"Joint effort, Janelle, or I go alone." He turned onto the entrance for Highway 50.

"Did you ask her about Enrique?"

"If I had, I would have had to explain about her grandson being missing." He flicked his light bar, clearing the fast lane for the Explorer. "I figured it would be better to tell her that in person."

"How did her number pop up from out of nowhere?"

"Remember Trish?" he asked. "The Stuarts' daughter?"

I tried to place her in the pantheon of Greenvillians. "Refresh my memory."

"Her folks own the place Mrs Lopez rented. Apparently Mrs Lopez called Trish yesterday asking for her security deposit. Trish remembered I'd been looking for the woman."

"So maybe Mrs Lopez is desperate enough for money to risk revisiting her past."

"Or whatever she was running from is no longer a threat," Ken suggested.

I still had the truck registration in my hand. "Can you check on ownership for me?" I explained about Sadie's trade.

He radioed in to central dispatch, repeating the license number I read off to him. Half a minute later, Ken relayed dispatch's response. "Ben Waring."

"Sadie's great-grandson?"

"Yeah. She's always bragging on him."

"Could we try the VIN?" Maybe Glenn had gotten new plates. Or switched them.

But the VIN came back the same, registered to Ben.

"Damn," I muttered. "So mystery man Glenn never transferred the truck into his name."

"He'll have to sooner or later. When's the registration due?"

I checked the slip. "August."

"When his registration expires, one of the deputies will catch up to him. Meantime, I'll put out a BOLO on the truck."

A "be on the lookout" was better than nothing, but I didn't have high hopes it would bear any fruit. I sank down in my seat, trying not to think about James, dead in the woods somewhere or Enrique, raffled off to some child molester.

Damn, why had I let those boys in?

CHAPTER 21

Mrs Lopez lived in a small duplex in the Arden Arcade area of Sacramento. The living room furniture was threadbare, the carpet worn and freckled with the black dots of cigarette burns, but it was clean and neat. The familiar photograph of Enrique hung on the wall.

Mrs Lopez was as tidy as her home, dark hair pulled back in a ponytail, slacks pressed, her shirt fresher than the one I'd dragged out of the Safeway bag. A young grandmother, probably in her mid-forties, she greeted us with a soft Spanish accent, a tray of cookies and a pot of coffee. We settled on the sofa while she perched on the edge of a well-worn easy chair.

"Have you heard from my daughter?" She picked up her coffee cup, her hands shaking. "Is Enrique with her?"

A lead ball dropped in my stomach. "We have some bad news, Mrs Lopez."

Her mouth clamped down as she steeled herself. "What is it?"

I glanced over at Ken, but he was leaving it to me. "Your daughter's dead. A drug overdose three months ago."

"I had a feeling." She blinked back tears. "There won't be a problem transferring Enrique from foster care, will there? Felicia intended to send him to me."

"Why didn't she?" I asked, putting off the inevitable.

She raised the coffee to her lips, but she barely sipped. "A week before I moved out of the Stuarts' place, Felicia called, said she'd changed her mind. She could take care of her own son." She shook her head. "Stupid girl."

Ken reached for a cookie. "Why no forwarding address, Mrs Lopez? We couldn't even find a PO box."

Color rose in her cheeks. "My ex-husband. It's better he doesn't know where I live. He's back in prison now, so I'm okay. I can take care of Enrique, no problem." She looked at me. "I can get custody, right?"

Better to rip the bandage off quickly. "Mrs Lopez, we don't know where Enrique is."

"What do you mean?" She stared at me, uncomprehending. "How can you not know?"

"He wasn't at the apartment when they found your daughter," I told her. "Social services has no record of him. If you don't have him, we don't know where he is."

The cup slipped from Mrs Lopez's fingers, shattering on the coffee table. As lousy as I was at comforting, I knew enough to grab her hand as she bent over sobbing.

As Ken mopped up spilled coffee from the table and carpet, my cell trilled out "Light My Fire." I would have ignored it, but caller ID said it was the office number. Which meant Sheri was calling me from the office on a Sunday.

Leaving Ken to try to soothe Mrs Lopez, I stepped outside. "What are you doing at work on your day off?"

"You asked about missing eight month-old babies in the Bay Area." I could hear the excitement in her voice.

I sat on the cement front steps. "And?"

"I kept striking out with Google, getting either too many hits or none at all. But then today, I'm out with my folks for brunch and the light bulb clicks on so I come into the office."

"Cut to the chase, Sheri."

"I'm getting there. I searched for abandoned babies, teen pregnancy. You know how California has that safe surrender baby law? Turns out a sixteen year-old – she lives in Kansas now, but they used to live in San Francisco – got pregnant, hid it for nine months, then gave birth in a public bathroom. She left the kid in the doorway of the New Holy Light Church. It was one of those storefront churches in the Tenderloin district. On Jones between Eddy and Turk."

The location tickled a brain cell. I put it aside for the moment. "When was this?"

"Eight and a half months ago."

Which fit the timeline to a T. "Is there a fire connection?"

"Big time," Sheri said. "Someone set a fire in the alley beside the church that night. Spread to the church itself, just about burned it to the ground. Naomi Simmons had left her baby on the front step, which didn't burn but was covered with shattered glass. At the least, they should have found a body. But there was nothing on the front step in the morning but rubble from the fire."

"So someone took the baby." I didn't want to think much past that revelation to who that someone might be.

"Apparently, the teen's family's got megabucks," Sheri told me. "Naomi came clean with her parents and now they want the little girl back, if she's still alive. Impassioned plea, promise of reward, etcetera."

"Go back to the fire. How'd it do so much damage to the church when it started in the alley?"

"Place was a former dry cleaners," Sheri said. "Leftover containers still squirreled away, chemicals spilled on the floor."

Which reminded me of the Nguyen's Laundromat. I felt a prickling up my spine. "Were you able to find out the ignition source?"

"I saw something about kerosene."

"That would be the accelerant."

"That's all I know," Sheri told me. "Kerosene on rags, set behind a dumpster."

"See what you can find out about the ignition source." I wasn't sure where that would take me, but more information wouldn't hurt.

I stepped back inside, where Mrs Lopez sat with Enrique's photo on her lap. Before we left, Ken murmured some encouraging words, promises he probably knew he wouldn't be able to keep.

As we drove back to the sheriff's office, I told him what I'd learned from Sheri. "The girl I spoke to at McDonald's saw a black infant in the car she spotted James in. Andros at the café said a woman in what was likely the same car might have been holding a baby."

"Damn." He didn't look any happier than I felt at the mounting body count of missing kids. "Listen, I've got to get something to eat. Why don't we head back to my place for some lunch?"

"Sure. But take me back to my car. I'll go check out first."

But what I really wanted to do was follow up on a radical idea. My nerves jangled as Ken dropped me off at the sheriff's office, an intriguing pattern coalescing in my conscious mind. I wanted to jump on my laptop immediately, but forced myself to pack up, forced myself to settle my thoughts. I was tempted to forget lunch with Ken so I could manipulate some data. But melding his thought processes with mine might get us to an answer quicker.

He'd made us each a grilled ham and cheese sandwich and had shaken a can of Pringles out onto a paper plate. Seated at the trestle table, I inhaled the sandwich and chips and guzzled the Sprite he'd poured for me.

"I want you to consider something," I said as I wiped my fingers on a paper napkin.

Giving me a fishy look, he swept up the plates he'd served the sandwiches on. "Okay."

"For the moment, I need you to go along with a far-fetched storyline."

He set the plates on the breakfast bar and dropped into a chair. "I'm listening."

Draining my glass of Sprite, I threw out my crazy-ass idea. "What if they're all connected?"

"By all, you mean..."

"The disappearances of James, Enrique, the baby. Even Brandon."

He narrowed his gaze. "James and the baby, I'll buy. But the other two..."

"They all have a fire connection." I ticked off on my fingers. "A fire set at a church where someone leaves a baby. The sofa set on fire in the apartment where Enrique lived. James disappears from a service station where a fire is set in the bathroom."

"But how do you leap to Brandon, a hundred and sixty miles away? That fire by the river could have been set by a careless camper, kids ditching school."

"Maybe. But we do have witness reports that put James and the baby here."

Ken tipped his head noncommittally in response to my argument. "How were the fires started?"

"Not sure about the church, other than kerosene on rags. At the service station, it was a little lighter fluid and a match. The paper towels were damp, so it didn't get very far before it was discovered. What about the dumpster at the Hangman's Tavern?"

"Some kind of accelerant," Ken said. "Could have been lighter fluid. Fire chief didn't go very far with it because there wasn't any property damage."

"It could have been kerosene at the church because the kidnapper was prepared. The service station and dumpster fires were more crimes of opportunity."

Ken rubbed his cheek, beard stubble scraping under his palm. "I'd be interested to know more about the fire at Enrique's apartment."

"I'll have Sheri pull the incident report." I fished an ice cube from my glass and chomped on it. "Until we find out otherwise, let's pretend the same person kidnapped all four children. We can see if the facts support that."

"Okay." He swept up the last three chips. "We have an eight-month-old African American baby girl. A three year-old Hispanic boy. An eleven year-old African American boy. An eight year-old white boy. Different races, different genders, different ages."

"James and the baby were seen together more than once. Each of the four has a link to Greenville."

He looked thoughtful as he sucked salt off his fingertips. "There is another common thread."

"What's that?"

"If we knew these kids had been kidnapped, law enforcement would be all over it. We'd bring in the FBI, we'd have Amber Alerts on the freeway, television and radio." He gestured with the last Pringle. "But these kids – an abandoned baby no one knew about, a drug addict's son everyone assumed was with his grandma, a presumed runaway, a boy we figure drowned in the river–"

I caught his drift. "They're completely under the radar."

"Lower priority."

"No reason for anyone to bust their butts looking for them. Or even know to look for them."

He picked up the empty glasses and carried them to the kitchen. "We are searching for Brandon."

"You're looking for his body," I pointed out. "And you would have gone on thinking you just hadn't found it yet if Dave the repairman didn't see the mystery woman. It wouldn't cross your mind that someone might have taken him. Someone who intended to keep him."

"Or kill him, if he wasn't already dead." Ken brought up the ugly possibility as he rinsed the glasses. "They might all be dead, buried somewhere on BLM land."

"Either way we've got to find this man and woman." I rose and leaned against the counter while he put the dishes in the dishwasher. "You think it's worthwhile now to do a more thorough search of the area where Brandon disappeared?"

"The dogs are still coming up empty. And while I'm willing to go along with your storyline as a theoretical exercise, I don't know that it's compelling enough to call out the troops."

I could have whined, pleaded with him, batted my eyes. Even if I'd had it in me, I doubted it would be effective.

"Then let's go back to your arson victims," I suggested. "Maybe if we think about something else, we'll get some new inspiration on the kidnappings."

"Go through the report folders again? I took them back to the office yesterday."

I shook my head. "Tell me what you know about these people. About their lives."

We returned to the table. I booted my laptop and brought up my notes file. I'd created a table listing dates in the first column, structure burned in the second, victims names in the third. I glanced down the list in time order – BLM, Sadie Parker, unnamed contractor, Westfields, McKays, caretaker Elvin Hughes, Markowitz, Abe and Mary Jacoby.

"So, what do you want?"

"Anything. Small town stuff. Secrets. Scandals."

His expression dubious, he sat back, staring out into space. "There was a scandal last year involving Mrs McKay. Something about her and the UPS man. Mr McKay was living at the Gold Rush Inn a few months until they worked it out."

I typed a note on a fresh page. "What else?"

He considered. "When the Westfields first arrived, people sniped about how they threw their money around, buying sixty-plus acres, building a gargantuan mansion, shelling out for a big flat screen from the electronics store."

"Good. What else?"

He rocked his head side to side as if to shake loose a mental tidbit. "Elvin Hughes is the biggest pisser and moaner about the Westfields. Complains about Abe and Mary too. Doesn't matter that the Westfields and Jacobys worked hard for what they own. Elvin can't stand the fact that they have so much and he has nothing."

"Didn't occur to you that he might be a suspect?"

"Elvin's in a wheelchair. His granddaughter shops for him and brings him supplies, takes him into town as needed."

I typed, glancing up to prod Ken further. He threw up his hands. "I don't know. Markowitz was a greedy bastard. The contractor has a temper. Punched his hand through a wall in the post office."

An envious man. A greedy one. A cheating wife. An angry contractor.

A deeply buried bit of trivia was tapping me on the shoulder. I shut my eyes, willing it to unearth itself.

I sat bolt upright. "The seven deadly sins."

"Say what?"

I ticked them off. "Lust, gluttony, greed, sloth, wrath, envy, pride."

Ken looked at me blankly a moment, then realization struck. "Mrs McKay committed the sin of lust."

"Markowitz filled the bill for greed. The contractor was wrathful. Elvin envious."

"You still have gluttony, sloth and pride," Ken pointed out.

"Both the Westfields and the Jacobys could be considered gluttonous, because between them, they own half the county." I noodled over the other two, remembered Sadie's great-grandson. "You told me Sadie was always bragging on Ben. That could pass as pride."

"There have been plenty of folks unhappy with the rundown state of that BLM land where the chicken coop burned. There are still a few other structures standing, just about ready to fall down."

The government too lazy to take care of its property. "Sloth."

He nodded agreement. "Which gives me a way to link the arsons. Except..."

"Except...?"

"Seven fires, seven sins," Ken said thoughtfully. "But then an eighth. And that shed makes nine. Which could mean..."

"He's started over again."

Ken grimaced. "So we could be looking at five more fires."

Not a pleasant prospect. "But maybe knowing how they're linked will help you catch him before that happens."

I wished I could say the same about my missing kids. I couldn't see a damn thing that pinned all four together. "Let me enter what we've learned, run it through ProSpy. Who knows what we might come up with?"

"I thought you were going home."

My one day of snooping around Greenville had morphed into a long weekend of examining the nasty underside of rocks. "I'll go back tomorrow. If I play around with the data, maybe I can substantiate my theory about the kids. At least enough to give you something more definitive for a search."

"Did you check out of your room already?"

"I'll check in again. It's not as if the Gold Rush Inn is swarming with tourists."

"Spend the night here." He shut the dishwasher door and swiped a rag across the tile counter. "You can work in the dining room. I've got some weeding to do in the yard and Cassie won't be home until five."

Working at Ken's versus spending the next several hours hunched over my laptop on a motel bed wasn't a difficult choice. "Where would I sleep?" With Cassie home, I assumed we'd be refraining from mattress Olympics.

"You can have my room. I'll take the sofa."

At six-foot-plus, he'd be gimpier than me in the morning. "Thanks for the noble gesture, but the sofa's fine with me."

He went upstairs to change into appropriate garb for weed pulling while I retrieved my computer from the car. Ken brought me another Sprite before he headed outside, looking buff and manly in T-shirt and jeans.

Using Ken's satellite network, I connected to the internet. Once ProSpy was ready, I entered the additional information I'd discovered about the kids, what we'd surmised about the fires. One of ProSpy's features allowed me to create a grid of what I knew about each of the four children versus the circumstances of their disappearance. I could then work through the grid as I would one of those logic puzzles with clues like the red-headed girl was three years older than the boy with the blue suspenders. Usually, if I stared at the grid long enough, something useful would pop out at me.

But I was still having trouble wrapping my mind around a woman being the perpetrator. Typically, women didn't abduct children except when it involved a custody dispute. And then it would be her own child she took, not a stranger's. And why would the guy set fires at the scene? To provide a distraction from the abduction?

So what would compel a woman to take four unrelated children? If it was Pickford or Beck, the answer would be easy. But although a female molester wasn't an impossible scenario, it also wasn't likely. And the wide range of ages, as well as the different genders, made an already unlikely scenario even more of a rarity.

Searches of the internet turned up nothing similar to what I was trying to tie together. I couldn't see anything linking these children except opportunity. The baby was easy – she'd been abandoned and this woman had found her. Even James made sense. Somehow my mystery woman came across him after he'd run away. Maybe she'd lured him into her car with a promise to take him home.

But what about Enrique? He wasn't abandoned on the street or a runaway. How had she come across him?

The brain cell that had stirred when Sheri had told me about New Holy Light Church suddenly woke up and stood at attention. Pulling the computer closer, I minimized ProSpy and brought up my notes. The church where the baby had been taken from was in the Tenderloin, between Eddy and Turk on Jones Street. The apartment where Enrique lived with his mother was down near Golden Gate, maybe a block and a half away.

If the mystery woman lived near enough to the church to have found the baby, maybe she lived close enough to Enrique's mother to have known her. Maybe she went over to Felicia's to borrow a cup of sugar or to shoot the breeze and discovered her dead and Enrique sobbing. Or another possibility – Enrique left the apartment after his mother died and mystery woman found him roaming the streets.

Ken wandered into the kitchen, face smeared with dirt, the back of his T-shirt sketched with a sweat map. He had grass stains on his knees and something green clinging to his backside, but damn, I wanted to roll him into bed.

He headed for the sink to wash up. "Making any progress?"

"More guesses and suppositions." Leaning back in my chair, I plopped my left leg on the table. Maybe he'd take the hint and give me another massage. "Turns out the church where Naomi left the baby was spitting distance from where Enrique lived."

He scrubbed his hands dry on a paper towel. "So your kidnapper had opportunity."

"It seems so," I said. "So let's say she scored a baby and a three year-old boy in the city. She and her husband leave town. James runs away that day and ends up at the Arco. Maybe mystery woman sees James there and nabs him."

Ken joined me at the table and, bless him, took my leg in his lap. "I can understand why she took them," he said as he dug in his thumbs. "But why keep them? Why not turn them over to the authorities?"

I tried not to melt into my chair. "Maybe she thinks she's rescuing them. If the mystery woman knew Felicia, maybe she knew about the grandmother. Maybe her intent was to take Enrique to Mrs Lopez."

"If they were good-hearted enough to do that, why take James to Greenville? At the least, I'd think they'd give him a ride home."

I tried to formulate an answer with Ken's magic fingers on my calf turning my brain to mush. "Maybe she thought he'd be better off with her."

"Maybe." He sounded almost convinced. "Then Brandon comes along."

Air gusted from my lungs as he ran the heel of his palm along my knotted muscle. "A real gift, washing up right in her two-thousand acre backyard. Although I don't understand why she'd want a dead boy."

Ken kneaded in silence. I could see some kind of calculation working in his brain.

"Is it enough?" I asked him.

He still didn't look completely convinced, but he nodded. "I'll have Sergeant Russell deploy foot and mounted teams. Not a whole lot of daylight left today by the time the teams get out there."

"You can't power through there with your four-wheel drive vehicles?"

He shook his head. "No roads near where Brandon washed up. The terrain's damn near impassable for even four-wheel drive. To our advantage, in a way. Wherever she's holed up, it has to be walking distance."

We heard Cassie's footsteps stomping on the front porch and this time, Ken had a chance to extricate himself from his compromising position. By the time she came in, Ken was on the phone and I was back at the computer, idly searching the missing children pages of Court TV's Crime Library. A few similar cases, but none that fit my specs in California.

Cassie's gaze passed over me without interest, then fell on Ken. No doubt reading his mind, she pulled a palm-sized instrument from her pocket and pricked her finger with the lancet. Checking the blood sugar result, she pressed a button on her insulin kit. By the time Ken hung up, he had nothing to yell at her for.

"Did you eat at the party?" he asked.

"It wasn't a party," Cassie said. "It was a Warcraft competition."

I could see him count to ten. "Don't make everything an argument. Did you eat?"

She shrugged. "There were chips and stuff. No real food."

"I want your help with dinner at five."

Her chin thrust toward me. "She staying?"

They both stared at me. I weighed the relative merits of a solitary meal at Emil's with a fun-packed emotion-fest here at Ken's. "Sure. Why not?"

In the end, Cassie made herself scarce, given a reprieve from dinner prep by my offer to play kitchen helper. She mostly kept her mouth shut during the meal while Ken and I discussed the SAR teams' game plan for a search pattern.

I bedded down on the sofa as promised, a long-sleeved Greenville Sheriff's Department T-shirt as a nightie. I didn't need it – I still had a few unpleasant options in the Safeway bag – but he offered and I couldn't seem to say no.

Fortunately, we had a built-in chastity belt in the form of Cassie. Uncle Ken and his quasi-paramour, Janelle, weren't getting any whoopee that night.

Just as well. He'd burrowed deep enough into the shell of my heart. Another night of intimacy, he might have taken up permanent residence.

••••

My body curled on Ken's cushy sofa, my nightmare theme de la noir was fire. It roared through my subconscious, horrifying and gratifying in turns. Fire of destruction, fire of passion, fire of expiation. I burned in a myriad of ways during the night, flesh melted from my bones, climax wrenched from my body, pain and exultation tangled like weeds in a forgotten wrecking yard.

Somewhere in the dark hours, I woke with a near epiphany, brilliant but dulled by drowsiness. Fires and missing children, seven deadly sins, a connect the dots picture I perched on the edge of recognizing. Sleep dragged me under before I could comprehend it fully, pushing me into conflagration again.

When morning light from the living room window poked at my eyelids, I squinted one eye open and tried to recapture the revelation my unconscious mind had offered up. Like dreams always do, the vague images scattered like smoke, too insubstantial to get a firm grip on. I had to hope something might trigger that same thought process in the waking hours. If it hadn't been total crap in the first place.

I listened to the quiet house, wondering if Ken or Cassie were awake yet. All those dreams of fire still teased me, making me edgy and unfulfilled.

Ken's footsteps on the stairs deep-sixed hopes for my version of a morning smoke. I shoved off the blanket and hot-footed it to the downstairs bathroom with my much-worn jeans and the last of the halfway decent T-shirts. Everything else in the plastic bag the thrift store would probably trash, or use to spiffy up the employee bathroom. Good thing I was going home today.

All changed and shiny clean, I joined Ken in the kitchen where he had a cup of coffee waiting for me. I gulped half of it down without speaking, letting caffeine course through my veins and jostle my brain cells.

I topped up my cup, added a scoop of creamer and a shovel full of sugar. "Did your deputies find anything interesting at Lucy's place?"

"A 20-yard dumpster full of crap," Ken said. "When they finally excavated enough to get to the basement, they just found more of the same."

"No sign that she might have been preparing to kidnap that kid? Toys, kiddy furniture?"

"Where would she have put it? You saw her place." Ken sipped his coffee. "Turns out Lucy was married once, had a baby girl forty years ago. The baby died of crib death as an infant. Husband left her soon after."

Which had probably been the trigger for whatever psychotic nightmare she was living in now. Oddly, pondering Lucy's tragedy sparked an idea, but I couldn't bring the notion to full consciousness.

Either it was important enough to come to me later or it would sink back into the great unconscious. "Then we go back to the question – if Lucy didn't take the kid, how'd she get her hands on him?"

Ken shrugged. "Maybe someone else took him, was feeling the heat and dumped Norberto at Lucy's."

"A cockeyed explanation." I finished the last of my coffee. "You'll keep me posted on what you find in the woods?"

"You don't want to wait around, see what they come up with?"

"Just let me know if you find James and Enrique." I set aside my coffee cup. "What's the word on Pickford? Was the photo enough to send him back?"

"That and an outstanding warrant on a DUI traffic stop." He stepped past me to the doorway. "Cassie! Let's go! You'll miss your bus."

No answer from above. Ken moved closer to the stairs. "Cassie! I have to get to work."

Her muffled voice drifted from upstairs. "Go ahead! You don't need to stay and babysit me."

It looked for a moment as if Ken intended to stomp up the stairs and drag Cassie down. He turned to me, the exasperation clear on his face. "What the hell takes her so long?"

"Girl stuff," I said, although I had very little personal experience with such mysteries.

I grabbed my computer bag from the trestle table. An image flickered in my mind, a scene from the feature film of my dreams. I couldn't capture it fully, but a shred of instinct lingered.

"Before I go, could I take another look at those arson reports, see if I spot any more details?" Maybe if I read the material again, something would spark that dim memory. Fires and missing kids, all tangled with sin.

"They're sitting on my desk," he said, still distracted by his niece.

"I'd just like a few minutes to look them over."

"Sure." Ken shouted up the stairs again. "Cassie! Lock up. And make sure you change your cartridge before you leave!"

"Okay, okay," Cassie yelled down.

"She'll miss the damn bus," Ken said as he walked behind me through the living room. "Then she'll be calling me asking for a ride."

"Maybe she'll surprise you." Of course, in my experience, teenage surprises were never pleasant.

He hesitated, his hand on the front door, staring back inside. Then he followed me down the porch steps and into town.

CHAPTER 22

Mama never should have stayed out so late. Somehow, the first purification hadn't been enough and she'd had to find the proper place to perform the ritual again. Still unsatisfied, the sense of sin still too powerful to ignore, she'd had to complete the ceremony a third time to quiet the feeling of wrongness.

After the third purification, she'd felt restless, unfinished. She knew she had to return to the children, that they needed her with time running so short. But she just drove, watching the stars vanish and the sky lighten. It was full daylight now, yet Mama couldn't let go of the sense that she'd left something undone.

She turned aimlessly, drove slowly through a neighborhood crowded with houses, children's toys strewn across lawns, flowerbeds full of so much color it made her heart ache. She knew the people in these houses were full of sin, that they passed their wickedness on to their children. But for a moment, she longed for the life they had.

A school bus was stopped up ahead, its red lights flashing. Mama pulled over, tried to see through the bus windows, to see the children inside. But the sun was so bright on the glass, she had to squeeze her eyes shut. She opened them again just as the bus was pulling away.

The paved road Mama had stopped on turned to gravel just beyond. A girl was running up the road toward Mama, waving her arms and yelling at the bus. When the bus kept going, the girl turned and saw Mama's truck. She smiled and walked over and Mama's heart stuttered in her chest. Blonde hair, blue eyes, perfect face.

Angela. Mama's sweet daughter had come back.

Angela opened the door, started to climb into the truck. Then she saw Mama.

"Sorry," Angela said. "I thought you were–"

Mama grabbed Angela's arm and yanked her inside. Stomping the accelerator, Mama drove away fast, the door slamming shut. Angela screamed, tried to grab the door handle, but Mama hung on tight to Angela's arm.

"Let me go," Angela pleaded. "Please, let me go."

She was crying and Mama couldn't bear it. She slapped Angela hard, once, twice. The second time Mama's daughter hit her head against the truck window. She was quiet after that. No more yelling, no more crying, leaving Mama to revel in her joy. Her oldest daughter had returned to her. Now her family was complete.

CHAPTER 23

An hour after Ken and I had arrived at the sheriff's office, I was still flipping through reports, coming up empty but unwilling to give it up as a lost effort. He'd left me in his office while he attended the morning briefing, then came back with the remains of a box of donuts.

Grasping at straws, I'd entered as many of the small details I could think of – the exact time each fire was discovered, the weather, the damn phase of the moon. I had run it all through ProSpy, but I didn't receive any more enlightenment than I had before.

The list of hits that ProSpy produced contained all the same suspects, plus the house fire in Victorville from a year and a half ago. Ken, leaning over my shoulder to pick out a donut, spotted the anomaly on the screen. "I thought you'd filtered that one out."

"Should have." I picked the glaze off an old-fashioned buttermilk. "It was declared accidental."

I studied the sparse details of the Victorville fire. It started in the early morning hours. Kerosene stored in the service porch beside the gas water heater was an accelerant.

Connect the dots. Dream shreds tried to coalesce in my mind. "I need to do a Google. Can I use the department network?"

"Use my computer." He woke his monitor from sleep mode, entered a password and brought up his internet browser.

I went to Google and typed in the search terms "Victorville" and "fire", then narrowed down the hits with the date listed on the hit ProSpy had given me. Google coughed up several citations, including one from the Victorville *Daily Press*.

I clicked on the listing and read it aloud. "'Five children died today when an early morning house fire destroyed their two bedroom home near Victorville. Their mother, Michelle Cresswell, daughter of a local pastor, suffered severe burns...' You have to register with the website to read the rest."

I debated whether to waste a few minutes creating an account on the newspaper's website, or just look for the article elsewhere.

Ken hovered over me. "I've got a meeting."

I decided to check another of the Google hits. "I'm good. You don't need to hang around."

"Will you be here when I get back?" he asked.

That should have been my cue to say my goodbyes, but that little brain cell was still rattling, suggesting to me I stay around awhile longer. Not to mention, I didn't want to leave without seeing him again. "I'll wait for you."

I went back to Google for more information on the Victorville fire. The other hits were even briefer accounts than the one from the *Daily Press*.

Ken's return distracted me before I could get back to the first article. "Forgot something," he said, grabbing a report from his desk.

A faint memory popped above the surface and sucker punched me. "Wait."

"I have to get back to–"

"*Wait*," I repeated as he started out the door.

He stopped, arching a brow at me. "The mayor's going to be ticked."

"*Listen*. The night of the dance, when I was talking with Rich McPherson, he started talking pretty crazy."

"He was drunk, Janelle."

I waved him to silence. "He said something about there being more than seven. That those are just the ones we count and the others are way worse."

Ken glared, waving a hand in a *go on* gesture.

"At the time, yeah, I just figure it was a drunk man raving. But what if it was sins he was talking about? As in seven deadly?"

A flicker of interest in Ken's eyes. "That's a pretty slim link."

"Don't you think it's worth going down and having a word with him?"

Ken tapped the report folder against his fingers. "I'll need ten minutes."

While he was gone, I tried to get back to the *Daily Press* website to set up an account. Just my luck, the site was down. I checked the site status every minute or so while I waited, but never got past the site unavailable message.

We zipped back to Main Street. Ken straddled two parking places in front of Greenville Electronics. A half-hour past opening time, the store sign read "closed," the door was locked, the lights off.

Ken rattled the glass front door. "McPherson! Are you in there?"

As we peered inside, Sadie emerged from the Greenville Gazette office across the street. "What's the ruckus, Ken?" she called out.

"Have you seen McPherson?" Ken asked.

"Not yet. You need to get in? Hang on." She disappeared inside the gazette office, emerging moments later with a ring of keys heavy enough to anchor a cruise ship.

Sadie started across the street. "Joe Templeton gave me the key two years ago when the creek flooded his store. For emergencies."

"You're not required to let me in," Ken told her, taking care of the legal necessities.

"Joe won't mind." Shaking out the proper key, she unlocked the door with a twist of her skinny wrist, then pushed it open.

Sadie retreated back to the Gazette while Ken and I went inside the electronics store. We headed for the back, Ken toward the storage room on the left, me toward the bathroom on the right.

Everything was tidy in the bathroom, seat down, toilet flushed. As I quickly scanned the TP-stacked shelves of an open cabinet, Ken called out, "Take a look at this."

At the back end of the storage room, overstocked crowded metal shelves. In the front, a flat screen monitor shared desk space with file folders and used paper coffee cups.

Ken gestured at the file folders. "Check out the names on the tabs."

Without touching them, I angled my head to read the ones that were visible. Peter McKay. William Markowitz. Sadie Parker. Jill Westfield.

Ken pulled a latex glove from his shirt pocket. Using it as a fingerprint shield, he fanned the folders on the desk, revealing a file for the Jacobys and Elvin Hughes, the caretaker.

A definitive link between McPherson and the fires.

The clatter of the back door lock pulled us both from the storage room. McPherson entered, newspaper under his arm and coffee in his hand. He froze a moment, then dropped the coffee and the newspaper and took off out the door again.

"Shit," Ken muttered as he ran for the door. He turned to toss me his keys. "Bring the truck around."

I made my version of a mad dash out the front of the store. In the Explorer, I gunned up Main Street and made two sharp right turns, ending up in the alley behind the storefronts. The row of buildings stretched along to the right, a steep bank leading down to Deer Creek on the left.

I spotted McPherson, nearly to the end of the block of buildings. He looked back over his shoulder at Ken in close pursuit and put on speed. When he reached the end of the alley, instead of turning back onto Main Street, he dove down the embankment toward the creek. Ken scrambled after him.

I slid out of the Explorer, hopping around the front of the truck before I decided Ken was doing a great job on his own. He caught up to McPherson before Rich slogged through the creek, took a moment to catch his breath, then strong-armed Rich back up the bank.

Ken muscled Rich around the Explorer and spreadeagled him against the side. After a quick search, Ken cuffed him. "Let's go back inside," Ken said between gasps.

While Ken escorted Rich, I parked the Explorer behind the store. I followed them inside and into the storage room.

Rich's eyes got big when he saw the folders spread out on his desk. Ken dumped him into the desk chair. "I think we've figured this all out, Rich. We just need you to fill in a few details."

Alarm blared in McPherson's clear, sober eyes. "I don't know what you mean."

"We know about the fires," I said.

I saw a hint of relief in his face. I didn't like it. What was I missing?

He bowed his head, evading Ken's gaze. "I didn't set any fires."

I pulled a scarred wooden chair over, then sat facing him. I took both his hands in mine. "You tried to tell me the night of the party, but I didn't listen."

"I was drunk." He tried to tug his hands free, but I held them tight.

"I think you're a good man, Rich. You want to do the right thing." I tipped my head to one side so I could meet McPherson's gaze. "You didn't set the fires, but you know something, don't you?"

He shook his head, but I saw the sheen of tears in his eyes. I let him have one hand free so he could dip his head and swipe at his nose.

Then I captured his hands again, gave them a gentle squeeze. "You want to get it off your chest, don't you, Rich?"

He gulped in a breath, a sob catching in his throat. "Yeah."

"Who started the fires?" I asked.

He gulped a couple of times, his Adam's apple bobbing. Then he gasped out, "My wife."

His wife. A female arsonist. Not unheard of, but unusual. The why of it blared at me, demanding an answer.

"Where is she?" Ken asked, voice as gentle as mine.

"I don't know." Rich twitched his shoulders. "She never came home last night."

That did not sound good. I didn't like the idea of this pyromaniac at large. "But you knew she was setting the fires."

Rich shrugged. "The nights I don't have too much to drink, she takes the truck after I get home. But she's always back by dawn."

Ken leaned in closer. "What happened this morning, Rich?"

"I waited for her, but when she didn't show up by eight, I walked to a neighbor's place a few miles away. He drove me into town."

"I'll need the make, model and year on your truck."

Rich gave him the info, and Ken radioed a BOLO to dispatch, then he returned his focus to Rich. "Let's talk about the fires."

Rich squirmed in his chair. "The cuffs hurt."

"I'll take them off if you promise to stay put," Ken said.

I put a hand on his shoulder. "And tell us what you know."

Rich bobbed his head in agreement. Ken unlocked the cuffs nodding at me to continue.

"How many fires has she set?" I asked.

"I don't know how many here."

How many *here*. "So she's set fires elsewhere," I prompted.

Rich wouldn't look at me. "She can't help it. After what happened with her daddy, then when the–" He bit the words off. "Burning things makes her feel better."

That sent a shiver down my back. I'd convinced myself of the same thing, although I limited the destruction to my own hide.

"What happened to her daddy?" I asked.

"When she was seven... she was with her daddy while he was burning leaves. Kerosene splashed on him somehow and he caught fire. Burned him bad."

"These files," Ken said, gesturing toward the desk. "Did you tell her where to burn?"

Rich seemed to collapse in on himself. Tears spilled down his cheeks. "She wanted to know who I talked to during the day. She'd ask me about them."

"To learn about their sins?" I asked.

He slumped further in the chair. "She idolized her daddy. When he preached, she sat in the front row, and her eyes never left him. Even with the scars the fire left."

"So he taught her about sin," I said.

"He was a good man," Rich said. "She just got it a little mixed up."

So mixed up, she felt a compulsion to burn, again and again.

Rich lifted his wrist, checking the time. "I have to make sure she got back okay."

"We'll be heading out there, soon," Ken said. "Where's the cabin?"

"South county," Rich said. "I can show you on a map, on the computer."

Rich moved his chair aside, making room for me to use the keyboard. I brought up a map of Greenville County. With Rich looking on, I zoomed in until he said stop, then he pointed to the screen. "Here. It's built up against a huge boulder, maybe twenty feet tall."

"I'll need directions," Ken said.

Rich gave Ken a sidelong look. "It'd be easier to show you."

"You can show us," Ken said, "but you'll stay in the car."

It crossed my mind that I could finish the Google search I'd started earlier, read the complete article from the *Daily Press*. Something kept nudging me to lay my hands back on that keyboard. Wisps of dreams, filled with fire and sin, momentarily fogged my mind.

"How about you talk to Ken now, Rich," I said. "I need to look for something on the internet."

"Sure. Okay." McPherson wiped away tears with the heel of his hand.

Ken continued my line of inquiry. "Tell us about the other fires. The ones that weren't set here."

"There were trash fires in the dumpster out behind our apartment. I tried to tell myself it was just kids." Rich glanced over at the screen as I set up an account at the *Daily Press*. I positioned myself to block his view.

"Where was this apartment?" Ken asked.

He looked at me, then away. "San Francisco."

A prickling danced up my spine, pulled me from the opening paragraphs of the article. "Where in San Francisco?"

He whispered, so softly I had to strain to hear. "Jones, near Golden Gate."

I locked gazes with Ken. He gave me a nod of encouragement. "What else did she burn there?" I asked. "Besides dumpsters?"

"A dry cleaner," Rich said, still trying to see the computer screen. I planted myself firmly in his way. "A church."

A roaring started up in my ears. "Was there a baby at the church?"

I might as well have struck McPherson with a sledgehammer. His mouth dropped open and he swayed in his chair. The waterworks turned on again, tears gushing down his cheeks.

My own knees trembled. Turning like an automaton, I scrolled down the page displaying the article and read about Glenn and Michelle Cresswell and the family they lost.

"Ken. Listen to this."

My stomach churned as I traced a finger down the third paragraph. "Killed in the fire were Lydia Cresswell, ten months old. Sean, Thomas and Glenn Jr, ages four, eight and ten."

Still caught up in Rich's admissions about the fires, Ken didn't get it at first. "I don't follow you."

I turned the screen toward him. "They're the same genders, nearly the same ages as James, Enrique, Brandon and the baby."

I scrolled down further, to the photograph of the family that accompanied the article. I clicked on it to enlarge it.

There were the five children with Mom and Dad, all of the young ones lost in the fire. The woman I didn't recognize, but the man's shaggy head of hair and full, bushy beard set off a rocket in my brain.

"It's Glenn," I blurted out.

"Who's Glenn?" Ken rose to better see the screen.

I stepped back to give him room. "The man Sadie Parker said traded his Volvo for her truck. The same man Andros over at Emil's Café and the girl at the McDonald's saw. Glenn who had James and the baby."

As Ken stared intently at the photograph, Rich covered his face with his hands. Ken knocked them away, compared the face on the screen with the man sitting in the chair.

"Oh my God," Ken said. "Rich is Glenn."

Now I could see it. The eyes were the same, never mind that the beard and hair obscured everything else.

I looked up at Ken, ramifications thundering down on me. "He has the kids. All of them."

Rich – Glenn – shook his head so hard, I half expected it to unscrew from his neck. Ken dragged his chair around and sat knee to knee with Glenn again. "Where are they?"

"I don't know what you're talking about." He wouldn't look at us, tears reddening his eyes, snot seeping from his nose.

"Those missing kids," Ken said. "We've got witnesses who saw them with you."

He shook his head some more, snot flying. "They're mistaken."

I dropped my hands on his shoulders, bending close to his ear. "Come on, Glenn. We know it all. About Michelle finding the baby at the church. Taking James from the Arco. And Enrique..."

Glenn slumped, elbows on knees, head bowed. I could almost feel his emotional meltdown through my hands; knew the moment his barriers shattered.

"At the cabin," he whispered hoarsely. "She keeps them at the cabin."

"Where?" Ken asked. "Are they safe?"

"They're in the basement." Cresswell sniffed, a wet, pitiful sound. "But they're all okay, I swear to you."

"She hasn't hurt them?" Ken asked, his fingers tightening.

Glenn swiped snot onto his arm. "I wouldn't let her hurt them."

I grabbed a handful of tissues from the desk and stuffed them in his hand. "But you left the kids alone this morning."

"Because I knew she'd be back," Glenn said. "I had to come in to work."

"But you're sure those kids are okay," I said. "You checked on them before you left?"

Glenn snorted into a tissue. "Junior would've yelled if there was a problem."

That was no damn answer. Ken pulled Glenn to his feet. "We'd better get out there, now. Hopefully before Michelle returns."

Ken stowed Glenn in the Explorer's cage. As he pulled out onto Main Street, he called Sadie at the *Gazette* to ask her to lock up the store. Then he radioed for backup to meet us at mile marker thirty-five where we'd be turning off the highway.

In my mind's eye, I saw Tommy Phillips in the back seat beside Glenn, directing his accusing stare at someone other than me for once.

"Tell us how it happened, Glenn," I said.

Now that the walls had broken down, Glenn seemed eager to talk. "When she found Lydia in San Francisco, I thought it would help."

Ken gunned up the entrance to Highway 50. "Why not take the baby to the authorities?"

"That girl didn't want her. What was the harm in Michelle keeping her?" Glenn asked. "I thought then maybe she'd stop..."

"Setting fires?" I asked. "But it didn't work out that way, did it? And now all those kids are at risk."

Cresswell swiped his snotty nose. "Michelle wouldn't hurt any of those kids. Not after what happened to her own."

What happened to her own. Had seeing her father badly burned when she was a child set a time bomb ticking inside Michelle? An emotional nuke that exploded when she lost all five of her children in a fire?

Either one might have been enough of a trigger to create Michelle Cresswell's fascination with burning. Combined, they would have been more than sufficient to pull the pin. Just as Lucy had become unhinged by the death of her baby.

Insight suddenly burst into my brain. "You took Norberto. Dropped him off at Lucy's."

He muttered his affirmative response so softly, I barely heard him.

"But why?" Ken asked.

I answered for Glenn. "To distract us. He'd heard the story about Lucy's baby, knew from his own wife how far into the deep end a woman could plunge after losing her kids."

"What about Enrique?" Ken asked.

For a moment, Glenn looked at me blankly. Then he said, "I never knew his real name. Michelle always called him Sean."

"How'd she find him?" I asked.

"His mother, Felicia, lived upstairs from us. Sometimes Michelle would take care of the boy when Felicia went out."

To get high, no doubt.

"Michelle would pretend he was our four year-old. Sometimes she'd end up keeping him a week at a time." Glenn wrapped his arms around himself. "Then she found Felicia dead. She ran and got me, all excited, saying we had Sean back."

Ken threw on his wig-wags to nudge traffic out of the Explorer's way. "So you just took him."

"I knew Michelle would take good care of him. She always took good care of the kids."

Except I still had an uneasy feeling about a woman who played with fire. My own dark urges toward self-abuse might have morphed into a compulsion to burn my own kids if I'd had young innocents under my control.

Ken slowed behind a slow moving truck, waiting with ill-concealed impatience for the driver to move aside. "How'd you get hold of James?"

"We stopped at a gas station to change the baby. I'd gone into the store for some juice for Sean. Somehow Michelle got James into the car, hid him under a blanket in the back seat. I didn't know he was there until we were nearly to Fairfield."

James had probably still been steamed at his stepdad, enough to get into the car, anyway. Later, when he'd changed his mind, it was too late. "He tried to bolt at the McDonalds?"

"I wanted to take him back home," Glenn said. "But Michelle insisted he was Junior, come back to us."

"What brought you to Greenville?" Ken asked.

"My family used to own the cabin, on leased BLM land. We broke in, cleaned the place up."

Michelle had three of her children back, she must have been jonesing big time for the other two. She needed more fires to take the edge off her grief, used the excuse of sin to justify the destruction. "How'd she know where to find Brandon?"

"She knew that cove in the river," Glenn said. "Would pull the dead things out and burn them."

A sickening lump settled in my stomach. "Did she burn Brandon?"

"No!" Glenn insisted. "I told you, he's safe. Just like the others."

"Have you seen Brandon?" Ken asked.

"Saturday morning. When I brought them their breakfast." Glenn turned away from me. "He was... sleeping."

My mind kept circling back to the fire that killed the Cresswell kids. Instinct drove me to ask the question. "Were there other fires in Victorville?"

He shredded the tissue in his hands. "I told you, we moved away from there after the kids died."

I turned in the seat to better see Glenn through the cage. "Were there fires *before* your house burned down?"

He looked at me, eyes wide, then dropped his gaze. His body had started to shake.

I leaned closer, right up against the wire mesh. "The fire that killed your kids wasn't the first, was it?"

His body vibrated. Another minute and the guy would disintegrate.

I pressed my hand against the mesh. "What did she burn before your house? A woodpile? Maybe someone's shed?"

"It wasn't her. It couldn't have been," Glenn insisted. "She only did it after they died."

"Come on, Glenn," I said gently. "You know better. Seeing her daddy burned that way messed her up. So she went out at night. Leave you and the kids sleeping, go out looking for a way to soothe that inner pain."

He flicked a sidelong glance at me, denial battling with stark reality in his face. "She was happy."

"Are you sure?" I asked. "All those children to take care of."

"I helped her when the baby had colic," Glenn said. "I'd walk Lydia at night when she cried. But Michelle loved our kids. She loved to show them off at church."

I thought of Holy Rock Baptist Church, sitting beside my mother in the pew. To my mother, religion offered redemption and forgiveness. But to some, God only represented damnation and punishment.

I had a feeling I knew which side of the fence Michelle Cresswell had fallen on. "Did Michelle ever punish the kids, Glenn?"

He hunched in the seat. "Sometimes kids need to be punished."

"Of course they do, Glenn." As I pressed my hand against the cage, my arm flexed, burn scars catching on the knit sleeve of my T-shirt. "What did Michelle punish the kids for?"

He squirmed. "When they broke the rules. When they were bad."

"The baby, too?" I nearly whispered the question. "Was the baby bad?"

The color left his face. "She said they sinned." He spoke so softly I could barely hear him.

"They sinned," I said aloud for Ken's benefit. "And she punished them. With fire."

His head bobbed, nose dripping. "She burned them."

Out of the corner of my eye, Ken's hands gripped so tight on the wheel, the tendons popped. His voice was hoarse when he asked, "How, Glenn?"

"She just made them... Hold a candle while it burned." Glenn wriggled, as if guilt was eating through him like a parasite. "But sometimes when it burned to the bottom..." He swallowed, and I could see his Adam's apple jiggle in his throat. "It was just their fingers. Their hands sometimes from melted wax."

The air in the Explorer seemed to thicken. Glenn had said he wouldn't let Michelle hurt them. That burning their fingers didn't qualify as "hurting them" set off a quiet rage inside me.

Wanting to grab Ken's shotgun and blow his head off, I spoke quietly. "Then she was only trying to purify them from sin, when she burned them all to death."

Glenn jolted, sitting upright. "She wouldn't. She couldn't." He shook his head, snot and tears spraying. "Not her babies."

"If she thought it was better for them, if she thought there was too much sin..."

He tipped his head up, met my gaze. "But now she has them back. She wouldn't do it again."

Ken and I exchanged a look and I saw in his face exactly what was going through my mind. The ticking time bomb of Michelle Cresswell was about to go nuclear. And four children would be caught in the explosion.

Ken stomped the gas, goosing the Explorer even faster. "Is your wife armed, Mr Cresswell?"

Glenn looked startled. "She doesn't like guns."

"What makes you so sure she won't hurt them?" I asked. "Like she did before?"

"Because they're not all there!" Glenn shouted. "Because she wants Angela first. She won't do anything until she has her." He collapsed forward, sobbing. I hoped guilt gutted him from the inside out.

"Which one's Angela?" Ken asked me, gaze out the window as he watched for mile marker 35.

"Their thirteen year-old."

"I don't know of any missing thirteen year-old girls."

"She might not be thirteen. Could be twelve or fourteen."

Ken's radio squawked. "Heinz."

"This is dispatch. What's your 10-20, Sheriff?"

"Highway 50," Ken told dispatch, "fifteen miles east of town."

"We have another arson. Possible fatality. EMT and deputy dispatched to the location."

Another arson. Michelle had been busy last night.

"Who's backing me up here?" Ken asked dispatch.

"Deputy Farrell and Deputy Braun are on their way. The other unit on duty rerouted to the arson scene."

Ken signed off with dispatch. "After the first seven fires, she started over."

"And probably won't stop until she reaches seven again. Or finds Angela."

Ken's radio crackled again. "This is central. There are two more arsons, with injuries. One in zone twenty-two, the other in thirteen."

"Damn it," Ken muttered. "Send Alex and Lisa out there. Soon as they're clear there, have them follow my GPS to my location. South county off mile marker thirty-five."

He signed off with dispatch. "That means no backup for at least an hour."

"How many deputies do you have on day shift?" I asked.

"One per zone. Sometimes they double-up as needed."

"Anyone else available from another zone?"

"Sure. But they're way the hell on the other side of the county."

He pulled over at the mile marker, in a slim turnout overlooking the river. A bridge crossed the river here, and an asphalt road led off into the trees.

"Three fires in one night," Ken said. "So she's up to five, counting the one at Abe and Mary's and that shed."

"Assuming Glenn is right, she won't do anything to those kids until she can find Angela."

"And we'll make damn sure she never does."

I jumped when Ken's phone rang, clipping my elbow on the truck door. "Heinz," he snapped into the cell.

His face clouded as the caller spoke. "No, she's not sick at home. Did she call and tell you that?" He pinched the bridge of his nose. "I'll track her down, Maude."

He stabbed the disconnect button, muttering a few creative words under his breath. "I have to send someone over to the house. It looks like Cassie's playing hooky."

My urgency ratcheted up a notch. "She never made it to school?"

Ken picked up on my edginess. "She probably just missed the bus. Thought she could get away with staying home."

"Angela was thirteen. Same age as Cassie." I just stared at him, waiting for him to reach the same conclusion I already had.

"Shit. Oh, shit."

He thrust the Explorer into gear and yanked the wheel to the right. With a squeal of tires we barreled across the bridge and up the narrow road.

CHAPTER 24

Mama still hadn't brought them breakfast. Before Mama had come home with the girl, Daddy had opened the door and looked inside, but he didn't bring them anything to eat either. As late as it was in the day, the baby was hungry and wet. She was crying so loud, James finally picked her up.

James rocked the baby in his arms and patted her back, but she just screamed louder. Sean, sitting on James's mattress, scrunched into the corner and covered his ears. James wished he could do the same.

Thomas lay on his own mattress, as quiet as ever under the blanket Mama had thrown over him. The girl was slumped beside Thomas, a big bruise on her head. Mama had said her name was Angela.

The box strapped to Angela's waist had started beeping a few minutes ago. She'd been kind of awake when Mama had first carried her into the basement, but she'd seemed dizzy and mixed up. Now she was breathing funny, really fast, and she'd fallen asleep.

James set the crying baby in her playpen, then went down on his knees beside Angela. He shook the girl's shoulder. "Are you okay? Hey!"

Angela didn't answer. As she breathed out, he smelled something sweet, like fruit. She felt hot, too, as if she had a fever.

The door rattled and Mama came inside. Not sure if he should be touching Angela, James quickly got to his feet. "Mama, the girl's real sick. She won't wake up."

Thomas wouldn't wake up, either, hadn't since he'd arrived. James knew why, but he was afraid to say anything to Mama about it.

Mama went down the stairs and dug through the junk under them. When she turned toward James, she had some long, skinny plastic things in her hand. James remembered his stepfather using those to hold together power cords and stuff in the house.

"It's time, Junior," Mama said as she lit a candle beside the mattress. "Time for heaven."

"What about the baby?" James asked. "I think she wants her bottle."

"It doesn't matter now, Junior." She dropped the plastic strips into his hand. "Mama needs you to tie them all up."

"No." James took a step back, dropping the ties. "I won't."

He didn't even see Mama's hand. He flew across the room, banging into the wall beside his mattress. Now Sean started to cry.

Mama stood over him. "Mama doesn't like bad boys."

She pulled a lighter from her pocket, then grabbed James's shirt to pull him up. She clicked on the lighter and shoved the burning flame right in his face.

"Be a good boy and tie them up," she told him, bringing the lighter close enough for James to feel the heat. "You have to be good to go to heaven."

James shook all over as he fumbled for the plastic strips. He did the baby first, putting a tie loosely on her little hands. Then he did Sean. The little boy just sat there, staring up at him.

James had to pull the blanket off Thomas to find his hands. His skin was cold and creepy, his wrist bent all weird. James managed to get a tie around both arms.

The girl was lying funny and Mama had to help James move her. Mama held her wrists side by side so James could wrap them with a tie.

Finally it was his turn. Mama tightened a tie around his wrists, then his ankles. She tied them both together.

She went under the stairs again and pulled out the plastic buckets filled with rags. She dumped out the rags and arranged them in three piles in a line, the first between James's mattress and the baby's playpen, the next a few feet away, the third between the mattresses and the stairs.

"Not enough." Mama pushed the rags into higher piles. "You be good, Junior. Mama has to go out."

Mama retrieved one more item from under the stairs and set it beside the rag piles. Then she hurried out of the basement.

When James read the label on the can, he finally understood. He was going to die down here.

CHAPTER 25

The asphalt road ended maybe a hundred yards in, replaced by board-edged gravel the Explorer roared up as easily as the paved surface. But after about three miles of back teeth rattling on the Ford's stiff shocks, the track narrowed and turned to dirt. Another three-quarters of a mile and tall grass nearly obliterated the going, the trees even tighter, the side view mirrors of the Explorer scraping on branches as it passed between them.

Ken's GPS reassured us that backup would be able to track us, even here in the back of beyond. We saw signs that another vehicle had gone boony crashing through the trees – broken branches, churned up undergrowth. Not the best commute for Glenn and it must have been a damned nightmare for Michelle to navigate in the dark, lit only by her zealot's fire.

Up and down a rise and there was the Chevy, parked catawampus against a downed pine tree that blocked what passed for a road through the forest. Which meant Michelle was at the cabin. If she did have Cassie – her Angela – she could go nuclear any moment.

Ken squeezed the Explorer in beside the pickup and reached across the front seat to open the glove box. He pulled out a Glock 26. "You still certified?"

"I get out to the gun range sometimes."

He dropped the gun in my hand. I pressed the magazine release and counted ten bullets.

"Careful," Ken said. "There's one chambered."

I slid the magazine back into place. In his cage with the doors locked, Glenn pressed his hands against the wire mesh. "Please don't hurt her."

"We'll do everything we can to keep everyone safe, Mr Cresswell, including your wife," Ken said. "But the safety of those kids is our first concern."

We climbed from the Explorer. Ken grabbed a portable radio and tossed it to me.

Before he shut the door, Ken leaned in to ask Glenn a last question. "Which way from here?"

A long beat of silence, Glenn's reluctance written in his face. Finally he said, "After you go over the tree, look for a pair of redwoods grown together. Take the left deer trail, then the next time it splits off, go left again."

Radio clipped to my front pocket and the Glock in the waistband of my jeans, I waited as Ken checked Glenn's truck. He opened the door and retrieved a purple backpack from the floor on the passenger's side. He stared at it, expressionless.

"Cassie's?" I asked.

"Yeah." He unzipped a side pocket. "Damn."

"What?" I asked, trying to see over his shoulder.

"The spare cartridge for Cassie's insulin kit."

"Maybe she put in a fresh one at home," I suggested.

"Not likely," he said as he dropped the backpack on the hood of the Explorer. "She probably ran out of time to change it and just stuffed it in her book bag."

We climbed over the two-foot diameter tree blocking the road. At the joined redwoods, we found the first deer trail split, then almost missed the second Y in the heavy brush. Once we'd continued on the leftmost track, I could see a granite face maybe a hundred yards ahead.

"Is that the boulder?" I asked.

Ken doubled his pace. Pine branches slapped me in the face, and poison oak clung to the trunk of every tree. Blackberries choked the space between the cedars, firs and pines, thorns reaching out to scratch my arms through my T-shirt.

As we approached the boulder, we slowed, moving carefully around its circumference. It loomed over a small clearing, the adjacent hillside swallowed by spiny brambles that had sent tendrils over the granite face itself.

"Where the hell is the cabin?" Ken said softly.

I edged farther around the boulder. A glint of glass through the thick vines caught my eye.

"Under that mess," I whispered.

Greenery enveloped the cabin like a shroud. If I hadn't seen the glimmer of glass, if Glenn hadn't told us it was here, I might have passed it right by.

Ken drew his Glock 22; I tugged the smaller 9mm out of my waistband. Keeping close to the boulder, we crept up to the cabin. The blackberry canes were thick as a man's thumb, the inch-long thorns scraping my skin as I squirmed between them. We approached at an oblique angle, staying out of direct view of the two front windows.

It looked as if the sturdy vines were all that kept the rotting wood of the cabin from collapsing. The glass had cracked in the leftmost window. Newer two by fours had been haphazardly nailed to the porch supports to keep the overhang from crashing down.

Plastered to the wall of the cabin, we stood quietly, listening. Nothing but wind sifting through the trees, the chatter of a squirrel.

The window nearest us was covered, the stained white cloth shifting slightly as air fingered its way through the cracked glass. Although the fabric was lightweight, the lack of light inside the cabin made it impossible to see if anyone was moving around in there.

Ken crouched below the window level to creep along the crumbling porch. He tried the door, but the knob wouldn't turn. I followed his path, then moved past him toward the side of the house opposite the boulder. As I sidled through the pocket of space between the cabin wall and the stickery overgrowth, I saw the second window was covered as well with the same pale cloth.

I spied Michelle's makeshift pyre, charred wood and what looked like blackened skulls set in a circle of rocks. I stopped short of a window at ground level and went down on one knee in the dirt, pulling my shirt free of thorns as I went. I worried I'd be hard-pressed to get to my feet quickly, but the window was so low, I had no other choice.

I could barely see through the scum on the basement window. The leafy vines blocked out most of the sunlight that filtered through the trees. As I used my sleeve to swab a corner of the window, someone moved inside, shifting into my field of view.

It was James. Crouched on the floor and trussed up like a turkey. I must have cast a shadow through the window because he craned his neck and looked up at me. I couldn't see all of the basement, but unless Michelle was hiding in a corner, she didn't seem to be inside.

Two figures lay opposite James. I recognized Cassie's white and pink sneakers and the jeans with a hole near the ankle. She lay still, whether asleep or something worse, I didn't know. I assumed it was Brandon lying beside her covered with a blanket. I couldn't see Enrique, had to hope he was in one of the corners I couldn't see.

James tried to struggle to his feet. I shook my head, waving my hands in the window to indicate I wanted him to stay put. Michele might be somewhere else in the cabin, could enter the basement at any moment. I didn't want anything James did to alert her to our presence.

I snagged the radio from my back pocket. "Ken? The kids are here."

A jay squawked, sailing from tree to tree above my head. A squirrel chattered in outrage. But no answer from Ken. I called into the radio again. "Ken?"

Something caught my eye inside the window and for a moment, I saw Tommy standing there in the basement, waving his arms, shouting at me. I gawked at the familiar hallucination, then shut my eyes to clear the brief insanity.

Metal pressed against the back of my neck. The bore of a Glock 22.

I froze. "Easy does it, Michelle."

The barrel dug a little deeper. "Drop the gun," she said.

I set the 9mm down beside me. Keeping Ken's Glock pressed against my skin, Michelle stepped around behind me and kicked the 9mm out of reach. "Get up. Slow."

Keeping my hands spread wide, I pushed to my feet. Michelle never let up the pressure. I tried not to think about the mess that Glock would make of my skull. Talk about a bad hair day.

I studied her out of the corner of my eye. I don't know what I expected – long, scraggly hair, missing teeth, red-rimmed eyes? But her dark brown hair was a tidy shoulder length, her dental work looked good and her blue gaze seemed calm and steady. The palm-sized burn scar on her right cheek had healed fairly well, the taut skin a slightly darker pink than her natural color.

A poke of the Glock's barrel turned me away from her. "Keep your eyes to yourself."

Michelle lowered the weapon to the middle of my back. Now I had a new mental image – my chest splattered all over the cabin's rough-hewn log walls. A nudge with the Glock propelled me toward the front of the cabin.

I hadn't heard gunfire, so however Michelle had incapacitated Ken, there was hope he was still alive. I forced myself not to think about the myriad of noiseless ways she could have killed him.

He was sprawled on the porch, under the cracked window. Blood stained his sandy hair, dripping from the side of his head down into his ear. A hefty four by four-sized chunk of tree limb lay beside him.

If he was bleeding, he was still alive. I shut my mind to any other possibility, keeping my focus on Michelle as she unlocked the cabin's door.

With Michelle's enforcer urging me on, I stumbled over the uneven threshold into the dim interior light. As I struggled to get my bearings, Michelle closed the door. Now the room was nearly dark, the broken-down sofa and chairs faint silhouettes in the shadows.

She grabbed a handful of my T-shirt and pulled me over to the cracked window. The Glock still against my spine, she yanked the covering from the window. Light filled the room, too bright after the dimness. The ugliness of the place wasn't improved with illumination now I could see the cruddy dishes in a wash pan, mouse droppings on the floor, layers of dust on everything.

"Hold this." She stuck the piece of stained dirty sheet in my hands, then guided me to the second window for the other scrap.

My arms full of disgusting percale, we wove our way through the obstacle course of detritus. Down a short hallway, she stopped me at a closed door. She reached around me with her ring of old fashioned latch keys and jabbed one into the lock.

"The sheriff has backup coming, Michelle. They'll be here any minute."

Michelle opened the door. "Mama was busy last night. She left a blessing on three houses."

"You burned them down."

"I purified them of their sins."

She nudged me through the door onto a small landing, then down the steps. I surveyed the dank basement – mattresses on the floor, a playpen in the corner, a candle burning between them. Enrique huddled in a corner on one of the mattresses, James beside him. The baby whimpering in the playpen. Brandon's body covered by a blanket on the other mattress. Cassie beside him, asleep, unconscious or dead, I didn't know, her insulin kit beeping its warning.

I could already smell the kerosene from the open can, but it didn't look as if she'd poured it yet. Three large mounds of rags were lined up between the kids' makeshift beds.

Michelle's funeral pyre for her beloved children. Born again to die again.

"Put them on the floor," she told me. I dropped the sheets beside the stairs.

The Glock pressing into my back, she turned me to face the cinderblock wall. One hand keeping the firearm in place, she dug through the jumble of crap under the stairs. She came up with a pair of gardening shears and a handful of plastic cable ties.

Michelle herded me over to the mattress where James sat. She cut James's restraints, then tucked the shears into a back pocket. "Hold out your hands so Junior can tie them."

I kept my hands to myself. "Is this how you burned your own kids, Michelle? Tied them up first? Or were they sleeping in their beds when you killed them?"

Michelle directed the Glock at James's head, those cold blue eyes on me. "Do as you're told."

I held my hands close to James, keeping my wrists angled to prevent him from tightening the ties too much. His head bowed, he fumbled with the cable tie. When he pulled the end of the plastic, he left it loose.

"Feet, too, Junior. Then tie them together."

He wrapped two long ties around my ankles. When he was done, he glanced up at me. I shrugged a shoulder in Michelle's field of view, blocking James's hands. He ran a tie through both the wrist and ankle restraints, but he only poked the tip through the locking mechanism. A good strong push with my feet and it would pop free.

Michelle wrapped another tie around James's hands, then snugged up the wrist and ankle ties. I held my breath, waiting for her to check the other tie, the one tethering hands to feet. But her gaze strayed to my wrist where my shirt had ridden up.

She tugged the sleeve farther up, exposing my scars. "It's hard to burn the sins away like that, one at a time."

A creepy little prickle danced its way up my spine. Not the sort of woman one wanted as a kindred spirit. "I'm a real klutz with a match."

She stared at me, that no-one's-home look in her eyes. "It's better to toss them on the fire all at once."

That might be exactly the kind of punishment I had coming, but these kids had done nothing to deserve that kind of agony. As Michelle turned her back on me to pick up the kerosene, I torqued my wrists, searching for some give in the plastic ties. There was none. But the ankles... I felt a slight give when I pushed my knees apart.

It gave me something to work on while I waited for her to put down the Glock, to figure out she couldn't start a fire with one hand. But for the moment, she seemed to have no difficulty adding the sheets to the rag piles and pouring kerosene onto them.

I fell back on my only option for the moment. Keep her talking while I worked on the ankle restraints. Pray that Ken might return from la-la land and rescue us. Or that the cavalry would arrive.

"Why'd you kill them, Michelle? Why'd you kill your babies?"

"I didn't kill them." She emptied the can in the third pile, then turned back toward the stairs. "I killed the sin. It was the only way I could send them to heaven."

"But they're not in heaven. They're here."

She brought out another can of kerosene. "God sent them back to me."

"To burn them again? But it didn't work, Michelle. Not if they've come back." Reasoning with a psychotic was a lost cause, but maybe it would keep her hands off the matches.

"The fire wasn't hot enough the first time. It didn't cleanse all their sins."

Cassie moaned and shifted on the mattress and relief shot through me. Still alive, then. I pushed harder on the cable ties around my ankle.

Michelle sprinkled the holy water of kerosene on the floor. "I have to be sure they stay in heaven this time."

The kerosene in one hand, the Glock in the other, she hesitated. I could see the fervor in her face, as if her gaze sought out the glory of her tyrannical god. It wasn't the one my mother had worshipped all those years ago, but a being entirely of Michelle's creation.

Finally, finally, she set the Glock down on the stairs. Her hand free, she pulled a lighter from her pocket. Using my thumbs, I'd worked the ankle ties down around one of my cross-trainers. Squirming, I pushed the shoes from my feet and the ties off my ankles.

Michelle clicked the lighter.

My left leg collapsed when I tried to stand, the pain in my calf shooting clear up to my molars. Scrabbling across the floor, kerosene wetting my shirt, my jeans, I head-butted Michelle off her feet. She dropped the lighter and it hit the concrete floor, the flame doused when the safety released. I rolled, knocking the lighter away. It skidded under the junk beneath the stairs.

I rolled back toward Michelle, catching her before she could get to her feet. Using both hands as a club, I punched her face, bloodying her nose. She struggled free, throwing me off her, scrambling away.

She stumbled into one of the rag piles, got her feet tangled in them, fell to her knees. I levered myself up, ignored the agony in my left leg and limped toward her. Stretched out on the floor, she reached for the candle. James flung his body down and blew hard at the flame. It shifted in the gust of air.

I grabbed Michelle by the waistband of her jeans and tried to pull her back. James squirmed closer, trying to get near enough to extinguish the flame. Michelle reached out, got her fingers on the candle, tipped it just as James blew hard again.

As the candle fell, it flickered out, a wisp of smoke trailing from the wick. The wick still glowed, but extinguished in the liquid kerosene.

Michelle dug another lighter from her pocket. I shook her, but she kept her grip long enough to hold the flame against a pile of kerosene-soaked rags. They burst into flame.

I kicked the rags aside, but the flames licked higher. My fingers still hooked in Michelle's waistband, I snagged the garden shears and tossed them at James.

Michelle got to her feet and kicked behind her, knocking me to the floor. My head whacked against the concrete, the pain stunning me. I stared at the flame burning in front of my nose.

And remembered that plastic melted. I held my bound wrists over the rag fire, let the flame burn the cable ties, felt it sear my skin. The ecstasy of exquisite pain distracted me for an instant, the sickness of my bliss not lost on me. For an eternal microsecond I considered the merits of death by fire. Then the cable ties parted and I rolled away from the flame.

Beside me, James had cut the ties from his hands and feet. "Get the others!" I yelled. He used the shears on Enrique, then turned to Cassie.

Using the wall for balance, I rose. And found myself again facing the bore of Ken's Glock 22.

"The fire will cleanse us all." Wild-eyed, Michelle waved the weapon in my general direction.

The flame that had freed me from my restraints had reached the closest mountain of rags. "I'm taking these kids out of here, Michelle."

"Your pain will be burned away."

"The hell it will!" I kicked the flaming rags toward Michelle, creating a path of fire between us. I dove for Enrique, grabbing him up.

Michelle pulled the trigger, the shot going wild and caroming off the cinderblock wall. "James, get the baby!" I could carry Cassie, but we'd have to leave Brandon's body behind.

As I bent to pick up Cassie, Michelle fired off another round. The bullet whistled past my ear and took another chunk of cinderblock from the wall. I didn't know what would get me first, fire or gun. The temperature in the room had risen from dank to unbearably hot and Michelle was going to figure out that Glock sooner or later.

I rose with Cassie slung over my shoulder, James behind me with the baby, Enrique beside him. Michelle was nowhere near being out of ammunition and I presented too damn wide a target. The fire had reached the mattresses and my escape path was dwindling fast.

She lifted the gun, held it steady. Beside me, James wound up like an all-star little league pitcher and flung something at Michelle. Her hands flew up to protect her face.

"What the hell was that?" I asked.

"Nails," James said.

Recovered from James's surprise attack, Michelle lowered the Glock again and aimed. An instant later, she hit the floor, writhing in pain.

Ken, taking the stairs two at a time, ripped the Taser wires from Michelle's back. He snatched up his Glock on the way down.

Dodging flames, he ran toward me. "I'll take Cassie. You get Enrique."

"I'm not leaving Brandon." I relinquished Ken's niece to him and scooped up the dead boy. With the body over my shoulder, I crouched to pull Enrique up to my hip. "What about Michelle?"

"I'll come back. We get the kids to safety first."

Ken went up the stairs first, James next. I followed, got up three steps. A hand clutched my left ankle, nearly pulled me off my feet.

I twisted and fell on my butt to keep from falling over. "Ken!"

He stopped at the top of the stairs. "Send Enrique up!"

I let him go. "*¡Corres!*"

He ran up to Ken. I kicked at Michelle, trying to dislodge her. She wouldn't let go. The fire had nearly reached the stairs.

I let Brandon's body slide onto the steps and swung at Michelle with both fists, striking the side of her head, her face. She dug her fingers in like claws and pulled me toward her.

Damned if I was going to burn to death, let her take me into her hell. I kicked hard with both feet, punching my left heel into her chin, my right into her chest. She flew backwards, bouncing off the wall then stumbling forward into the fire.

The flames enveloped her body at once and she screamed, a hideous, blood-chilling sound I'd heard only in nightmares. I grabbed up Brandon's body and scrabbled up the stairs, my left leg barely holding me, my socks catching on the splintered wood as the steps collapsed behind me. I hit the top step running, my path through the cabin a blur.

Kid Deputy was just outside the door, ready to take Brandon from me, to prop me across his shoulder as we got clear of the growing conflagration. Three other deputies ran toward us through the woods and I could hear the whine of fire engine sirens in the distance.

When Ken started toward the cabin, I waved him off. "She's gone," I told him. "You can't save her."

I can't say I was a hundred percent certain that was true. But in either case, I didn't feel a whit of guilt telling Ken to stand down.

CHAPTER 26

That afternoon and evening was like the mother of all family reunions at the Greenville Sheriff's Office. Ken rode to the hospital with Cassie, assigning Deputy Farrell and me welcoming committee duties for the parents and guardians trickling in.

Mrs Lopez showed up first to claim Enrique, letters from her daughter in hand to authorize her to pick up the boy. Glenda Madison arrived around six that evening. She'd gotten stopped just west of Davis for speeding, but a call to Ken greased the skids and sent her on her way. Her Heimlich-strength hugs and effusive thanks actually put a lump in my throat. Imagining Kid Deputy laughing at me was all that kept me from blubbering like a girl.

Shortly after Ken called from the hospital to tell us Cassie had been stabilized, the Thompsons turned up to ID and claim their dead boy. After they'd seen his small body in the morgue, Brandon's mother thanked me over and over for finding him.

Her gratitude was hard enough to accept, but when she said, "I knew it. I knew he was gone. I felt it," I nearly lost it all over again.

While Deputy Farrell and I waited for the arrival of the baby's grandparents, Lucy Polovko brought us a tidbit of after the fact enlightenment. Come to reclaim some detritus Ken's deputies had taken from her shack as evidence, she was rambling again about Baba Yaga the witch when I had an "Aha!" moment. Digging out what lucidity I could from Loony Lucy, I managed to correlate the fire-loving Baba Yaga's visit with one of Michelle's conflagrations.

Glenn Cresswell was put on suicide watch in the Greenville County jail until the Sacramento FBI could send someone to come pick him up. Glenn's hold on sanity might have been firmer than his wife's before she died, but he'd lost a few French fries from his Happy Meal since then.

Finally, just past midnight, it was the baby's turn. Mr and Mrs Simmons showed up with their daughter, Naomi, having expedited an overnight DNA test at a Sacramento lab. Once they'd confirmed the baby was their granddaughter, they pulled more strings to have her promptly released to them from foster care. By 3am the infant was in the arms of her dazed teen mom, and under the watchful eyes of her determined grandparents.

I called Ken at the hospital to update him. His voice sounded rough and exhausted over the phone. "Cassie's out of danger," he told me. "Nurses are nagging me to go home and get some rest. Thought I would."

I could hear the implicit invitation in his tone. "Sounds like a good idea."

Implicit turned explicit, his gravelly voice X-rated. "I'll sleep better if you're there with me."

Far too tempting. To have him hold me, so I could let loose the tears I'd been fighting back. So I could somehow expiate my grief and guilt over Brandon's loss. "It would be better if I didn't."

After several long beats of silence, he said, "Don't leave without saying goodbye. Please."

I pressed the heel of my hand into my forehead, gritting my teeth against welling emotion. "Meet you for breakfast at Emil's?"

We set a time, then I disconnected. I hustled out of the sheriff's station to my car, then let the ugly sobs rip from my throat. When I was done, I swabbed the wet from my eyes with the hem of my grody T-shirt, then drove to the Gold Rush Inn.

When I got to Emil's after a few restless hours sleep, he was waiting for me in a booth. There were two cups of coffee on the table, mine properly dosed with sugar and creamer. It was lukewarm – I'd slept through my phone's alarm and was ten minutes late – but I gulped it down to forestall the conversation I knew was coming.

If I'd hoped to slurp up one cup of java then get on the road, I was disappointed when Diana made her way over with two plates piled high with breakfast. A stack of pancakes and scrambled eggs for Ken and a greasy Hangtown Fry for me, an omelette packed with oysters and bacon. A guilty pleasure of mine, and of course he knew it.

Ken drowned his flapjacks in syrup, then set the pitcher aside. He speared me with his irresistible blue gaze. "You could stay, you know."

I ducked my head to address my Fry, but damn, a part of me wanted to. To risk the crap I would make both our lives. "That's not a good idea."

He carefully cut a bite of pancakes. "Why not?"

I tried to craft a lie that would make him mad, that would forever cut him off from me. Nothing but the bare-knuckle truth came to mind.

"Because I'm sick, Ken. Sick in the mind, sick in the heart, sick in the soul." My throat tightened. "Putrid sick."

"No. You're not."

"You don't know a tenth of what goes on inside me. What I keep on a leash. I take up with you, let the prison walls soften up, and all that sickness escapes. All over you and me both." I felt the hard knot of it burn inside me. "It's better to keep it inside."

His mouth tightened in a hard line. He didn't believe that I was so irretrievable, but he at least understood the magnitude of the barriers between us. "You think you might go back to it? Finding lost kids?"

I'd considered it. Except for Brandon, the kids were safe, back where they belonged. Happy ending all around. Nearly.

"I don't think so," I said finally. "It's better if I don't care too much."

"Better for who?" he asked, then he waved away the question, and changed the subject. "Are you sure you don't want me there when you do it?"

"I'm sure. The fire marshal's got it all set up. We won't need you." That was part of the ugliness I didn't want to risk him seeing. I wasn't entirely sure how it would be for me.

I forced myself to finish the breakfast he'd bought me. When he walked me to my car, I let him hug me, kiss my cheek. I promised I'd keep in touch, although it was a foolhardy commitment.

I drove off, avoiding a glance in the rear view mirror; didn't want that last look at him.

I traced the familiar path over to Lime Kiln, turned at the weathered sign lettered with the name "Watkins." Parked my Escort out of the way of the two fire engines, the fire truck, and battalion chief's Expedition. Someone had brush-hogged blackberry brambles and manzanita for thirty feet on all four sides.

Peterson approached as I eased myself from my car. "It's all ready," he said.

Someone had already been inside pouring a trail of gasoline throughout the interior. It had taken some arm-twisting, but the fire marshal agreed to let me toss the Molotov cocktail. After all, it was my property I was letting them burn for their training exercise.

With firefighters at the ready to constrain the fire to the old cabin, Peterson lit the wick of the gas-filled beer bottle. I allowed myself only an instant to admire the flame before I flung it through the cabin's open door. The fire took hold with startling rapidity, greedily licking at the floor and spreading toward the door and windows. My heart lifted at the sight of the brilliant sherbet orange flames, the deep black smoke. I imagined my father inside, burning to death. Other than Michelle, he was the only human being on the planet I would have wished that torture.

But it wasn't my father I saw inside in the last moments of the holocaust, just before the company started their planned suppression. It was Tommy, looking like he was standing in a protective halo of white light. His sad eyes softened as they stared at me and for the first time in eight years, that vision smiled at me.

I staggered back, terrified and jubilant all at once. Stared, thunderstruck, as Tommy vanished in a cloud of steam. As the smoke thrust its tail into the sky, I imagined that towhead boy following it up to heaven.

ACKNOWLEDGMENTS

Many thanks to the El Dorado County Sheriff's Department, particularly retired Lieutenant Kevin House and Detective Laura Bradshaw. Thanks for your input into *Clean Burn* and for making the Citizens Academy such a fun and informative experience. Also, a big thank you to arson investigator John Beaver for being so generous with your time, for loaning me your reference books, and for answering so many of my questions about fire.

ABOUT THE AUTHOR

Writing has been Karen Sandler's passion since the fourth grade. She took a circuitous route to the writing profession, however. Rather than major in English, she studied mathematics, physics and computer science. After earning a BA in math and and an MS in computer science from UCLA, Karen worked as a software engineer for nearly fifteen years. With a move from the Los Angeles area to Northern California, in 1995 Karen optioned her first screenplay, and in 1997 she sold her first novel to Kensington Publishing, with several more novels following thereafter. Karen's first young adult book, *Tankborn*, a dystopian science fiction, was released in September 2011 by Tu Books.

karensandler.net
twitter.com/karensandler

Murder. Vice. Pollution. Delays on the Tube. Some things never change...

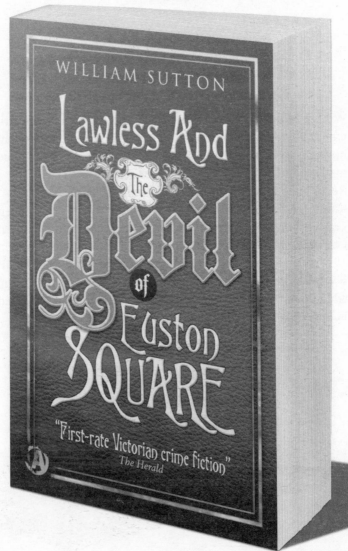

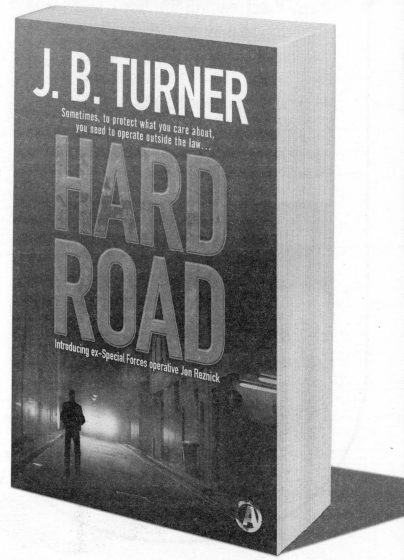

"Sometimes, to protect what you love, you need to operate outside the law..."